THE
UND[...]
YEARS

Shamini Flint

Published by Heliconia Press

ISBN No: 978-981-07-2061-2

With the support of

NATIONAL ARTS COUNCIL
SINGAPORE

The Undone Years

Cover design by Martin Bradley

Printed in Singapore

Printed on sustainably sourced paper.

'Looking back over the years, I have always been careful not to fall into the trap of romanticising the past. There has, after all, been very little in my life that would inspire the mendacity of nostalgia.'

– Chin Peng,
Secretary General,
Malayan Communist Party

Dear Yolanda,
With best wishes!
Shan —
2012

"Strange, friend," I said, "Here is no cause to mourn."
"None," said the other, "Save the undone years.'

- **Wilfred Owen**

For Mr. and Mrs. Pancharatnam –
for sharing their memories of the war

For Mr. and Mrs. Thomas Cheryan –
who made school holidays fun on their estate home

MALAYA
31 August 1945

The platform was a rough construction of wooden planks raised six feet off the ground. The grass underneath had wilted to a patchy brown. Crowds had gathered early. The people jostled for vantage – men, women and a few children supported on their father's shoulders or clutching their mother's hand in a tight, scared grip. Muddy patches had formed in the long grass of the school field and the fetid smell of damp earth mixed with that of rancid sweat.

Matthew stood near the front. Beads of perspiration formed parallel lines along his hairline and upper lip. He was greeted with smiles and a few slaps on the back. If anyone wondered why a British soldier in full uniform was attending an execution organised by the Malayan communists, they didn't ask. Matthew's eyes searched the crowd restlessly but there was no sign of Rajan. He was not surprised. Vengeance had never motivated his friend, although he had as much cause as any to hate the man for whom they were waiting.

The communists, wearing the uniforms of the Malayan People's Anti-Japanese Army, or MPAJA, formed a circle around the platform facing outwards. Crowd control, Matthew guessed; the crowd's mood was calm but the sight of Colonel Onada might provoke an outpouring of rage. Matthew wondered whether the soldiers would turn to watch the death of a man they abhorred or whether they had the discipline to continue to observe the masses of people standing bareheaded under the blistering afternoon sun. He suspected the latter. The soldiers seemed a well-trained lot. Red-faced in the heat, their eyes flickered around the gathering multitude looking for signs of trouble.

There was a sudden howling and a baying, a collective spontaneous sound. Matthew peered over the crowd as it parted like the Red Sea before Moses. The condemned man was escorted towards the platform. Soldiers created a passage, using their bodies as shields. The crowd hissed and spat. Women wept. The Japanese man appeared oblivious to the waves of hatred. He was dressed in white robes, the swathes of cloth emphasising his lack of height. Onada's hands were tied with a piece of twine behind his back.

There were more jeers and catcalls. Matthew also sensed apprehension. The man they hated was in shackles, surrounded by soldiers of the MPAJA. He was dressed in sacrificial robes. Yet the terror he had engendered in the three-and-a-half long years of the Japanese Occupation of Malaya was hard to forget. The people wanted justice, vengeance, closure – but they still feared, against all the evidence, that this man might yet turn the tables on his captors. A man on the edge of the crowd vomited against the foot of a tree; his noodle breakfast looked like rotting worms in the sunshine.

The soldiers stopped at the base of the platform. A single fighter – Matthew saw that it was Keng Lian – escorted Onada up the rough steps, one hand on his arm to help him maintain his balance. Major Chung clambered on to the platform, to face the assembly. He said, 'The Malayan People's Anti-Japanese Army, as the interim administrators of Malaya subsequent to the surrender of Japanese forces by the Emperor Hirohito, has sentenced Colonel Onada of the Japanese Imperial Army to death for his crimes against the people of Malaya.'

The crowd broke into a cheer. Major Chung walked down the stairs again. He had not even glanced at the prisoner.

Keng Lian removed a short double-edged knife from his belt and sliced through the twine binding the prisoner's hands. The Japanese rubbed his wrists, trying to get the circulation moving again. His face remained impassive. Keng Lian held out the knife hilt first to the prisoner. Onada accepted the weapon without blinking. Keng Lian strolled down and stood next to Matthew. He was grinning, his khaki cap with the three stars pushed high on his forehead. Matthew envied him his satisfaction in victory and vengeance. For Matthew, nothing was ever going to be that simple again.

Onada held up the dirk and bowed low. The crowd had fallen silent, unsure why the Japanese colonel had been given a weapon. Onada let his robes fall open. He was wearing nothing under them but long shorts. The Japanese man turned the knife, holding it with both hands, and plunged it into his stomach right up to the hilt. There were gasps from the crowd. He dragged the blade across in a six-inch horizontal cut. Blood spurted from the wound. A woman screamed. Again, Onada plunged the knife into his belly. This time he drew the blade down so that the two cuts formed a cross.

Matthew heard someone whisper, '*Sepukku ...*'

Onada fell to his knees. His eyes were glassy. He opened his mouth to speak. No words came. Colonel Onada, head of the Johore branch of the Kempetai, toppled forward. Keng Lian ran up to the stage and turned the man over with a heavy boot. Matthew could see that Onada was still alive, though barely. Here, in Malaya, there were no seconds to quicken the end, no one ready to sever head from body with a single stroke of a sword. Frothy blood leaked from his mouth and great rivers of blood seeped into the porous wood from his stomach wounds, staining it dark red. Keng Lian watched impassively until Onada's pupils dilated and his trembling hands were motionless. He knelt down and felt for a pulse.

Then he stood up and held his machine gun triumphantly over his head with both hands. 'Comrades, the butcher of Johore is dead!' he shouted. 'The butcher of Johore is dead!'

CHAPTER 1

How to begin this letter to you, my dear old friend? What will you think when you receive it? It's been so long. I remember when we first met in the summer of 1939 when I visited Malaya for the first time. I was so pleased that there was someone of my age on the estate. You were the best tutor I could have found to introduce me to life on the plantation. The best streams to fish in, the trees with the juiciest golden mangoes!

I know I should have written to you a long time ago. I comfort myself that you would have moved on with your life – that there was no need to rake up the past. Deep down I always knew that I was too ashamed to write, too ashamed to tell you the truth about those last days.

As I gaze down at these sheets of thin lined paper, my hand hovers uncertainly, clutching the pen as if it were a lifeline. I used to have a strong, white hand and a firm handshake. Where did these liver spots come from? And the nails – long, grimy and a pale blue, as if the life that is ebbing away from me has already fled from these extremities. I hope that age has treated you more kindly than me, dear friend.

Looking at my hands, I wonder – is it possible that parts of us die first?

If so, a big part of me died in Malaya in 1945.

The rough grass was cut short, the work done by wiry men rhythmically swinging scythes. Andrew Coleman was dressed in traditional planter garb – knee-length baggy shorts and a white short-sleeved shirt. His brawny arms, the tan line visible when his shirt sleeves flapped in the breeze, cradled a shotgun. The planter's belly strained at his shirt. Small islands of white flesh were visible between the buttons. Large sweat patches formed crescents under each armpit and long socks hugged muscular calves. His feet were in heavy muddy boots.

As his son watched, wishing he had the same easy strength with a weapon, Coleman raised the gun and looked down the double barrel. He trained the weapon on a target in the distance. The gun barrel moved swiftly but he did not pull the trigger. He let the gun slip so the end was pointing downwards.

'Damn, he's disappeared again.'

Matthew nodded. He was a slim teenager with light, clear blue eyes. His fine blonde hair was parted in a ruler-straight line and combed into a slick yellow helmet.

'Can you spot the bastard, Matthew?'

His son trained his younger, sharper eyes on the durian trees in the distance. He shook his head. 'I can't see him, father.'

Andrew abruptly raised the shotgun in a fluid gesture.

He pulled the trigger. Matthew jumped at the loud report. The butt of the gun kicked into his father's shoulder. The older man did not flinch.

'Got him!' he exclaimed.

'Are you quite sure, father? I didn't see anything.'

'Go and have a look.'

Matthew headed towards the thick hedge and the row of durian trees on the other side. The trees were heavy with spiky fruit. The aroma was nauseating to the boy who had just arrived from England. He wrinkled his freckled nose in disgust. Matthew walked forward cautiously, nervous of the venomous snakes his mother assured him lurked in every crevice and under every bush. A light wind rustled the silvery leaves. He glanced up, anxious not to have his skull crushed by the heavy fruit. The previous day, he had tried the rich, yellow flesh, the same colour as his hair, for the first time and placed a curious thin hand on the fruit's razor sharp spikes.

Matthew grinned at the memory. He would tell his science teacher that Newton would never have discovered gravity if he'd been sitting under a durian tree.

He turned to look back and saw his father's broad silhouette against the massive black and white estate house. Shuttered windows ran the length of the upstairs. All the windows were open but fine mosquito netting was fixed to the frames. The green netting gave the house a sightless appearance. It reminded Matthew of his grandmother's cataract-filled eyes. Thick square whitewashed pillars stood at the four corners of the veranda. Red tiles framed the inverted 'v' of the high roofs. Lawns ran down in all directions from the house to the edge of the fruit groves. Beyond that, in every direction, rubber trees spread out in neat, orderly, well-spaced rows like soldiers lined up on a parade ground.

Matthew turned towards the trees. He wiped away the sweat that was trickling down his forehead and stinging his eyes. He picked up a stick and rummaged around the dry leaves and twigs under the trees.

'Is this what you're looking for?'

Matthew jumped with fright.

There was a quick, infectious chuckle. A boy of about his own age appeared from behind the blotchy grey trunk of a rubber tree. He was holding a dead squirrel by the tail. Blood dripped from the wounds made by the shotgun pellets. The planter's son felt ill. He had never seen death before.

'It won't fruit again,' remarked the slim Indian youth in a cheerful lilting voice, looking away politely to avoid the sight of the white boy's discomfiture.

Matthew was curious enough to ask, 'What won't?'

'That tree – the manager shot the squirrel in that tree. My Amma says that a tree that has seen blood spilt won't fruit.'

'That's rubbish,' said Matthew, recovering his equilibrium.

The Indian shrugged and laughed, his white, even teeth bright against his dark face. 'You're probably right!'

The other boy stuck out a hand. 'I'm Matthew.'

'Are you the manager's son? From England?'

Matthew nodded.

'I'm Rajan,' said the boy and shook Matthew's hand. His

clasp was firm and dry despite the sweltering heat.

'Are you a tapper?' asked Matthew.

Rajan shook his head emphatically.

'No, no! The tappers are all Tamils. My family is Malayalee, from Trivandrum in Kerala. My father is the *kerani* of the estate.'

'*Kerani?*'

'He works in the office,' explained Rajan, shoving his fists into his pockets. Matthew guessed that he didn't have a very clear idea what his father did. 'But our family are not tappers … only the Tamils are tappers,' he added.

Matthew nodded. He wasn't sure what a *kerani* was, or what a tapper really did for that matter, but he understood the implicit hierarchy in Rajan's explanation.

'Come and meet my father,' he urged.

Rajan shook his head. 'I'm not allowed around the big house. My father doesn't like it.'

'It's all right if you're with me.'

Andrew Coleman's booming voice could be heard shouting for his son to return.

Matthew grabbed Rajan by the arm and dragged him towards his father.

'And who do we have here?' asked Coleman. His smile, behind a thick salt-and-pepper moustache, exposed square yellow teeth that gave his friendliness a predatory edge. Rajan did not smile back although he ducked his head in a small bow. A planter being friendly to a native was not an invitation for reciprocity.

'Rajan, sir; my father is the *kerani.*'

'Ahhh! My clerk, Thomas, you mean? Fine fellow. Don't know what we'd do without him, eh?'

He put out his hand.

Rajan did the same. He was still holding the dead squirrel.

There was a moment's silence and then Andrew Coleman burst into loud laughter. The boys followed suit, Rajan with relief and Matthew with pleasure.

'So, you found the pest that's been eating my fruit!'

'Rajan says that the tree won't fruit again – the one where you shot the squirrel.' Matthew's thick brows were raised with scepticism.

'Is that so, young man?'

'I don't really believe it, sir. But it's what my mother says …'

Coleman snorted. 'Old wives' tales!'

'Yes, sir.'

'So you're going to keep my son company while he's on holiday?'

Rajan nodded.

'Are you at the estate Tamil school?' asked Andrew Coleman.

'No, sir. I go to the Methodist Boys' school in town.'

'I might have guessed. Thomas wouldn't want his son fraternising with the labour lines. Well, I'll leave you young fellows to get acquainted.'

He turned and panted up the hill, leaving them eyeing each other warily.

***

'I'm fifteen,' said Matthew by way of an opening gambit.

'Fourteen,' confessed Rajan, annoyed at being the younger. He knew he had already, if temporarily, conceded the role of leader in their band of two. Seniority was paramount, every year the equivalent of a stripe.

'So what do you do for fun around here?' asked Matthew, shoving his hands into his pockets.

'Do you like fishing?'

'Of course.'

'I know a good place, where the river pools under a rain tree. There's a jetty and the fish are always hungry.'

'Let me get my rod,' said Matthew. 'I'll be back in a jiffy.'

Rajan slipped back under cover of the boundary fruit trees. He felt exposed on the lawn, half expecting a gardener to come and send him on his way. Maybe even the manager himself. It was not unlikely that he would change his mind about his son befriending a native. He hadn't seemed fickle – a big, bluff, straightforward sort of man – but one never knew with the whites. His father said that the colonials were as changeable as the weather.

Matthew's jiffy – whatever that was – took approximately five minutes and when he returned, puffing slightly as if he had hurried for fear his new companion would be swallowed up by the trees, he was carrying a shiny red rod taller than himself.

'Do you need to get yours?' asked Matthew.

Rajan suppressed an envious thought and shook his head. He pushed his unruly hair away from his forehead and said, 'I have everything I need down by the river.'

Any embarrassment he felt over the spool of wire around a rusty condensed milk tin that he produced from under a bush was put to rest a few hours later as he looked into the laden bucket where round-mouthed fish gasped for air. He took one out and efficiently gutted it with a small sharp knife.

Matthew, cutting his line for the umpteenth time, grimaced. 'This rod is useless. 'I didn't catch anything at all!'

Rajan nodded sympathetically. Inside, he couldn't help feeling a little smug. Matthew might be a year older but he hadn't spent that time learning anything useful like how to catch or clean a fish.

'I'll give you some of mine to take back,' he offered. 'Maybe your mother will cook them for dinner. They taste really good fresh like this.'

Matthew's blue eyes twinkled. 'My mother doesn't know where the kitchen is,' he remarked, opening up the gulf between them again. But he bridged it with his next words. 'Maybe next time you can help me make one of those.' He nodded at Rajan's fishing contraption. 'Then I might actually hook a fish.'

CHAPTER 2

I'm not sure that you realised at the time but Mother was not that keen on our friendship. Father didn't mind. He was a lot less fussy about people 'knowing their place'. Besides, he understood that your family weren't labourers. But to her dying day my mother was unable to tell the difference between a Tamil, a Malayalee or a Telugu. To be frank, I think she struggled with the Malays and Chinese too!

Were your parents unhappy about our friendship? If they weren't keen on me, they were much better at disguising it. I won't forget how often your mum would hustle me into your home and feed me – if I close my eyes I can still smell her cooking. My taste buds are gone. All this damned medication. But remembering your mother's fish curry is almost like being able to taste again.

'I don't like Matthew hanging around that boy.'

Sarah Coleman's lips were pursed and her silver blonde hair primped. Her floral cotton dress, so fresh in the morning, was clinging to her like a lover. She glared at her husband when he did not agree with her immediately. She despised her beefy spouse. Did he have to be such a caricature of a planter, she wondered, with his bloodshot eyes, booming voice and thin grey hair arranged damply across his sunburnt scalp? Mind you, they were all like that, or became like that after a few years in Malaya.

She remembered when Andrew had first asked her to marry him. He had painted a picture of gracious living in a tropical paradise, of afternoon teas with the other planters' wives, of dozens of servants to do her bidding and a magnificent house to set off her fragile beauty. He hadn't mentioned the energy-sapping heat that left her listless yet restless, the mind-numbing pettiness of the planters' wives, the swarms of mosquitoes that formed a thick cloud around her head at dusk and the frightful stink from the rubber factory when the winds changed.

Her tone clipped, Sarah Coleman said again, 'I don't like Matthew hanging around with that boy.'

'He's harmless,' said Andrew.

'He's a native!'

'Thomas is a good worker. The son's at the Methodist Boys' school in town. He's good company for Matthew.'

'I thought he'd spend more time with me.'

Andrew Coleman said, with rough sympathy, 'Boys prefer company their own age. He doesn't mean to ignore you or hurt your feelings.'

Sarah could not stand it that this man she detested was feeling sorry for her. She stood up abruptly, wriggling her narrow shoulders. Her dress was stuck to her back with perspiration.

'I'm going to lunch at the Pickfords,' she snapped, and marched out of the room, her heels clicking on the patterned tiles.

***

'Rubber seeds make perfect bullets,' explained Rajan holding out a fistful to his new friend.

Matthew fingered a smooth brown seed with intricate whorls on its surface. It was hard and light, perfect for their slingshots.

They practiced for a while, aiming at empty whisky bottles recovered from the pantry cabinet in the big house.

'We need a moving target,' said Matthew.

Rajan grinned. He was always ready for mischief. 'I know the perfect one.'

The boys marched through the rubber trees with their slingshots ready. They reached the outskirts of the assistant manager's bungalow. It was a single-storey sprawling building with quarters for the servants jutting out the back.

'Whose house is this?' asked Matthew in a whisper as they crouched in the greenery, the scent of jasmine strong in their nostrils.

'The Assistant Manager, Mr. Johnson. Have you met him yet?'

Matthew shook his head. He pinched his nose hard between thumb and forefinger. The intense aroma of tropical flowers was making him feel sneezy. He didn't want to give away their hiding place.

'Nobody likes him. I heard my father say that he invites young Tamil women from the labour lines – the pretty ones – to live with him.'

'Sounds like a good target,' agreed Matthew.

Rajan beckoned for Matthew to follow him. They crawled forward on all fours to a spreading, umbrella-shaped rain tree overlooking the driveway. Rajan climbed up efficiently, using the long hanging vines for support. He avoided the orchid plants that nestled in the forks. With one arm looped around a tree branch, he gave Matthew a hand up.

They slid forward on their bellies until they had a good vantage point, hidden by the thick leaves but with a clear view of the front porch and the Austin motor car parked in front.

The boys waited for their prey, trying to avoid fidgeting as the minutes passed.

Matthew was so stiff he was afraid he wouldn't be able to hold on to his branch for much longer. The rough bark was scratching his arms and legs. 'Rajan, this is boring,' he whispered.

Rajan raised a thin long finger to his lips. The front door opened and a tall man with short mousy brown hair and protuberant blue eyes ambled out. He was tanned but not to the leathery darkness of Matthew's own father. He looked both younger and fitter than Andrew Coleman, a newcomer still to the energy-sapping tropics.

Rajan slipped a rubber seed into the band, and gently

drew his slingshot back. He winked at Matthew, aimed carefully and let fly. Both boys ducked. The assistant manager yelped in pain, a hand going to his forehead.

The brown youth and the white one grinned at each other. Even white teeth gleamed green in the reflected light of their treetop hideout. When they heard the car leave, they slid down and ran back into the cover of the rubber trees, giggling all the way.

***

'I don't like you spending so much time with the manager's son.'

'But why, Amma?'

'It is not fitting.'

'He's good fun – I am teaching him about living on an estate.'

'Bah! What could you teach him? His life and yours have nothing in common. He is the son of the manager. You are the son of the *kerani*.'

'Leave the boy alone,' said Thomas, glaring at the plump woman with jet black hair and pinprick eyes narrowed by rolls of fat. She was perspiring.

Thomas was always surprised that, with the amount she sweated, his wife did not lose some of her layers of wobbly flesh. But she was an excellent cook who, unlike many women whose hours in the kitchen resulted in a sharp loss of appetite, adored her own cooking. Thomas didn't blame her. Her dishes were delicious – the red-hot fish curry with the special dried tamarind that had to be brought from India by newcomers and lent the dish that sour, tangy aftertaste that lingered in the mouth; *avial* – mixed vegetables cooked with scraped coconut from the tall palm in the garden; *katchia moru,* a thick yellow soup so rich and tasty that he would drown his plate of steamed rice in the stuff. But he didn't put on weight because he was disciplined in the amount he consumed. His wife, however, would complete her vast cooking exercise and eat a large lunch with him and Rajan. Sated, she would sit in her rattan easy chair, fanning herself frantically with an open palm until she dozed off, waking with a start to begin preparing a sumptuous dinner, perhaps shouting at him to wring the neck of a plump chicken.

'I do not like it,' insisted Mrs. Thomas in a rare show of defiance. She usually altered her opinions to conform to her husband's.

A single vertical line formed between Thomas's eyebrows. 'Do you think our son is not good enough to spend time with that boy?'

'I think that no good can come of changing the natural order of things.' She dabbed her forehead with the *pallu* of her pink *saree* with the paisley border.

'I tell you that my son is the *equal* of that boy.'

Thomas snuffed out his evil-smelling pipe with a hint of regret but an overwhelming sense of the benefits of self-discipline over self-indulgence. He rose to his feet and watched his wife heave herself out of the easy chair. The sweat-stained armpits of her *saree* blouse were visible as she levered herself up, the rolls of fat under her arms swinging with effort.

'I don't want to discuss the matter anymore,' he said.

He spoke English at home as a point of principle although both he and his wife were from the same fishing village in India. She preferred Malayalam, was more comfortable in her native tongue. Quite often their conversations were carried out with each speaking a different language.

Thomas was determined that his son should speak English as naturally as an Englishman. Unfortunately, there was nothing he could do to soften the lilting Indian cadences of Rajan's accent or erase the colloquialisms picked up from the Chinese and Malay boys at his school. However, it was some small comfort that there were plenty of middle-rung civil service positions to be had for good English speakers in the British administration in Malaya. Thomas desperately hoped his son would grow up to have one of those jobs in the towns and cities. He didn't want the boy stuck on a plantation at the beck and call of a single white rajah whose whims were more than commands – they were commandments.

'I'll go and come now,' said the *kerani*. He spoke in English, knowing even as he did so that his sentence construction owed more to his native tongue.

'I will see you in the evening.'

This brief exchange had not varied in their fifteen years of marriage and Thomas did not expect it ever would.

He walked with a small step but an upright posture towards his motorbike. He tucked his trousers into his black socks to avoid catching them in the spokes. Thomas knew it lent him a comic air but he had decided early on that this was preferable to getting grease marks on his trousers. The breeze from his steady pace failed to ruffle his grey hair, which was slicked back firmly with hair cream that functioned, once it was dry, like glue.

He saw his son trot out of the house as he rode past and nodded in acknowledgment of his cheerful wave. Rajan never walked when he could run, he thought to himself with a feigned irritability that was an inadequate disguise for the pride he felt in the boy.

Smart, tall, handsome, English-speaking, fraternising on equal terms with the manager's son – Rajan was destined for great things. Thomas was sure of it, with the fierce patriarchal certainty that only fathers from the Indian sub-continent could achieve when contemplating their only sons.

***

Thomas reached the estate office. It was a long, low building made of whitewashed brick divided up into the manager's office at one end and the assistant's at the other. A bigger room in the centre, furnished with tables, chairs and a single fan overhead, was for the clerical staff.

In this middle room, Thomas was the most senior and important personage, treated with respect and even deference. His quiet, brittle manner instilled trepidation and uncertainty in his underlings.

Thomas's own pride of position was severely curtailed by being separated only by a thin wall from his superiors on either side. A stentorian yell would signal that his manager wanted to see him in the next room. Never once in the five years they had worked together had the Englishman felt it necessary to walk the twenty feet from his desk to the door of the adjoining office.

This afternoon, sated with lunch but not sleepy with over-eating, Thomas opened his diary and glanced at his schedule for the afternoon. It was a part of his routine from which he never deviated.

He saw that he had an appointment with the Chinese contractor, Chan, who supplied the electrical equipment used on the estate. A generator had broken down. Thomas had been assured that a repair job was a false economy. Now he was meeting the contractor to place an order if the price was right – this too having been prudently checked with the competitors. Once Thomas was satisfied, he would escort the man to see the boss. Only the estate manager had the authority to purchase such an expensive piece of equipment. However, this was a formality. Andrew Coleman had never contradicted a suggestion from Thomas in their entire acquaintance.

The contractor marched in at exactly two-thirty. His shirt bore the reddish marks of driving on the clay tracks from the main road to the estate offices.

'Mr. Thomas, I bring you all the quotes you wanted.'

'Very good, Chan. Please come and sit down. Would you like a cup of tea?'

'No, no.' Chan handed over the slim file with generator specifications and Thomas accepted it and made a show of studying it.

'This one is the best generator on the market. I guarantee it,' said Chan.

The contractor wore black-rimmed glasses and looked both honest and sincere. Thomas did not know him well enough to be sure that he possessed either of these attributes. 'I am sure you are right,' he said, but his tone was non-committal.

'And the price is very good for you because you are an old customer of our company.'

Thomas was amused to hear 'very' spoken to rhyme with 'smelly'. Then he remembered his earlier concerns about his own son's accent. His eyebrows, tufty and grey, moved slightly closer together.

'You want me to reduce the price, Mr. Thomas?'

'You can do that?'

'Maybe another ten percent?'

'I will put your proposal to Mr. Coleman, the manager.'

Chan knew this was his cue to stand and he did, scraping his wooden chair backwards against the grey cement floor.

Thomas led the way and knocked on the adjacent door.

Andrew Coleman was slumped in his chair. His eyes were shut and his chest rose and fell with the regularity of a metronome. At the second knock, Coleman opened his eyes and looked blearily across the room, blinking a few times to regain focus.

He beckoned his clerk forward who in turn ushered Chan in.

'Chan,' said Coleman. 'Good to see you. What are you selling us today?'

'A generator, sir.'

'Excellent. I assume Thomas has made my decision for me?'

'I have assessed the available models and compared prices, sir, and have my recommendations for you.'

'As I said, you've made my decision,' chortled the planter. 'We all know that the whites just pretend to run the show, eh! But it's you natives with your native cunning who are really in charge!'

Thomas essayed a stiff smile.

Coleman dug his elbow into Chan's ribs, causing the plump man to wince. 'I don't think my chief clerk finds me amusing!'

Tired of his own attempts at humour, the planter turned sullen.

'What do I sign?' he snapped.

Thomas slipped a sheet of paper in front of him and held out a pen. Coleman leaned over and scrawled his name, large and aggressive, across the bottom of the page, and tossed the pen back on the table. 'You can go now. I have work to do,' he said.

Thomas collected the papers and the pen and led the way out. He did not look back but Chan couldn't resist. Andrew Coleman had already shut his eyes, this time with his feet on the table for greater comfort.

'You're not angry?'

'What do you mean?'

'You're not angry that you do all the work and he sleeps?' Chan gesticulated so violently with his head to indicate the room they had just left that one thick lock of shiny black hair was dislodged from his careful coiffure. 'If I were you, my blood would be hot!'

Thomas looked quizzically at the other man, taken aback by this directness. 'He's not that bad. He hates paperwork but he runs the estate quite well – he knows his rubber trees.'

'You're a good man, Thomas.'

The *kerani* smiled and the emotion reached his eyes. 'Thank you. I do my job.'

A young girl was leaning against the contractor's ancient Morris. She straightened up as the men came out of the building.

'My daughter, Mei Ling,' said Chan and beckoned to the girl. She came over and shook hands, muttering a polite salutation.

Thomas saw that she was older than she had appeared at first. Perhaps fourteen, his son's age. A quick smile revealed a dimple in her left cheek.

Thomas could sense Chan's pride. It reminded him of his own feelings earlier that afternoon when thinking about Rajan. He smiled a genuine smile for the second time that day. It was a new record for the *kerani*, who kept his emotions on a tight rein.

The men shook hands and felt an unexpected camaraderie.

Thomas was still staring after the car when his son appeared at his elbow. He looked down at the boy in surprise. It was unheard of for Rajan to seek him out at work – the family knew better than to do that.

'What are you doing here? Did your mother send you?'

'No, Pappa.'

'Then why?'

'Who was that?'

'What?' asked his father, still waiting for bad news and unable to fathom the conversational turn.

'Who was that in the car?'

'Mr. Chan, the contractor. Why?'

'I mean the girl. Who was the girl?'

'His daughter. I can't remember her name. What are you doing here?'

The increasingly cross tone finally got through to Rajan.

'Me? Oh! I came to ask your permission to go to dinner at the manager's bungalow tonight.'

'They invited you for dinner?'

'Yes.'

'What did your mother say?'

'She said to ask you.'

Thomas nodded.

He remembered his earlier pride at the thought of his son hobnobbing on equal terms with the son of the manager. Then he remembered his shame and the Chinese man's pity when that same manager had treated him with such contempt.

No white man would ever treat an Asian as an equal. Deep down, Thomas knew it all too well. They were so certain of their own superiority. His son too was destined to be a second-class citizen, fetching and carrying, nodding and agreeing, smoothing the way for his masters.

'Well, can I go?' asked Rajan, shifting from foot to foot

impatiently. The boy who never stood still, thought his father.

'Yes, you can go – but just this once.'

Thomas knew what the boy would have said if he had tried to articulate his own uncertainties – *Oh, Pappa, it's just dinner!*

***

Rajan walked at a slower pace than he was accustomed towards the mansion on the hill. It was not because he felt any trepidation about his invitation to dine with Matthew's family. It was just that Amma had urged him to arrive at the manager's bungalow looking as neat as when he had left his own home. His hair had been vigorously combed and smelt faintly of coconut oil. He had washed the back of his neck and behind his ears. His mother had starched his blue shirt to an uncomfortable stiffness and ironed it until even the memories of creases had been erased. His sandals had been wiped clean with a damp cloth and his shorts were freshly laundered, the pockets empty instead of bulging with a day's collection of string, stones and rubber seeds.

Rajan knew that, if he ran, he would sweat through the starch on his shirt, his shoes would get dusty and his hair would be in disarray. So he sauntered along slowly and regretted the necessity. A flash of lightning lit up the horizon. He counted to three and the air shuddered with a clap of thunder. The storm was close. Rajan looked upwards with a grin. If it came to a choice between arriving soaked or merely dishevelled, he would opt for the latter. But although the sky was leaden, he had a few minutes left. The house at the apex of the rolling lawns was already visible.

Matthew was waiting for him in the huge entrance hall, flanked on either side by living rooms and the dining room. A door at the end led to the mysterious nether quarters where the staff lurked. Matthew beckoned to Rajan to join him in racing up the glossy hardwood stairs to the upper storey. After a brief hesitation, Rajan followed him.

'Where are your parents? Should I say "hello" to them first?'

'No need,' said Matthew.

Rajan did not grudge Matthew his position of authority in his own domain. It was just a fleeting pleasure in having the upper hand when usually it was he, Rajan, familiar with every tree and stream and secret on the estate, who was the leader in their relationship.

Matthew led the way to his bedroom and stood aside to let his friend in first. Rajan's brown eyes widened in amazement. The room was bigger than his entire house. The floor, polished strips of wood, was worn to a smooth finish by the tread of servants. The glass windows were tall and narrow and had wooden shutters as well as net screens to keep the mosquitoes out. As an extra defence against malaria, thin wisps of smoke curled upwards from spiral green mosquito coils resting in tin lids. A ceiling fan spun furiously but the room was cool without its efforts; the high ceilings and big windows ensured it. The oppressive humidity from the looming storm was hardly noticeable. The painted shelves were full of neatly arranged sports equipment and an enormous quantity of books.

'I don't even *have* a book – or any of these other things either,' exclaimed Rajan.

'What do you mean?'

The Indian gestured at the shelves.

'Not even a football?' demanded Mathhew.

Rajan grinned. 'I had one, but I kicked it into the refuse pond near the rubber factory. My father won't buy me another one.'

'You can borrow my things if you like.'

Rajan guessed Matthew was embarrassed at his possessions so he was trying to sound offhand and casual. 'We should play football tomorrow,' he said.

'All right, but not near the rubber refuse pond.'

Both boys laughed.

The manager's son looked at the alarm clock on his bedside table and said, 'We ought to go down to dinner.'

***

Andrew Coleman was standing on a handwoven Persian carpet, a crystal beaker of clear liquid in his hand. His wife sat in a large red leather armchair, holding a long-stemmed glass of red wine. The rain was pelting down outside. It muffled the voices of the couple. This was not of any real significance as neither was saying much or listening with any interest or enthusiasm to what the other had to say.

The boys walked in, Matthew leading the way, and

Rajan feeling intimidated for the first time that day. Andrew Coleman boomed in a welcoming voice, foghorn loud, 'Well, young Thomas, good to have you with us this evening.'

'Thank you, sir.'

Matthew turned to his mother and said, 'This is my friend, Rajan, mother.'

Sarah Coleman held out a thin languid hand which Rajan took nervously. He tried to hide his dismay. The dry skin on her bony hand felt like the abandoned snake skins that he and Matthew collected around the estate.

He said, as his mother had coached him, 'Thank you for inviting me to dinner. My Amma ... my mother, I mean ... thanks you also.'

'How kind of her,' she murmured.

Matthew rolled his eyes at Rajan outside his mother's line of vision.

Rajan was concerned that Matthew's mother was not well. He was not to know that the role she had chosen to play that evening was that of long-suffering invalid. Matthew had sheepishly explained once that his mother was a bit moody. As Mrs. Coleman slumped back in her chair, Rajan decided that Matthew had not been exaggerating. He might be socially inferior, live in a very small house and not have any books – or anything else that Matthew had, for that matter – but at least his mother smiled and sliced fruit for Matthew when he came to Rajan's home.

'Come on, then! Let's eat,' said Andrew Coleman and Rajan was grateful.

The dining table had been laid with knives, forks, spoons,

dessert spoons, dinner plates and side plates, and an array of food on china serving dishes. Rajan was grateful that his school, anglophile and training Malayans for the civil service, had instructed them in the niceties of handling cutlery. He was not an expert but at least he was not completely ignorant of the use of the startling array of silver catching the light from the flickering candelabra in the centre of the table.

The food consisted largely of salads and potatoes. Rajan remembered his mother saying that the white madams didn't bother to cook their food.

A servant appeared dressed in white trousers and bush jacket. He silently placed a shallow china bowl of hot soup in front of the diners. Rajan waited for the manager to say grace as his father did before dinner in their home, simple and somewhat perfunctory, but never overlooked.

It was a custom not followed in the manager's home. Andrew Coleman lifted his spoon, said, 'Tuck in!' and then having deposited a smattering of soup on his iron grey moustache, beamed at the boys.

Matthew and Rajan discussed their plans for the next day to go fishing in one of the streams on the plantation. Matthew's mother sat and ate in silence. Andrew Coleman occasionally jumped in with reminiscences about fishing as a lad in England. The boys listened with polite interest, and, when the size of the fish he had caught became magnified through the bottom of his glass, with disbelief.

Rajan was feeling quite pleased with himself for negotiating the pitfalls of dinner at the manager's bungalow when he was served a large slice of meat. He looked at it with trepidation. Meat was cut up and curried in his home so this dish was disconcerting. He watched Matthew slice a corner of his steak and slip it into his mouth, chewing with evident relish. Rajan followed suit and was horrified to see red blood seep on to his plate. The others were eating without any complaints. Should he mention that his dinner wasn't cooked? Would it sound rude? He had no idea. One thing was absolutely clear in his mind. There was no way he could eat it. The blood mixed with the oil on his plate made him feel nauseous. It reminded him of the blood oozing through the brown fur of the squirrel the manager had shot on the day, some months back, that he had first met Matthew.

Andrew Coleman noticed that Rajan was not eating. 'Anything the matter, boy?'

Sarah Coleman looked up from her plate for the first time. She raised an inquiring plucked eyebrow.

'Don't you like it? It's pretty good,' said Matthew.

'I'm sorry. It's just that mine doesn't appear to be cooked. When I cut it, all this blood spilt out.'

Andrew Coleman burst into a loud guffaw. His wife smiled thinly. Even Matthew grinned.

Rajan tried to look indifferent to being the butt of a joke.

Andrew Coleman took pity on the confused youth and said, 'It's just *rare*.'

Rajan was mystified. It was beef, wasn't it? Cows weren't rare.

'Rare just means it's not very well-cooked,' explained Matthew. 'That's the way we like to eat it. That's not the way your mother cooks it?'

Rajan shook his head mutely. He thought that his Amma had been quite right. The wives of the white managers were too lazy even to cook their meals.

CHAPTER 3

I was so pleased when I was sent to a boarding school in Penang after war broke out in Europe. Not that my parents had any doubts that Britain would prevail. They just felt the journey to and fro England would be perilous.

It meant I was back at Kuala Reman estate every hols – Penang was just a train ride away. It was great to renew our hunting and fishing expeditions and listen to Das, the conductor, spin tall tales. I recall we never let off picking on the assistant manager either. Do you remember when I came to you with a handful of round pellets, convinced they were perfect bullets for the slingshots? You told me the pellets were goat droppings!

It was that following summer, the summer of 1940, when Mei Ling moved to the estate. If I close my eyes I can still see her determined chin and reluctant smile – I don't doubt you can too. How long did we have together, the three of us?

The conductor of the estate, Das, was a tall Tamil from Madras. He had been fortunate to receive an education at a charity school for orphans. The school was run by missionaries so he was English-speaking and numerate when he caught the boat to Malaya. He arrived at Port Swettenham with all his possessions in a small cardboard case, accompanied by the big, black aggressive crows that had come across on his ship. Das had nothing to look back on or regret in India and an uncertain future ahead of him. But he was a determined young man and his language skills placed him in great demand on the white-run rubber estates. He was soon the conductor of one of the largest plantations in the country, the Kuala Reman estate.

He worked hard at his job of supervising the workers, smoothed the relations between his loud paymaster and his fellow Tamils on the labour lines, ruled over his kingdom with a benevolent hand but was quick to assert his authority when a tapper fell behind on his daily collection quota of rubber.

Das believed firmly in the essential uprightness of his colonial masters. He was certain of their goodwill – after all, hadn't they plucked him from an uncertain fate as a Madras street child and given him skills that now commanded a good wage, a house of his own and the prospect of a wife to care for his needs?

But Das also felt sympathy for the tappers trapped in their single wooden rooms, working from dawn to dusk with aggressive rubber quotas to meet. The workers sent their children to the estate school. Lessons were conducted only in Tamil so that the next generation was ill-equipped to escape. The children of tappers were soon on the plantations themselves, walking up and down the neatly planted rows, tipping latex into buckets, carrying the buckets to a collection point and then starting again – dull, repetitive, backbreaking work. Das's concern for the tappers led him to ask the manager for improvements in their condition. Usually, his requests fell on deaf ears.

'With the monsoon rains coming, sir – the labour quarters need some repairs.'

'Where's the money to come from for luxuries, eh, Das? You know with the war in Europe we need to squeeze every last drop of rubber out of these damn trees and use every last drop of blood to get it!'

'But if the tappers fall ill, our productivity will fall, sir. And there is no way of getting any new staff. There is less traffic from India because of the war.'

'How about poaching some workers from the other estates?' asked Coleman.

'We would have to pay them more, sir.'

Das held his breath as the manager looked at him thoughtfully. Had he been persuasive enough? He was most successful at getting concessions out of management when he spelt out the need in terms of their own self-interest.

'All right, damn it. Ask Thomas to find someone cheap. He knows every cutthroat contractor in town and most of them owe him favours.'

'Yes, sir,' said Das, careful to keep the grin off his face.

***

'So, Comrade Chan, do you still enjoy your role as a generator salesman?

'What do you think? Driving around the estates, kowtowing to the know-nothing whites, discounting prices – wasting my time.'

His Malayan Communist Party, or MCP, party bosses nodded and smiled. 'We think you should get closer to the workers. In your present role, you do not have the opportunity to build up relationships.'

Chan was more than willing. 'In a tin mine?' he asked.

The Malayan tin mines employed thousands of migrant Chinese workers and he knew the Johore branch of the Party, in conjunction with the other branches, was working hard to infiltrate the workers' unions.

'We don't want to waste your contacts in the estates. And we have had less success in converting the Tamil workers to our cause.'

Chan nodded. It made sense. Even better than that, he knew of an opening. On his last visit to the Kuala Reman estate, the chief clerk, Thomas had complained loudly about the man who ran the single plantation shop.

'I think I know just the place,' he said, beaming at his superiors.

It didn't take him long to drop a few hints to Thomas who, predictably, had taken ownership of the idea, decided it had been his in the first place, and offered Chan the opportunity to take over.

Das had concurred. But later, to Chan's surprise, he took him aside and said bluntly, 'I know you're a good and honest man, Chan. But I also know that you're a communist.

Chan eyed him warily. It was illegal to be a member of

the MCP and members were thrown in jail or deported immediately by the British.

'What are you going to do about it?'

'Nothing – it's none of my business. If you can persuade the Tamils to stand up for themselves, you have my blessing.'

'Will you help?'

Das shrugged his bony shoulders. 'Maybe.'

'What if Coleman finds out? You could get in trouble too.' Chan was determined to spell out the risks.

Das winked. 'But I know nothing of your activities, or the communist party in Johore!'

***

The sundry shop had been neglected by the previous owner. More concerned with the betting syndicates he controlled, and heavily involved in the various clan disputes in the Chinese community, he had been distracted from his obligations on the estate. As a consequence, the shelves in the small tin-roofed shop were almost bare, the canned goods dusty, the bread stale and the building dingy.

With the help of his wife and daughter, Chan carried the products outside and made an orderly stack on the grey cement porch. They lugged the shelves on to the road as well, and his daughter wiped them down with rags. When she had finished, Mei Ling sat cross-legged in front of the tower of goods and separated those that were old, expired, mouldy or otherwise damaged from the few bits and pieces that were salvageable. Her father washed out the floor of the shop with buckets of soapy water and a hardy *lidi* broom made from the leaf ribs of the coconut palm, the thin strips bound together tightly with a piece of string.

'Chan?'

He looked up and saw Thomas peering into the front of the shop. Chan dropped the *lidi* broom and walked out into the sunshine, blinking a little against the glare after being in the gloomy interior of his new premises. Thomas looked as cool and immaculate as ever in his grey trousers and white shirt, the outline of the singlet he wore to absorb the inevitable perspiration visible through the thin cotton.

'My wife has made some tea and I have brought you my son to help.'

Chan smiled at his friend. 'Both are welcome.'

Outside, Rajan watched the women work. He could see his father stare into the dim interior of the shop and heard him say something. He had been reluctant to come along, unwilling to be offered up as an additional pair of hands on this precious holiday afternoon. He had a plan to meet Matthew and ride their bicycles to the nearest village for ice balls. But when his father expected something of him, Rajan knew better than to argue. It was not that he feared punishment, although he had felt the strap often enough growing up. Rajan sensed that he was bound up in his father's expectations on a visceral level. Any genuine rebellion would break the old man's heart.

He recognised Mei Ling. 'You were here last year,' he said.

She glanced at the Indian boy. Her thick fringe was

44

plastered to her forehead and her pale skin was flushed as she worked in the sun sorting the goods.

'You came with your father. I saw you.'

She nodded and spoke in a voice that caught him by surprise. It was low and husky. 'Yes, I came with my father when he was still working as a generator salesman.' When Rajan did not reply she smiled a little and said, 'I'm surprised you remember. It was almost a year ago.'

'My father has asked me to help. What can I do?'

She patted a spot on the ground next to her, inviting him to sit down. 'You can sort these things out.'

Rajan sat down, unconsciously mimicked her cross-legged posture and reached for a tin of sardines.

A shadow fell across them.

'I thought we were going for ice balls?' said Matthew.

'I'm sorry, Matthew. My father asked me to help here.'

Mei Ling tucked her hair behind her ears and smiled warmly at the young Englishman. 'We could always use more help!'

Matthew blushed. Unlike Rajan, the rush of blood to his face was clearly visible. Rajan smirked. Matthew was so shy that being addressed directly by a pretty girl was too much for him. He guessed that the manager's son would take to his heels.

But he had underestimated his friend.

'I'd like to help. What can I do?'

Mei Ling nodded at the pile of cans. 'You can help us sort these out.'

As Matthew sat down and tried to fold his long legs, not

as adept as the Asians at sitting on the floor, she said, 'I am Mei Ling.'

'I'm Matthew.'

Rajan felt an unexpected stab of resentment as his best friend beamed at the daughter of the new sundry shop owner.

***

A few weeks later, the two boys strolled towards the river to their favourite fishing haunt. It made a change, realised Matthew. Since Mei Ling had moved to the estate, the three of them – Rajan, Mei Ling and he – spent almost all their free time together. Unlike most fathers, Chan was a lenient parent who did not mind his daughter making friends, even with boys. It was his political beliefs, Mei Ling had explained – as far as he was concerned, everyone was equal and entitled to the same choices. Mei Ling herself went to school in town and spent most afternoons poring over her books.

'What do you think of her?' Matthew asked the question casually.

'Who?'

'Are you living on a different estate from me? There's only Mei Ling right?'

'She seems like a good person – friendly. A bit bossy.'

'I don't care what she's like – I mean what do you think of her? You know – whether she's your sort of girl.' Matthew waved his hands in the air, simulating the curves of a woman, exaggerating them slightly.

Rajain bit his lower lip.

'I knew you liked her,' crowed Matthew.

'I don't really know many girls,' confessed Rajan.

'Back in Penang, I know quite a few – from the girls' boarding school down the road.' Matthew's tone was professorial. He added, and this time there was only excitement. 'There's one girl, if you pay her, she'll let you see her breasts.'

'Did you do that?'

'Of course.' It was a lie but there was no need for Rajan to know. Once in a while it was good to have the upper hand, even if he was talking to his best friend.

They were approaching the fishing hole in companionable silence when Rajan put up his hand.

'What is it?'

'I hear something.'

Matthew didn't doubt him. Rajan's sensitivity to any slight change in his environment still astonished him although they had known each other for while now. Rajan dropped to a crouch and Matthew immediately followed suit. There was no reason really except that they were young and it was natural to fall into roles. Right now, they were stalking unknown prey. It could be a *musang*, the civet cat that menaced the chicken population on the estate, a bad-tempered sunbear or even a worker on a secret tryst with a girl. Matthew felt in his pocket for his slingshot. It might even be the assistant manager.

They crawled forward slowly. Rajan parted the leaves

with slender quiet hands, gesturing for Matthew to have the first look. Matthew peered through the bushes and turned red to the roots of his hair, the colour infusing the back of his neck as well.

'What is it?' whispered Rajan.

Matthew raised a finger to his mouth but didn't move or say anything.

Rajan pushed forward until his face was right next to Matthew's peering through the gap.

'Mei Ling,' he breathed.

The Chinese girl, more woman than girl – that much was clear to see – walked out of the water. She was naked except for the sarong around her waist. Water dripped from her hair and down her body. A small pile of clothes by the river indicated that she had decided to go for a swim in that secluded spot.

'We shouldn't be here,' muttered Rajan. 'It's not right.'

Matthew waved a hand at his companion, urging him to be quiet. There was no way he was going to look away. He noted that, despite his scruples, Rajan had not been able to tear his gaze away either.

Slowly, without any urgency, Mei Ling slipped on her skirt and buttoned up her blouse. She flipped her long straight hair over her head and shook it out thoroughly, combing it with long fingers. She slipped on a pair of shoes and walked away slowly. They could hear that she was humming, content after her swim.

Matthew shifted his weight, sat down with his back against a rock and sighed theatrically. 'I think I'm in love!'

'Me too,' whispered the Indian teenager.

***

'I don't like you always being with that girl,' said Rajan's mother.

'What do you mean?'

'Always you're with that Chinese girl from the shop. Before that you were with the manager's son. Why can't you spend time with your own kind?'

'They are my own kind,' snapped Rajan. 'They're young people, the same as me.'

'I got used to your being friends with the manager's son – but I will never get used to that Chinese girl.'

'My friends have names, Amma. Mei Ling and Matthew, not "the manager's son" and "that Chinese girl".'

'You're not too old to feel my belt, Rajan. So be polite to your mother.'

Rajan turned around to face his father. 'And do you agree, Pappa? Do you feel the same way?'

There was a heavy sigh from the older man, so much alike in appearance to his son and so very different in temperament. 'Blood calls to blood, son.'

'And what does that mean?' It was the rudest Rajan had ever been to his father and a small part of him was shocked. But he was too annoyed to pull back. His parents were never happy unless he was toeing the line, keeping up appearances, sticking to his own kind. And what had it got them? A lifetime of servitude and loneliness – his father bowing and scraping before Andrew Coleman, and his mother waiting for the weekly visit of the clerk's wife from a neighbouring estate. And because he had spread his net a little further, he was being subjected to this ridiculous lecture.

'We can only be sure that we have the same values if we stick to our own people,' explained Thomas.

'But you like Mr. Chan!'

'I do – but I do not know him that well.'

'That's a choice *you've* made – I don't see why I should keep my distance from Mei Ling.'

'I will never accept a Chinese girl into the family,' said his mother.

Now they were getting to the crux – this had always been about their chief fear, that Rajan might decide to marry outside their race, not the fact that he was often to be found on the front step of Chan's shop, sipping hot tea and listening to Mei Ling as she expounded her views – derived from her father, he assumed – on the war in Europe and Japanese actions in China.

'I'm only sixteen, Amma – and we're just friends.'

His mother was staring at him, trying to read the truth in his eyes. Rajan forced himself to meet her gaze but he knew that he was not telling the whole truth. His fondness for 'that Chinese girl' had grown into something deeper than friendship. Not that his parents had anything to worry about. He would never find the courage to say anything to Mei Ling. He was too afraid of rejection.

Mrs. Thomas spoke with gloomy comfort. 'Well, I'm sure that horrible woman in the big house is even more worried about her son and that little minx than I'm worried about you.'

***

In this, Mrs. Thomas had been feasting on false comfort. Sarah Coleman was not concerned about any potential or existing relationship between Matthew and Mei Ling. But this was because she was ignorant of the time the two spent together, although usually it was in a trio with Rajan. Further, it would never have crossed her mind that a son of hers would consider a liaison with a native of Malaya, whether Chinese or anything else. He had formed an unhealthy friendship with the clerk's son but, to give Matthew his due, he had not picked up any dirty, ill-bred habits.

Sarah Coleman was nervy and short-tempered but her son was not the cause. She tried to read the papers but the news about the war in Europe was so bad she couldn't continue. The reports were probably wrong anyway, she thought with disgust. And what about the Japanese? They had shown by their attacks on China and Korea that they had territorial ambitions. Her husband was dismissive of the threat. But if he was right, why did that policeman Murray keep coming around with dire warnings? He was here now, singing the same song he had done for months.

'I'm telling you, Coleman, we need a back-up plan,' urged the policeman. His young Malay sidekick, smart in his uniform, stood next to him. They were both members of the colonial police force. The Scot was red-haired with a great big square head, jug ears and green cat-like eyes. His skin was blotchy and peeling, unsuited to the heat of Malaya. By contrast, the young policeman looked like an aristocrat. His long lean face with flaring nostrils and thin lips was completely expressionless as he listened to his superior officer.

'I think you're mad,' said Andrew Coleman. 'You know the Japanese are useless soldiers – they can't even beat the Chinese and they've been trying for years. And,' he leaned forward conspiratorially, 'I've been told they can't fight at night.'

'Who can't fight at night?'

'The Japanese! Their eyesight is bad. Our lads would soon sort them out.'

'That sort of silly tale is precisely why they're going to catch us out.'

Coleman looked sulky, like an overgrown schoolboy. He turned to the Malay policeman, 'What do you think?' he demanded.

'I believe in the British troops, sir.'

'Well, so do I,' said Andrew Coleman, thumping the table with a calloused hand.

Murray scowled at his independent-minded sidekick and motioned for him to leave the room.

'We need contingency planning. We've got to set up some sort of defensive perimeter around the estate – train the Tamils to use firearms. Otherwise there'll be no resistance at all from the civilian population if Japan does invade.'

'Give the Tamils weapons training? Don't you think

I have enough trouble running this estate without having to worry about one of them taking a potshot at me when they've had their skinful of toddy?'

'You're so damned cocksure. But we're suffering terrible losses in Europe. Japan is making huge inroads in Asia.'

'Singapore is impregnable. Surely you can't think Fortress Singapore will be lost?'

'I don't think it. I fear it.'

'Nobody else does.'

'Wars are not won by assuming that the best possible outcome will materialise!'

Sarah Coleman asked, her voice reedy with panic, 'But why do you think these people will side with us in the first place?'

The men looked at her in astonishment. 'Which people?' asked Coleman.

'The natives! They might turn on us, support the Japanese.'

'Nonsense,' said Murray. 'Why would they do that? We've brought huge advantages to this place, done our best to improve the lot of these people. We've made Malaya one vast success story.'

'They can't stand us,' insisted Sarah Coleman.

'You don't really believe that, do you?' asked the Scottish policeman.

'I do. What's more – I know that I'm right!'

'But how can you say that?' asked Andrew Coleman, looking at his wife helplessly.

'Do you really think these men who tap the rubber and

their wives who work in our kitchens love their British masters?'

'The Chinese have no reason to love the Japanese. They won't work with them,' said Murray.

'That's right,' agreed Sarah Coleman. 'They won't. But they're all bloody communists now, so they won't be working for us either. They'll be looking out for themselves and no one else.' She glared at the two men who had fallen silent in the face of her implacable certainty. 'A contingency plan to give the Tamils weapons?' she snorted. 'Only if you want to be shot while you sleep.'

***

Rajan felt guilty. He had arranged to meet Mei Ling and walk down to the village with her. She had some errands to run for her father. But when Matthew had suggested they go fishing, he hadn't told him about his plans. Instead, he had found himself lying – telling his best friend that he had chores at home. He just didn't feel like having Matthew come too. Now he stamped his way through the undergrowth, annoyed with himself for misleading Matthew but thrilled that he would have Mei Ling to himself for a few hours.

She was waiting for him, a tapping foot betraying her usual impatience. He smiled a little – he was a punctual youth, but she was always early.

'Is Matthew coming with us?'

Immediately, frown lines appeared on his forehead.

'Why?' he demanded.

She looked surprised at his trenchant question but answered equably, 'Just thought he might like to come with us, that's all. He usually does.'

'He's busy.'

More lies. What was the matter with him? Rajan would have trusted Matthew with his life – but not, he realised sheepishly, with his girl. His girl? He was getting ahead of himself but he discovered that he liked the idea. Mei Ling was smiling back at him, her expression cheerful and open.

He had to ask, fearing her answer, knowing he was acting like a fool. 'Do you wish he was here?'

She laughed suddenly. 'You are in a funny mood today.' And when he didn't respond, she added, 'No, no, you know my politics and my father's – we have spoken of it often enough. I am quite happy to go for a walk with the *kerani*'s son. The manager's son is too high up in the world for me.'

Rajan grinned happily down at Mei Ling, noticing for the first time that he was a whole head taller than her. 'On the way back from town, I want to show you something,' he said.

He was as good as his word. As they made their way slowly back to the estate, sauntering along the dirt tracks, he suddenly beckoned to her and led the way between the trees.

'What is it?' she asked.

'I told you – I have something to show you.' He walked ahead until they reached the banks of a slow moving river that reminded Rajan of a well-fed python. He reached under a bush, found the end of a rope and hauled out a small skiff, flat-bottomed and worn.

He gestured for Mei Ling to get in.

'I don't want to go for a swim,' she warned.

Rajan laughed. 'It's safe, I promise.'

She got in carefully, tucked her legs under her and trailed a hand in the water.

'There might be crocodiles,' he said.

She pulled her hand back and scowled at Rajan, who was grinning at her.

Rajan could never understand how anyone who spent so much time on an estate could know so little about the environment around her. But he knew Mei Ling walked along oblivious to her surroundings, her mind grappling with some idea she had found in a book that her father had given her. Rajan had read one or two – fortunately most of them were in Chinese and therefore inaccessible to him – putting up with Matthew's friendly teasing at his newfound interest in political tracts, to try and keep up. He had almost laughed out loud from time to time. Women's rights and workers' rights? A world in which his mother thought herself the equal of his father and his father the equal of the white manager? That would be the day.

'So, why are we going on a boat trip?' asked Mei Ling. Her words were impatient but her tone languid. The timelessness of the river was having a soothing effect, even on the young rebel.

'Just wait,' he said in a hushed tone.

'It's getting dark,' she complained, lowering her tone

instinctively to match his.

'It's almost time,' he replied and almost before the words had been swallowed up by the darkness, millions of pinpoints of light suddenly dotted the heavy foliage along the river banks and floated above the waters.

'What is it?' breathed Mei Ling.

He could see that her eyes were wide with wonderment, the whites almost as bright as the fairy lights.

'Fireflies,' he explained. 'They come out at night along this part of the river.'

She smiled at him and he smiled back, wondering whether he dared reach over and take her hand.

***

'A spot of fishing?' suggested Matthew. 'I think the fish are hungry today.' He was lying under a *dedap* tree, his head pillowed on his hands. A velvety red flower fell on his chest and he brushed it away with a lazy hand.

'I said I'd call in on Mei Ling,' confessed Rajan.

Matthew sat up at this. 'What in the world for?' he demanded. 'So you can sit and listen to her spout communist nonsense with a daft look on your face?'

'I do not,' retorted Rajan. 'She's just interested in politics, that's all.'

'I know what *you're* interested in …'

'It's not like that.'

'I bet it isn't. Don't tell me you look at her and think about Malayan politics. You're thinking about what we saw that time at the fishing hole!'

'We shouldn't have looked. We should have left.'

'What? And missed the show? Don't be such a prude. It was good fun.'

'That doesn't make it right.'

'It doesn't make it wrong either,' said Matthew. 'You've been such a bore. Most of the summer you've been hanging around with Mei Ling instead of me.'

'Don't be silly. We're all three friends, aren't we?'

'I'm the bloody spare wheel, more like.'

'Look, why don't you come with me?' asked Rajan, remembering all the times he had sneaked off with Mei Ling that holiday, consciously excluding his best friend. He got to his feet, dusted himself off and leaned over, hand extended, to drag Matthew to his feet too.

'Maybe I will come along,' said Matthew, accepting the proffered hand. 'But I promise you I won't be listening to Mei Ling's daft theories – I'll just be looking, and remembering …'

Rajan didn't like Matthew's sly, lascivious tone. He didn't mind it particularly when they were talking about the girls in Penang or some actress featured in the local newspapers. But it wasn't right when it was about Mei Ling.

'Maybe I'll suggest we all go for a swim together – I bet you'd like that,' continued Matthew.

Rajan grabbed his friend by the shoulders and shook him. 'Stop it! Stop talking about Mei Ling like that.'

'Make me.'

In a moment the two friends were in the dust, wrestling

furiously. Matthew was taller and stronger but Rajan had a wiry strength that he was putting to good use. It was over as quickly as it had begun. Rajan managed to push him off. Matthew rolled over on his back and lay still, staring up at the pattern of leaves against the blue sky. Rajan could hear him panting next to him but the other boy had recognised the implicit truce as well.

'I'm sorry,' said Matthew. 'I just wanted to get back at you for spending so much time with Mei Ling.'

'You're my best friend, Matthew,' said Rajan. 'You know that!'

The slim Englishman with the bright blue eyes nodded reluctantly. 'I guess you're right.' He added, unable to keep the bitter note out of his voice, 'But it was better before she came here.'

'You know you don't mean that.'

Matthew did not respond for a moment despite Rajan's reproachful tone. At last he sat up and slapped Rajan on the back. 'Let's face it – she'd never agree to a swim anyway!'

'Well, what are we waiting for?' grinned Rajan. 'Let's visit Mei Ling and find out how the war in China is going!'

CHAPTER 4

December 8, 1941, a date that will live on in infamy. That's what Roosevelt said after the Japs attacked Pearl Harbor. But the attack on the Americans meant nothing to us. Do you remember – it was that same day that the Japanese invaded Malaya? They landed in Kota Bahru and started advancing down the Peninsula on their damned bicycles. No one, it seems, in the entire British Army, had anticipated that the Japanese might attack from the north, approaching Singapore through Malaya.

My mother insisted that we evacuate. You must believe that I would have preferred to stay. Malaya was my home – you were my family. In many ways, it seems to me that everything that came next, that tore our lives apart, that turned you and me from brothers to strangers, can be traced back to that day.

The Scots policeman sped up the driveway, yelling the news even as he leapt out of the Land Rover. He was scarlet-faced with anger and excitement, his accent reverting to its original Glaswegian under the pressure of circumstances.

'They landed in Kota Bahru last night! The Nips have landed in Kota Bahru!'

'I don't believe you.' Andrew Coleman was pale with shock under his tan.

'It's true. I heard it on the official wires.'

'What's going on? What's happened?' Sarah Coleman hurried into the room.

'Murray says the Japanese have landed in Kota Bahru.' Coleman could not state it as a fact – it was still an opinion, the policeman's opinion. There was room for doubt, for him to change his mind, for it all to turn out to be some gross error.

Sarah Coleman screamed, a shrill animal sound. She flew at her husband, pummelling him with angry balled fists. He grabbed her wrists and held her away from him, uncertain what to do. Matthew was watching from the doorway, his face frozen in shock. The planter shifted his grip until he held his wife's hands with one of his own. He used the other to slap her across the cheek. He hit her hard, harder than he meant to because he was off balance. The imprint of four beefy fingers was clear and red against her wan cheek. Matthew rushed to his mother and she turned and collapsed into her sixteen-year-old son's arms. In that instant she ceased to be his carer and he became hers. The natural order of things had been reversed by the shock of the moment, by the onset of war.

Matthew glared at his father, tears in his eyes. 'Why did you do that? What's happened?'

Andrew Coleman was unconsciously flexing his hand.

He looked at his son, opened his mouth to speak and closed it again.

Again, it was the Scot who delivered the news. 'The Japanese have invaded Malaya.'

The boy asked the first coherent question of the evening. 'Will they succeed?'

Andrew Coleman was all bristling moustache and bluster. 'Of course not, my boy! Singapore will reinforce the troops we have along the Peninsula. We'll soon have the buggers on the run.'

'They flattened Pearl Harbor,' said Murray.

'But they caught the Americans napping!'

'I fear they've caught us napping too.'

A silence followed this statement.

'We have to get out. We need to get to Penang … or Singapore!' Sarah Coleman was still holding her cheek where she had been struck.

'I don't think there's any need to panic, ma'am. We'll have plenty of warning if we need to evacuate.'

'I'm leaving in the morning and I'm taking Matthew with me!'

'So soon?' asked Matthew, turning to his father for confirmation.

Andrew Coleman was still struggling with the news, uncertain what was the best course of action. He regretted that he had not listened to the policeman and organised some sort of defence.

'Yes, in the morning,' said Sarah.

All those present realised that there was no arguing with

her. Her mind was made up.

'I can't leave so soon,' exclaimed Andrew.

'I don't care,' said his wife, seventeen years of bitterness contained in the swift look she gave him.

'I have to tell Rajan,' said Matthew.

Sarah Coleman opened her mouth to protest, to insist that he stayed at home, safe by her side, until they could flee together but the boy had sprinted out of the open doors on to the veranda and down the grassy verge, his shirt-tails flapping behind him, before she had a chance to speak.

Sarah Coleman turned to her husband and said crisply, her immediate panic channelled into a steely resolve to keep Matthew safe, 'I'll need the car, a driver, a couple of guards and all the money you have.'

Coleman nodded. His eyes were bloodshot, the pupils dilated in panic. 'All right. But I have to pay the staff. I don't know what's going to happen to them …'

'I don't care!' snapped Sarah Coleman.

***

'Rajan!'

The boy with the fishing line turned his head and grinned at his friend. It was late evening. The sky was a cloudy purple, the trees black solid shapes. He had not been expecting Matthew out again.

He nodded towards a spool lying further up the bank.

'One more for you.'

Matthew shook his head, his fine hair dark with sweat.

His friend noticed for the first time that Matthew was as pale as the underbelly of a fish and out of breath from running.

'What is it?' he asked, flicking his line out of the water, the earthworm still wound around the hook. His bucket was empty beside him. The fish were not biting – although, he thought ruefully, as he scratched the welts on his arm, the mosquitoes certainly were.

Matthew was still panting. He bent over and put his hands on his knees, trying to steady himself.

Rajan got to his feet. He had never seen his friend like this, ashen, worried, silent. He asked again, 'Is anything the matter?'

'The Japanese have landed in Kota Bahru.'

'I don't understand.'

'The Japanese – they've attacked Malaya. They're on their way south, towards Penang and the rest of the country.'

'My father says that the British will have no problem defeating them. It will all be over in a few days.'

Matthew shook his head, trying to make his friend see. 'You don't understand. My mother wants to evacuate.'

'What do you mean?'

'We have to leave – before the Japanese get here. My father still has work to do. But Mother says she and I are leaving in the morning.'

'But where are you going?'

'Singapore, I expect … then on a ship back to England or wherever we can get safe passage.'

'You're running away?'

'Damn it, Rajan! It's war. The Japanese are not going to be very nice to any of the British they find hanging around.'

'What about the rest of us?'

Matthew was silent. He looked down at his feet. At last, he said, 'I don't know.'

'We have nowhere to go – this is our home.'

He looked at Matthew who had come to warn him, or to confess that he was not going to be a friend – not now, not this time with the Japanese advancing on their bicycles down the coast.

'You're really going?' he asked.

'I have no choice.' Matthew added, and it sounded as if he meant it, 'I would prefer to stay, you know that.'

The Indian boy nodded.

Matthew held out a hand. Rajan hesitated for one long moment, their friendship hanging on the distance between them. Finally, he shook his friend's hand.

'Good luck. I'll see you when this is over,' said the English youth.

Rajan glanced around, his hand still clasping Matthew's.

The light was fading. The rubber trees were swaying gently. An ochre leaf swirled in a spiral, caught up in a gust that also brought the familiar stench of processed rubber. He blinked once, expecting the scene to change – that there would be some portent, some acknowledgment in the surroundings of the tumultuous news. A bullfrog croaked, a melancholy but profoundly ordinary sound. Nature was unmoved.

'I have to tell my father!' exclaimed Rajan suddenly. He looked at his best friend. 'Good luck to you too,' he added, his voice breaking slightly. He spun round and ran into the darkness and was soon lost in the deepening shadows of dusk evolving into night. Matthew turned away and trudged back towards the big house.

Rajan reached home and shouted for his father. There was no response and he ran into the bedrooms looking for him. He found his mother sitting on the bed in the spare room, a dumpy Buddha-like figure with tears running down her cheeks.

Rajan stopped at the door abruptly. He put one hand on the frame and asked, 'You've heard the news?'

She stared at him, unseeing, blinded by her tears.

'You've heard the news?' he asked again.

She nodded once and dabbed her eyes on the long train of her *saree*. Rajan thought that it was a useful piece of clothing that could double as a handkerchief and then wondered that his mind had space for such trivia.

'Where is Pappa?'

'Gone out.'

'Where has he gone? I must see him. Tell him!'

'He knows. He has gone to discuss with the other men what to do. Das came with the news. He heard it on the radio.'

Rajan knew that 'other men' could only mean Das, Chan and the hospital assistant, Ibrahim. No one else would be considered useful or worthy by his father. The only other person whose views would interest him would be the manager but he would not presume to seek out Andrew Coleman.

Rajan patted his mother on the arm and then sped out of the house. Night had fallen. The only noise was the raspy, echoing sound of the cicadas in their ear-hurting, night-time chorus.

He found his father where he expected to find him – outside the sundry shop with Chan and Das. Mei Ling was sitting on a low wooden stool listening intently to what the men were saying. Her heart-shaped face was serious and she was chewing on her lower lip. Rajan slowed down to a walk and approached the men.

His father looked up, saw him. 'Don't bother me now, Rajan,' he said reflexively.

Rajan nodded but was unable to keep from blurting out, 'Matthew is leaving!'

'How do you know that, boy?' asked Chan, his tone sharp and anxious.

'He told me. Matthew just told me.'

'What about the manager?' It was Das, his tall lanky frame silhouetted against the entrance to the shop so that it seemed to Rajan that a shadow had suddenly found its voice.

'He's staying for now.'

'I told you what would happen!' Despite his words, there was no triumph in Chan's voice. Whatever it was he felt vindicated about, it did not give him pleasure.

Rajan moved around to stand next to Mei Ling. He glanced down at her once and saw that her expression was one of fierce concentration, her eyebrows drawn together to form a single line. She showed none of the fear and uncertainty he was feeling. He straightened up and tried to emulate her attitude. He could almost feel his spine stiffen, as if it was something that could be achieved by an act of will.

'It is right that they evacuate the women and children. The British will not get any mercy from the Japanese.' Das sounded defensive.

Chan turned his head and aimed a globule of frothy saliva on to the red dirt next to his feet. 'You think *we* will get mercy?' he snapped. 'You have heard what they have done in China? The Japanese are a cruel people. They will destroy Malaya and we will have no way to defend ourselves because our so-called masters will have run for their lives.'

Thomas spoke, his voice a thin sound, without texture. 'I think the Japanese will not be so bad. They are Asians like us. They have come to liberate us – that is what they say, anyway. Maybe we should give them the benefit of the doubt.'

'If you believe that you're a fool!' snapped Chan.

Rajan was shocked by the attack on his father. He felt Mei Ling quiver beside him as if the words had run through her veins like a mild electric shock.

'Let's not quarrel amongst ourselves,' said Das, always the peacemaker. 'We need to stick together.'

'I'm sorry, Thomas,' apologised Chan.

Rajan saw his father nod in the dim light although he could sense from his ramrod straight posture that his anger with the other man had not ebbed. With the insight that the young can bring to an adult dispute, Rajan realised that Chan was lashing out in fear. He was terrified of the Japanese, terrified of the news, terrified for his family.

Rajan felt his own heart turn over with fear for the girl beside him.

'Chan, you will be a target.' Das spoke with sympathy.

Rajan didn't understand the remark. Why Chan? What about the rest of them?

'I know.'

'What will you do?' asked Das

'I heard from the communist leadership that they're going to co-operate with the British to defend Malaya. There is a school that has been set up for military training. I've been asked to go. I will do it. I will fight the Japanese if given an opportunity.'

Rajan couldn't believe his ears. Mei Ling's father was going to take up arms against the Japanese? But that was the surest way of ensuring that the Japanese would single out his family for retaliation. If even a tenth of the stories Mei Ling had told him that summer about the Japanese in China were true, they would not balk at collective punishment.

'What about your *family*?'

It took Rajan an instant to realise he had spoken. His tongue had acted independently of his brain. His father glared at him for intruding into the adult conversation. The words were spoken though and he did not regret it.

'I don't know,' said Chan. 'If we lose, I don't know what will happen.'

'Are you sure you're doing the right thing? Isn't it better to lie low and see how things turn out?' asked Thomas.

Rajan guessed that the courage of the slightly overweight, middle-aged Chinese man had impressed him.

'I cannot do it,' said Chan. He grinned at the other men, square white teeth gleaming like the Cheshire cat, 'There's always place for one more – do either of you want to come along and learn how to fire a gun?'

Das laughed. 'I'd shoot my foot off on the first day!'

They all chuckled. The big Indian was known for the clumsiness that sometimes turned his size and strength against him so that he was a walking liability to his own wellbeing.

'How about you, Thomas?' asked Chan.

'I choose to believe that the Japanese will not be as bad as the British. I will wait to be proved wrong,' replied the *kerani*.

CHAPTER 5

In the end, despite Mother's worries, it was an uneventful trip to Singapore. We rode in my father's Austin. Our driver was competent, the roads were empty. My clearest memory is of boredom on the drive south punctuated with the excitement of watching truckloads of Australian troops being moved north to defend the Jitra line in Kedah. The men were cheerful, returning my waves and smiling and chatting amongst themselves. It made me feel more confident.

We had to wait a few weeks in Singapore. We were billeted in government quarters. Mother wouldn't let me go out much. We needed to stay put for news on whether we had a passage on any of the boats leaving. No one was being given much notice of evacuation.

I remember her sitting in the front room, neatly dressed in one of her floral frocks, her two hands wrapped around a mug of tea, staring down the driveway all day. She grew old before my eyes and there was nothing I could do. A first indication, I suppose, of the helplessness that war brings. It was a lesson I was taught over and over again.

Matthew sat outdoors. He leaned against a pillar, staring at the plumes of smoke that were spiralling into the air in the distance. They looked like smoke signals, he decided, communicating the news that Singapore, under constant attack from Japanese warplanes, was burning.

The newspapers and radio stations in Singapore were putting a brave face on the war in Malaya, talking up the troops and emphasising their valour in battle. Matthew read the papers every day and fed his mother snippets of information like an intravenous drip feed to a terminally ill patient, trying to bolster her confidence in the outcome.

But the armies of refugees, mostly Chinese, pouring into Singapore told a different story. They spoke in hushed tones of the Japanese troops racing down the only road from north to south, defeating demoralised British and Indian troops. Where there were pockets of stiff resistance, the Japanese cut into the jungles or the rubber estates and circled past the troops, cutting off their supply lines so that they had no option but to surrender.

There was no attempt to hide the news of the sinking of the *Prince of Wales* and the *Repulse* just outside Kuantan. The two warships had steamed north to intercept the Japanese, unaware that all the airfields in northern Malaya were already in Japanese hands. The aircraft carrier that had been intended to escort the ships had run aground before reaching Singapore. In the absence of air cover, the two ships were both sunk with great loss of life. Matthew saw grown men weep when they heard the news of the sinking of the flagships of the British Navy. His mother was hysterical.

Finally, a young trooper, his uniform dusty and his face streaked with soot, came cycling up the driveway. Matthew's mother rushed out, her skirts billowing and her face damp with sweat. Her mouth opened although no words were forthcoming. She didn't dare speak and find out that yet again there was no way off the increasingly vulnerable island. But this time it was good news.

'There's passage on a troopship leaving tomorrow,' said the messenger.

'Where to?'

'Heading for Colombo.'

Matthew nodded. 'We'll be there.'

***

'We must destroy the rubber trees,' said Coleman, eyeing his subordinates warily. He did not expect his news to go down well.

'What do you mean?' asked Thomas.

'We must slash the trees. Otherwise the Japanese will exploit the rubber for their war effort.'

Andrew Coleman's face was mottled and his voice hoarse. In a mere few weeks, the Japanese had pedalled halfway to Singapore. Accurate information was hard to come by. Coleman had continued running the estate, relieved that he had fallen in with Sarah's wish to take Matthew away so soon after the Japanese invasion. She had been more accurate than him about the speed of the advance. At least he had the comfort of knowing his son was safe.

Andrew knew he would have to get out soon if he was to make it to Singapore safely. He no longer doubted that the battle for Malaya was over. The Japanese were going to emerge victorious. But Fortress Singapore was impregnable. He was confident of that. All he had to do was make sure that he had the resources to get there. Some of the other planters had already abandoned their estates. His own assistant manager planned to set out that day.

Coleman had waited for news of whether the British expected to launch an operation to recapture Malaya in the short term, in which case there was no point sabotaging the rubber trees. But no word had come from anyone with even a semblance of authority. Murray was his only contact, even if he was just a colonial policeman, and he insisted that the Japanese would have a free hand. The war was lost. The trees should be sabotaged.

'But they are our livelihood,' protested Thomas.

Andrew Coleman leaned forward, his stubby fingers splayed on the surface of the desk. 'This is a British-owned and British-run plantation, and it will not be turned over to the Japanese!'

Das interjected, scowling at Thomas to be quiet. 'Sir, I understand why you wish to slash the trees. It will halt production. But the Japanese might retaliate against the workers if the property is destroyed.'

'That is a risk that must be taken.' Coleman took a deep breath and added with forced calm, 'The Japanese won't even bother to take over the estate if the trees are ruined. It will work out better for the workers this way. They will be left alone.'

'But we will not be able to earn a living if the rubber trees are destroyed,' explained Das, still trying to be reasonable.

Rajan appeared at the door of the office and the men turned to look at him.

'What is it, son?'

'I just wanted to know from the manager if there was any news of Matthew.'

Coleman was touched by the boy's distress. 'No, I'm afraid not. I know they got to Singapore.'

Rajan nodded. He already knew that.

'But there's been no news since. I assume that they're waiting for transport to get them out of Singapore,' continued Coleman.

'Your son is in Singapore waiting to escape. Soon you will do the same thing. But your legacy to us is to destroy my only way of feeding my family, my son?' Thomas walked over to the manager, so much bigger than him, and pointed a thin finger at him from a distance of a few feet. 'Let me tell you this. I am not going to do what you ask. I will *not* ruin the trees.'

***

The assistant manager, Johnson, was glad to be on his way. He straddled his motorbike, his leather suitcase strapped on the back. There were no four-wheeled vehicles to spare for his expedition south. The manager had insisted the Land Rover be left for his use. It was a dangerous business, trying to get to Singapore. The last he had heard, the Japanese had reached Kuala Lumpur. Johnson was reasonably confident there was still time for him to make his escape. He rode slowly through the estate. The sky was a metallic grey. The air was completely still, presaging the high swirling winds of a tropical rainstorm that would rip the leaves off trees and obscure the way with driving sheets of rain.

He saw a tapper by the side of the road. The man was signalling furiously, waving his wiry arms in a frantic windmill. Johnson was in two minds as to whether to stop. He wanted to be on the main road before the storm broke. The dirt track became a muddy river in heavy rain.

It was probably a message from the manager. It might even be about the war situation. Johnson pulled up, spraying dirt on the labourer who put up his hands to protect his face.

'What is it?' he snapped in Tamil.

'It is about my daughter, sir.'

'What about her?'

'She has been living with you these last few months.'

Johnson scowled. So this was Shanti's father – a fine time for him to crawl out from the rubber trees. He probably wanted money. He waited for the request, folding his arms to signal that it would be refused.

'Shanti is pregnant.'

Johnson rubbed his eyes with the palms of his hands. This was a damned nuisance. He didn't want to leave any half-breeds running around to embarrass him when the war was over. The father would have his wish. He would have to pay for the problem to go away.

'How much do you need?' he demanded.

Shanti's father looked at him impassively. Under the dark skies, his skin was shiny ebony. The whites of his eyes gleamed.

Johnson could not see any resemblance to the dainty young woman who had caught his eye on the plantation. Shanti had thick black hair in a single plait, plump cheeks and a flirtatious smile.

He said impatiently, 'I'm in a hurry – how much will it cost to get rid of the child?'

There was no answer from the other man.

Individual drops of rain fell like large teardrops. Johnson glanced up at the sky. He said sharply, 'I have to go.'

The tapper shook his head. He held up his staff and pointed it at the Englishman. 'You have ruined my daughter.'

'I've offered you money. What more do you want?'

The Tamil man's curly black hair unfurled under the weight of the rain but his eyes remained fixed on the planter. 'There is nothing you can do that will return my daughter to me.'

'Have it your way. I must go.'

He revved his motorbike.

Quick as lightning, the tapper stabbed the staff into the spokes of the front wheel.

The bike flipped over and Johnson flew over the handlebars. He lay on the ground, shaken.

Shanti's father walked over to him. Johnson raised himself on one elbow and shouted, 'What do you think you're doing?'

'I am here to see that you pay for what you did to my

Shanti.'

Johnson tried to get up, but his right knee buckled under him.

The tapper took two steps forward, the rain coursing down his face like tears. He swung the staff and hit the man across the forehead. There was a resounding crack, echoed by a burst of thunder.

Johnson fell forward into the mud, his arms sprawled out in front of him.

The Tamil turned the body over. He raised one eyelid and peered at the glassy pale blue eye of the assistant manager. He smiled. In the new world order, with the Japanese coming, revenge was possible even for an estate coolie.

***

Coleman marched towards the labour lines. He passed gardeners pruning the lush, green hedges and tappers, buckets of latex balanced on each end of a pole on their shoulders. They inclined their heads respectfully. There was no insubordination here. The manager continued past the small dispensary and saw a few workers huddled along the benches, wrapped in old sarongs and layers of clothes for warmth. Malaria, he guessed. It was the bane of the workers and endemic in all the plantations.

Das had suggested a hardship fund to help the families of those who were unable to work from malaria but he had resisted the idea. Coleman remembered telling Das that he didn't want to foster a culture of dependence. Coleman headed towards the rows of one-room dwellings in parallel lines that formed the workers quarters, noting the cement floors, corrugated zinc roofs and damp patches on the walls and ceilings for the first time. Perhaps he should have done more to make the place habitable.

It was the middle of the day so most of the men and women were out in the plantation, tipping the latex into tin buckets and rushing them towards central collection areas to make sure they hit their quota for the day. Failure to do so led to the withholding of wages. A few very young children were running around naked in the dusty front yards of their dwellings. Women watched them while they washed clothes vigorously, scrubbing them against ridged pieces of wood in large basins. Coleman supposed that the older children were at the Tamil language school or working. With the huge demand for rubber because of the war in Europe there had been an acute labour shortage. Coleman had turned a blind eye, despite Das's protests, to younger children being sent out to tap rubber.

The sun came out from behind a cloud. The air shimmered with heat. Coleman felt his brow pop with beads of sweat. A few trickled into his eyes making them smart. He wiped his eyes with his knuckles like a small child and continued to wait. It was almost time for lunch and the workers would soon be back for their *tiffin*, a mountain of rice with a curry.

He had decided to bypass his *kerani* and the foreman. He would instruct the workers to destroy the trees directly. Coleman had no fear of being disobeyed. Tamil workers were the labourers of choice on the estates because of their willingness to do repetitive chores, their docility and their obedience to authority. The planters from Ceylon and Burma had admired these traits and when they had been called away from their tea estates to run the rubber plantations of Malaya, they had turned to the same source of workers. Andrew Coleman did not expect trouble.

A few men drifted in and Coleman shouted to them in Tamil, 'All of you, come here. I have something to tell you.'

The men gathered, promptly joined by the rest of the workforce. The Tamils were dark and wiry, their muscles like ropes under the skin. They wore vests and sarongs tucked above their knees. Their sunburnt faces were shiny with sweat, their hands calloused and clothes splattered with latex. The men were curious to hear what the manager had to say to them without his usual intermediary, the conductor, Das.

'The Japanese have invaded Malaya.'

There was a rush of murmurs through the crowd, like wind in the trees. They had heard the news but now the white manager was here to confirm it in person.

'The Japanese, they want the rubber from the plantations so that they can win this war against Britain.'

There were nods at this.

'War requires sacrifice ... we must destroy the trees.'

There were loud gasps of shock at this and one or two exclamations of 'No!'

'I am ordering you to slash the trees. That is your work this afternoon.'

'That is their work this afternoon ... what is their work tomorrow?'

Coleman turned around. It was Das who had approached so silently that no one had noticed him, so engrossed were the labourers in what the manager was saying.

'Stay out of this, Das!' barked Coleman in English.

'I'm sorry, sir. I cannot let you do this.'

'They will obey me,' said Coleman.

Das turned to the labourers and spoke loudly, 'If we slash the trees, we will have no work tomorrow or the next day or the day after that. We do not know how long the Japanese will be here or what they will want from us. The British are leaving. Many have left already. Our manager will soon be gone. Are we to be left with nothing?'

'Is it true that you will be going?' It was one of the men in the front row asking the question of the manager but looking from one man to the other for an answer. It was inconceivable to them that Das and the manager should be speaking with different voices, disagreeing on what should be done. The manager was the boss. The conductor was his eyes, ears and right arm.

'I have to go,' said Coleman. 'It's not safe for us in Malaya anymore.'

'It is not safe for *any* of us.' Das turned to the Tamils. 'Go back to your work. We will not slash the trees. They are our livelihood.'

There was a muttering amongst the men. A few looked at the manager, apprehension and uncertainty reflected in their sooty eyes. Slowly they dispersed, walking away to their homes to have some lunch and get back to work.

Coleman watched them go. He thought about using the

rifle he had slung over his shoulder to shoot one of them. To make the point that he was serious and consequences would flow from their failure to follow his instructions. He could do it with impunity. It was a wartime situation and these men were hindering the defensive efforts.

Coleman noticed Das watching him as though able to guess the tactics he was contemplating. Coleman slung his gun off his shoulder and trained it on the man who had defied his attempt to sabotage the estate.

'I should kill you for your work today. You are a traitor to Britain.'

'You may be right. But your way would make me a traitor to my people.'

Coleman hesitated and then let the gun barrel dip. 'When I get back, I will see you punished for this.'

If Das was relieved to see that the manager had decided against summary justice, he did not show it. Instead, he inclined his head to acknowledge the promise.

'Despite that, sir, I truly hope that Britain wins this war and that you return to Malaya to take over this estate again.'

***

Rajan caught up with his father and grabbed his arm, tugging on it to get his attention.

'What is it, son?'

'What's going to happen to us?'

'What do you mean?'

'You disobeyed the manager, Mr. Coleman. What will he

do to you … to us? Will you lose your job?'

'I don't know, Rajan. There's not much he can do now and the job isn't worth much. If the British ever come back to Malaya … then I don't know. He will not easily forget or forgive what I did today.'

'Pappa, Mr. Chan says that the Japanese are *worse* than the British.' The boy's voice was soft.

'I know that. The Chinese in Nanking and elsewhere have suffered terribly at the hands of the Japanese.'

'So why are we siding with them?'

'We are *not* siding with them. We are just waiting to see what happens. The Japanese may not treat the Indians in Malaya as badly as the Chinese. They are very keen for Indians to rebel against the British in India.' He laughed although there was no genuine humour in it. 'It would make it very difficult for the British if the jewel of their Empire turned against them. After all, many of their troops are Indian. Even here in Malaya, it is the Indians who bear the brunt of the fighting.'

Rajan nodded. It was the Third Indian Division – a source of pride but also worry to his father – that was the first line of defence against the Japanese.

'In fact, the Japanese will definitely treat the Indians well. Can you imagine it if they persuade the soldiers from India to change sides?'

'Would they do that?'

Thomas shrugged his narrow shoulders to express his ignorance, 'I have no idea. Anyway, it means that we should not assume that the Japanese are our enemies.'

Rajan did not often contradict his father. He was full of respect for the stern, neatly dressed man who effectively ran the estate but, for the sake of his family, kept his opinions to himself to *kowtow* to his white masters. Until today. His father had rebelled against Coleman and now he was going to contradict his father. Perhaps it was a sign of things to come.

'What about the Chans?' asked Rajan.

'What about them?'

'Mr. Chan has gone.'

Thomas sighed. 'Yes, he has gone to join the fight against the Japanese.'

'Because he knows the Chinese in Malaya will not be well-treated!'

Thomas put a hand on his son's shoulder. It was a gesture of affection and solidarity so rare that Rajan could not remember his ever having done it before. Rajan felt a lump in his throat and swallowed hard. This was not a time to show weakness. Thomas, who had suffered so much humiliation at the hands of the British, had adopted some of their cultural tenets as the standard of behaviour he expected, and a stiff upper lip was the least of what he demanded of himself – and his son. Expressed emotion reflected, in his view, a lack of moral courage.

'Yes, that is partly the reason. But Chan is also a brave man who feels he must defend Malaya against this invasion even if it means siding with the British for once,' explained Thomas.

Rajan said, his tone subdued, 'I am worried about Mei

Ling … and the rest of the family.'

'If the Japanese find out about Chan's activities – well, it could be hard for them,' agreed Thomas.

'Pappa,' said Rajan, finally screwing up the courage to explain what was bothering him, 'If we know that the Japanese are going to be cruel to the Chinese, including people we know, I think we should destroy the rubber trees. We have to be loyal to our friends.'

Thomas's mood changed and he cuffed the youth on the side of the head. 'We have to do what is best for *our* family – and I will decide what that is.'

***

Chan was not impressed by his training or the equipment he'd been given. He thought wistfully that at least his wife would be pleased. On the limited rations they were being fed at the Special Training School 101 that had been established in Kuala Lumpur, he would soon lose his comfortable paunch.

'I am determined – do you hear me? – determined to turn you lot into a fighting force that will take on the Nips in the unlikely event of a British defeat in Malaya.'

Captain Chapman, the British soldier in charge of the camp, was an optimist, decided Chan, if he thought he could turn the ragtag bunch of communists at his disposal into a threat. The captain was sweating in the sunshine, lecturing his thirsty-looking troops with a combination of bravado and desperation. Chapman wanted his Chinese charges to take on the Japanese. Chan was not so sanguine. He was one of the older comrades and did not feel that a couple of weeks being taught how to use grenades and plant roadside bombs was going to turn the course of the war. They didn't even have uniforms, just the clothes they had arrived in. Although there were weapons, they had to turn them in every evening. Their British trainers wanted them to fight but they still didn't want to go to bed at night knowing that the commies were armed. Chan didn't really blame them. There was no love lost between the British and the Malayan communists. A number of his companions at the training camp had arrived directly from a British jail. Still, in light of how badly the war was going and with the decimation of their forces in northern Malaya, the British were going to have to make up their minds to trust them.

'After all,' said Chan to one of the other raw recruits resting under an acacia tree on the school field in Kuala Lumpur when the training was finally over for the day, 'My enemy's enemy is my friend!'

His companion grinned, exposing teeth that were brown from chewing tobacco. 'For me, I am pleased to get out of jail. I am happy to fight the Japanese. After we beat the Japanese, we must fight the British again.'

Chan laughed. 'You are thinking a long way ahead, my friend.'

**

Coleman had sent the family ahead in the polished, black Austin with the red leather seats. He took the plantation

Land Rover. It didn't belong to him but there was no one left to protest.

He explained to Murray that the workers had refused to destroy the trees. The Scotsman was less shocked than Coleman expected.

'I've heard a few stories like that,' he said. 'Your wife was right – these people have no reason to love us.'

'I don't accept that. We made Malaya what it is. The lack of gratitude is absolutely shocking.'

'My policemen have stayed loyal. But they're mostly Malay.'

'Should we ask them to help destroy the trees? Can you spare any men?' asked Coleman.

The policeman shook his head. 'I don't think that would be a good idea. If the workers resist, we could set off a civil war right here.'

'They won't fight,' said Coleman.

'I don't suppose you thought they would disobey an order from you either.'

Coleman chewed on the straggly ends of his moustache but didn't retaliate. It was true. He hadn't anticipated the rebellion on the estates. He remembered the insubordination of Thomas and Das and felt a vein start to throb in his forehead.

Murray looked at him in alarm. 'What's the matter? You don't look well.'

'It's nothing. Just remembering Das and Thomas – they were the ringleaders.'

'I always thought you had Thomas well and truly under your thumb.'

'It's Das who shocked me most,' complained Coleman. 'I was sure, with his background, that he would have shown more loyalty.'

'Background?'

'He was brought up by English missionaries in Madras.'

Murray cracked his knuckles.

Coleman noticed for the first time that he looked exhausted. 'Has it been rough?' he asked.

'A bit,' admitted the policeman. 'The Japanese are overrunning the Peninsula. It's a struggle to get the evacuees out. And orders from on top are to give assistance only to *white* British residents, not Eurasians. That's causing a lot of anger. Some of these Eurasians have British passports!'

'Well, you'll be glad to know that I don't need your help. I'm going to drive this Land Rover right down to Singapore, find my family and get on a ship out of there.'

'That's a good plan. I hope you have better luck than poor Johnson.'

'Yes, that was bloody unlucky – coming off his bike and cracking his skull even before he got off the plantation. He was a fool to keep going in the storm. The tracks are treacherous in the wet.'

'You'd better get going,' warned Murray. 'I've heard that the Japs have reached Muar. Gemas has fallen.'

Coleman didn't need further encouragement. He jumped quickly into his vehicle. His small bag of personal belongings was in the back. He'd been warned that there was no point bringing anything more. Singapore was bursting at the seams.

Coleman stared out of the window at his sprawling home of the last few years. 'I suppose the Japanese manager will move in ... it will be easy to take over the trappings – not so easy to make this place work. They have no experience in running rubber plantations.'

Murray did not respond to these words shouted over the engine noise. Instead he put up his hand in a gesture of farewell. This was not the time to point out to the incensed Englishman that his rebellious subordinates, not him, had been running the estate for years.

***

Coleman's journey began uneventfully. He drove down the laterite roads. Crimson dust clung to his tyres and covered the windscreen in a thin layer of grime. In half an hour he had reached the outskirts of the estate and swung the vehicle on to the main road towards the South. He'd been driving for an hour when to his surprise, a soldier suddenly emerged from the foliage.

He hesitated for one long second and then pulled over.

'Thanks, mate,' said the trooper. Blood seeped from a bandage around his head. He was covered in mud and grease and limped painfully. 'When I saw that you were a white fella, I decided it was the last chance to save my skin.'

'What's happening?' asked Coleman, glancing quickly at the soldier and then back up the road.

'We put up a bit of a stand at Muar – with the Indians – but ran out of ammo and food. No planes to re-supply us. Finally, we were told it was every man for himself. I volunteered to stay behind with the injured … to look after them until they could surrender.' He shook his head at the memory and Coleman had a sudden vision of torn and burnt flesh. 'When I heard the Japanese advancing, I made for cover – I thought I might get another chance to fight if I made a break for it.'

Coleman nodded approvingly but the soldier had not finished. 'I saw what they did.'

'What?'

'The Nips … they kicked and beat the injured men. I mean, they were harmless … and then they bayoneted those that were still alive. They poured petrol on the corpses and torched them.'

Coleman was silent. He felt sick to his stomach. The soldier next to him had tears running down his cheeks that left clear streaks on his sooty face. The planter pretended not to notice. His lips were set in a thin line. So these were the people from whom the *kerani* and conductor of his estate were hoping for decent treatment? They were in for a nasty shock.

***

Mei Ling was frantic with worry about her father. He had been gone for a couple of weeks and Mei Ling knew that she might never see him again. He was embarking on a new and dangerous path even for a secret communist. Mei Ling had been weaned on stories of rampaging Japanese troops raping Chinese women, murdering civilians and imposing their will on their captured subjects with direct brutal cruelty. But all that was left of her family to face the Japanese and deal with any collective punishment they might mete out if they got wind of her father's activities, was her mother and herself – two women.

Her reverie on the front step of the sundry shop was interrupted by a familiar soft-spoken voice.

'Worried about your father?' asked Rajan.

She pushed the shiny black hair that hung down from a middle parting away from her face, tucking it behind both ears. The hair cascaded back. Her small ears were not sufficient to hold back the tide.

'Yes, we've not heard anything since he left.'

'I'm sure he's all right,' said Rajan with an optimism he didn't feel.

He paused, staring at the young girl, trying to make out her delicate features in the shadows of the gloomy evening. He added, his voice quivering with a sudden high tide of emotion as he imagined the dangers Mei Ling would face when the Japanese arrived, 'You must do everything possible to stay safe. Trust no one!'

'No one? Not even you?'

His lips curved and then his face grew serious again. 'You shouldn't even trust me. I would never intentionally betray you, you know that. But the less people who know about your father, the better.'

'I hate it! I hate having to keep it a secret that my father is a brave and decent man. Everyone should know that he has gone to fight while others stay behind.'

Rajan, the thought of his own father foremost, was defensive. 'I admire your father and what he's doing. But have you considered that maybe the Japanese are not as bad as they are painted? How do we know that they will be worse than the British?'

His voice was raised and his clenched fists were shoved deep into his pockets as he continued, determined to advance all the arguments he could to justify the position of his family, 'My father has suffered under the British. Why should he fight for them now?'

'I see that,' said Mei Ling. 'I can understand why your father hates the British. They don't treat us Asians as equals. My father says that the communists are different. They believe that no one is superior just because of the colour of their skin …'

Rajan smiled a little at the idealism on display. He held out a hand and took one of Mei Ling's in his. They looked down at the contrasting shades. Rajan was the same colour as *teh tarik*, the strong brew made from tea dust and tossed until frothy. Mei Ling's skin was almost translucent. He could see the fine tracing of blue veins on the back of her hand. But there was none of the pinkness of a Caucasian. She was a pale yellow, like sunlight when dawn was breaking.

'The Japanese may be Asian – but I fear you're right and we have not done well in exchanging the British for them,' he admitted.

Mei Ling did not say anything. She was looking at their hands, mesmerised by the different colours.

Rajan was still arguing with himself, 'The British are not

all that bad anyway. Matthew is a good person.'

This last statement caught her attention. She tugged at her hand, releasing it from his grip. 'You're a fool to trust Matthew. I know he is your friend but at the end of the day, he believes he is better than you because he is white and you are not.'

Rajan shook his head firmly. 'No, you are wrong.'

'You're being naïve.'

'I thought communists didn't judge people by skin colour.' His tone was ironic. He added, trying to extricate the sliver of doubt she had planted under his skin. 'I would trust Matthew with my life.'

'I hope you never have to,' she said and walked away, disappearing into the darkness like a phantom.

Rajan watched her go, regret tinged with anxiety.

A few short weeks earlier, he had known with utmost certainty what each day would bring, the fishing, the chores, the friendship with Matthew, the offering to nip down to the shop for his mother so that he could smile and exchange a few words with the beautiful daughter of the shopkeeper. Now the future was hidden behind an opaque wall. He did not know where Matthew was and whether he was safe. He did not know if Mei Ling was going to be all right. The manager had left, as had Mr. Chan – both headed south, one to fight, one to flee. And one day soon, the Japanese would come. That, like Venus low in the evening sky, was the only certain point on the horizon.

CHAPTER 6

We finally got passes to escape on the Empress of Japan, a big ocean liner turned into a troop ship. (I read later, I've no idea if it's true, that Churchill personally changed her name to the Empress of Scotland.) The Empress had brought a huge number of troops to Singapore – presumably just in time for the surrender, poor bastards.

It was almost impossible to get to the ship. The Japanese knew that evacuations were taking place. The docks were being bombed and strafed. All the godowns were on fire. There were ships and small craft and Chinese junks trying to get away, weaving through Japanese minefields. People went down with their ships or were killed when the bombs struck or just drowned as they tried to make it to shore. I remember men and women in the water. They were on fire and screaming except that you couldn't hear them. I still wake up with nightmares of that soundless screaming except that in my dreams I'm drowning in the fiery water with them.

The ship was beautiful even in its wartime livery; an

enormous ocean liner painted a military grey. The *Empress of Japan* had three massive funnels that leaned back slightly as if they doubted the direction in which they were being propelled. Matthew could see the gun turrets poking out like needles in a pincushion. Propping up his mother who was sobbing like a child, he felt light-headed with relief. Surely it was possible to get away on a ship so big and so sleek. She looked unsinkable. He could imagine her in happier times, sailing across the Pacific, puffing smoke through her funnels against a calm sea and blue skies. The image faded. His mother grabbed him by the hand and dragged him forward through the crush.

Matthew kept his eyes firmly on the ship. He saw a puff of smoke and then fire break out on the deck of the *Empress*. He fought his way forward, holding on to his mother's arm and hustling her towards the vessel. It must have been a direct hit by one of the Zeroes flying overhead, delivering its deadly cargo with gleeful wantonness. He could see men on deck scurrying around trying to put the fires out. He hoped it wasn't serious. He had no idea what they would do if this last escape route was blocked.

There were more than a thousand women and children crammed on the deck of the ship. Matthew did his best to be useful, helping families with the small bag of possessions they had been allowed to bring onboard and trying to herd children towards their mothers so that they did not get separated on the heaving deck of the ship. He was rewarded with a small smile from a young mother. A sickly three-year-old threw up all over his shoes.

To Matthew's surprise, the troop decks were covered in an assortment of mattresses that must have been collected from all over Singapore. Women and children commandeered various corners of the bedding and huddled together, watching the horizon for the diamond shaped formation of approaching Japanese bombers.

Sarah Coleman was assigned a berth on one of the upper decks. It had originally been a two-person cabin in the days when the *Empress of Japan* was the fastest passenger ship on the high seas but now six women, two children and a baby were crammed inside. Matthew was not given a spot. As a teenage boy he was expected to make the best of it and bed down where he could. After all, he was not much younger than the eighteen-year-old gunners manning the ship's defences.

He wondered how long the war would last. Long enough for him to enlist? Matthew was suddenly afraid. He had seen the troops retreating to Singapore. They had been tired, wounded, bedraggled and dispirited. They all had tales to share of the Japanese with their jungle warfare experience and their air superiority. Their voices would lower as they spoke of wounded comrades left behind to become prisoners of war. Would he have the courage of the young men around him? The few troops on board wore hats set at jaunty angles, gritted cigarettes between tobacco-stained teeth and shouted cheerful insults at each other as they waited for their fragile passengers to be loaded onboard.

He heard the engines rumble. The *Empress of Japan* was on her way, led out by a minesweeper shining a red light to guide the liner out to sea. It was terrifying to think that their voyage might not even last long enough for the coastline of Singapore to disappear. Matthew looked back. The whole city was burning. Flames were leaping high in the sky, lighting the blackness of night with an evil reddish glow. The moon and stars were hidden by the thick pall of smoke that hung over the island like a dirty blanket. Soot and ash filled his nostrils.

But at least the ship was on its way.

***

Coleman brought his vehicle to a screeching halt at a military checkpoint just before the Causeway. In the dark hours before dawn he could not identify the nationality of the soldiers. He stopped the vehicle and walked forward. He heard a broad Scottish lilt. It reminded him of Murray who had been right about so many things in the lead up to war. Coleman wondered where he was and spared an instant to hope he had escaped.

The guards had their guns trained on him as he strode towards them. He said, 'I'm Andrew Coleman, a planter from north Johore. I need to get into Singapore. I have a young Aussie sapper in the car, badly injured. He needs help.'

'You must have the luck of the devil to have made it here!' exclaimed one of the men guarding the checkpoint.

'I've been driving with my lights off in the dark. Could barely see my hands in front of my face, let alone the road –

but then the moon came out and it's been a clear night. The Japs must be getting their beauty sleep.'

There were nods all around at this. 'We've been sitting here waiting for an air attack all night. The Australian troops are making their way to Singapore. We're going to blow the Causeway once the Argylls are across.'

'Blow the Causeway? My God, man – what are you saying? Is the fight for Malaya over?'

'The fight for bloody Malaya was over before it began,' said a surly veteran. 'We've just been providing the Japanese with target practice.'

Coleman could see that all the men were battle scarred and battle weary, their tired eyes visible above the glow of cigarettes.

'What about Singapore?' he asked.

'What about it?'

'Can it be held?'

'Anything's possible, I suppose.'

A young soldier came up and said, 'The Australians are across, sir.'

'It's our turn, laddies,' said the sergeant. 'But we'd better let him,' he nodded at Coleman, 'over first before we blow a great big hole in the last road to Singapore.'

'There must be so many left behind …'

'Aye, I think you're right about that. We've been waiting for some of the Indians but they never showed up.'

Coleman ran back to the vehicle, hopped in, gunned the engine and drove quickly over the Causeway. One of the soldiers gave him a casual salute and he returned it. His companion was asleep and muttering under his breath.

The planter turned around to face the Causeway now behind him. The remnants of the Argyll and Sutherland Highlanders battalion had fallen in and were being conducted across the narrow bridge by two regimental pipers. He did not know the tune they were playing but the melancholy call felt appropriate for this last retreat from Malaya. Andrew Coleman just hoped and prayed that Singapore could be held.

***

It was an anti-climax. They did not arrive in large numbers or armed to the teeth. They were not the caricature of British propaganda. Rajan had been unconsciously expecting a short, buck-toothed, bow-legged creature to strut in and demand obeisance from the men and favours from the women. Instead, six Japanese soldiers arrived on black bicycles. When they reached the estate offices, they hopped off the bikes and arranged them in a neat row, handlebars all turned in the same direction. The men appeared hot and bothered, fidgeting in their uniforms. Rajan, hiding behind the massive fissured trunk of a *tembusu* tree, was not surprised. If they had cycled all the way from the nearest town in the heat of the late morning, it was no wonder they were flushed and sweaty. Their uniforms were light khaki with buttons down the front, collars bearing red insignia, and large pockets on each breast. He saw that their peaked caps had flaps hanging down over their necks to protect them from the sun. The trousers, tucked into brown leather lace-up boots, were clean but faded. They had been worn for quite a long time – probably the whole Malaya campaign at least, guessed Rajan.

The men turned to go into the office where Rajan knew his father was working, or more accurately, waiting.

The first man to reach the door shouted something in Japanese. Rajan could not hear the response. The soldier beckoned and Thomas came out slowly, squinting against the sun. As always, he was as neat as a pin, his trouser crease crisp and his hair slicked back.

One of the men said something in Japanese and Thomas shook his head, gesturing with his hands, palms upwards, fingers splayed, to indicate that he had not understood. The Japanese soldier in the lead beckoned to one of his men. He came forward and said in Malay, his voice rough and guttural, his cadences at odds with the lyrical language he spoke crudely but clearly.

'You must bow,' barked the interpreter.

Thomas's brows knitted together, his Adam's apple bobbed up and down as he swallowed hard. 'I beg your pardon?'

The soldier kicked him in the back of the knees. His legs buckled. Thomas collapsed.

'You must bow before Colonel Hidojo!' screamed the interpreter.

Rajan sprinted from his jungle hideout to his father's side. 'What are you doing to my father? Leave him alone.'

He glared at the soldier who had been identified as the

colonel and saw that he was smooth shaven, with a pencil thin moustache tracing his upper lip. His flat brown eyes narrowed as he looked at the young man who had emerged so suddenly from the bushes.

Thomas scrambled to his feet and grabbed his son by the shoulder. He said, 'It's all right. I didn't understand.'

Thomas turned to the colonel and bowed deeply from the waist down.

The man said something in Japanese and the interpreter said, 'Good! Now you understand. All workers must bow when they see a Japanese soldier. If you show disrespect to the soldier and therefore to the Emperor Hirohito, you will be severely punished.'

Again the colonel said something but this time there was a thin-lipped smirk on his face.

'This boy is your son? He is brave. The Japanese admire courage.'

The Japanese officer took a step forward and slapped Rajan across the cheek with an open, calloused hand.

'You have courage. You must also have respect for your superiors. Let that be a lesson to you.'

Rajan held his bruised face with the palm of one hand. His jaw throbbed and his eyes were watering from the impact. He was angrier than he had ever been in his life. His father tightened his grip on the boy's shoulder to remind Rajan, who was on the verge of throwing caution to the wind and launching himself at the colonel, that any foolhardy act of defiance would have consequences for both of them. Rajan lowered his heavy eyelids like a veil so that the Japanese could not see the burning resentment in his eyes, and bowed slowly and carefully, making a performance of his subservience.

The men chuckled.

'We welcome you to this estate. Please tell me what you need,' said Thomas and only Rajan could guess his apprehension for his son in that moment.

'Where is the British manager?'

'He has left.'

'Is the estate damaged?'

'No, sir. But the manager destroyed some of the machinery in the factory.'

'Can it be fixed?'

'Yes. But we need to call in a skilled person.'

'Do it!'

Thomas bowed to acknowledge the instruction.

'Where is the manager's bungalow?'

'I will take you there.'

There was a quick nod of approval from the colonel.

Thomas said to Rajan, speaking Malayalam in a hurried undertone, the loose skin on his throat quivering with suppressed panic, 'I will go with the soldiers. You go home.'

Rajan realised that his father had offered to escort the Japanese to the manager's home as a means of separating him from the group. He didn't want to leave. His presence might act as a restraint on the soldiers. 'I'll stay with you,' he whispered.

His father shook his head.

'Go son, right now.'

Rajan bowed to the soldiers and ran away as fast as he could. When he finally stopped, heart thumping in his chest and his hands clammy with sweat, both from his run and a gut wrenching fear, he saw that he had run in the direction of Mei Ling's home.

***

Thomas indicated his motorcycle and the colonel nodded. He was about to get on when the soldier shook his head. He grabbed the handles and slung a booted leg over the seat. He sat down and said something that provoked a guffaw of laughter from the troops.

'*You* can ride the bicycle,' said the interpreter.

Thomas nodded at once. He was in no position to protest the swap. He climbed on the bicycle and pedalled away. The soldiers followed suit. The colonel revved the bike and did wheelies from time to time to express his pleasure in no longer having to use pedal power. If the other ranks resented his mobility as they pressed their bulging thighs into action, they were careful not to show it.

Thomas realised at once that the manager's bungalow had been looted. He had no idea who could have done it. It was widely known that the manager had left and Thomas regretted not posting a guard. It had been an oversight and he feared that the Japanese would want to exact punishment for it. The colonel paced around the bungalow, noting the missing furniture and the broken windows. The looters had been vandals too. Thomas suspected youth from the towns.

No one else would have acted in such a cavalier manner.

'Who has done this?'

The interpreter spoke but Thomas addressed his reply to the colonel. 'I do not know, sir.' After all, three-way conversations were what he was accustomed to. Had he not been the mouthpiece for the white manager in the same way that this interpreter was for the colonel? Here the necessity was the language barrier. Previously, it had been the need of the white manager to insulate himself from the natives.

'You should have prevented it.'

'I'm sorry, sir.'

'In Japan, we do not treat mistakes lightly. This is why the Imperial Army has swept all before it.'

Thomas inclined his head to acknowledge the criticism.

'I will move in here tomorrow. Have it cleaned. My men will have the quarters around the back.'

'I will arrange it, sir.'

'Gather the workers tomorrow morning at nine. I will address them all.'

'As you wish, Colonel.'

'And show my men where the flagpole is.'

The colonel held out his hand and a folded cloth was placed in his hand. He bowed to it and passed it back to the soldier.

Thomas remembered when the Union Jack had fluttered merrily in the breeze and the way it hung limp on a sultry day, the vibrant colours of empire fading in the tropical sun.

He watched the Japanese soldier run up their flag with reverent ceremony. As if the Emperor controlled the weather, a strong wind gusted and the flag was spread against the blazing afternoon sky. Thomas noticed the soldiers duck their heads and he too executed a deep bow. His knee was sore where he had been kicked. He did not intend to provoke another display of anger. As he gazed at the Japanese flag with its crimson circle he was reminded not so much of the rising sun but of blood spilt. There had been so much of that in Malaya already and he feared much more to come. His thoughts turned to Chan. He fervently hoped he was all right.

It was important to Thomas at that moment that someone had determined of his own free will that he would not bow to this flag or the soldiers that marched behind it.

CHAPTER 7

My father never talked much about his experiences. He did tell me that an Australian sapper he picked up on the way to Singapore was killed in the Alexandra Barracks Hospital massacre. Did you hear about that? The Japanese killed the medical staff and the patients. I think of that soldier sometimes, even though I never knew him. His fate seemed so cruel and arbitrary, even in a time of war.

I heard later that Mei Ling's father made his way down to Singapore and took part in that battle. I don't know if that was true but I guess it might have been. I've done a lot of reading over the years on the fall of Singapore. I am painfully aware of how our lives would have turned out so differently if only the Allies had been able to hold it. Perhaps it is an abdication of responsibility but I often wish that, in a universe of infinite outcomes, the fates didn't provide me with the set of circumstances that tempted me to behave as I did.

Chan found his way to the Singapore volunteer army under the command of Colonel Dalley. He was given a blue uniform, a triangular piece of red cloth to tie to his right arm and yellow cloth to wear around his head. It was the best that the British could provide. There were no helmets or boots available. Chan was wearing sturdy boots that he had found abandoned by the road on his way to Singapore. They were too tight for him and chafed his heels and toes but as he looked at his fellow soldiers; communists like him, supporters of the Kuomintang, students, clerks and general workers in their canvas shoes or rubber slippers, he felt lucky to be so well-shod.

Having received some rudiments of military training in Kuala Lumpur, Chan was promoted to major in the volunteer army. To his astonishment, each volunteer was issued with an outdated hunting rifle and twenty-four bullets.

'We need better weapons than this!' he protested. 'The Japanese will destroy us.'

The British officer sighed. 'That's all we have at the moment. You'll have to make every bullet count!'

A Chinese volunteer, so young he had a sprinkling of teenage acne on his face, said, 'I have come to fight the Japanese and I will do it with my bare hands if I have to!'

There were cheers from the waiting men.

'Let us hope it doesn't come to that,' replied the British major.

Chan did not comment. He didn't want to dampen the morale of troops under his command but he did not relish the prospect of a glorious death once his twenty-four bullets had been spent.

Chan was ordered to march to the front line at Jurong. The company of fifty men under his command waded through the swamp. They walked knee deep in mud, raising each foot high to take a step as the mud clung to their legs. The cheap blue trousers, caked with mud, tugged at the hair on Chan's legs. It was not possible to use the roads. There were regular air patrols by the Japanese. The main roads were also subject to artillery fire from the Johore side of the Causeway. The primary victims of the whistling shells were refugees.

Chan led his men north until they reached a rubber estate that faced out to sea. They took up positions and waited for the inevitable Japanese attack. Except for the drone of aircraft overhead, the dull thud of distant explosions and the sharper sounds of artillery fire, the company of men hiding in the rubber estates had a quiet afternoon. They drank water from their leather canteens and ate army rations sparingly. As evening approached, the Japanese searchlights cut through the dusk like immense glowing swords. Chan urged his men to stay calm. He took a few souls with him towards the beach. He was worried that, from their position inland, they might not see any Japanese landing until it was too late to defend against it or send a warning back to headquarters. The men crept between the spindly-leaved *casuarina* trees that lined the coast like sentries. They wrapped themselves in large coconut fronds and crawled forward on their bellies, hoping to look like detritus on the beach.

A small flotilla of rubber dinghies filled with Japanese

soldiers was coming around a rocky outcrop. Chan could not tell if it was an advance patrol or a major landing. He did not have much time to decide. There was sand in his mouth from keeping low to the beach. The thumping of his heart was echoed by the drumming of blood in his ears.

Chan motioned with his hand to the others. He hoped that his inexperienced young troops would recognise it as a sign to hold steady, not to open fire. Not yet anyway. He had to know what this advance party was about. Chan had been briefed by Colonel Dalley that Indian and Australian troops as well as other volunteers were ranged out on either side of him, defending the whole northern shore of Singapore. The Causeway had been blown up. That was expected to delay the Japanese advance for a few days. There was no point launching into a skirmish, getting his men killed and failing to warn the rest of the defensive forces that the invasion was underway. If need be, he would retreat and sound the alarm. However, if this group of soldiers was the sum total of the advance, he would attack.

He counted five dinghies with about ten soldiers in each. The moon had come out from behind a cloud. The faces of the Japanese glowed pale under their caps. He could see the sharp outlines of rifles with bayonets as they came closer to the beach. He knew he was running out of time to signal a retreat. They would be massacred if he waited much longer. At last, he decided that there were no more troops – these were out on some sort of reconnoitering mission. He, Chan, was going to make sure that they were not permitted to make their way back to Japanese headquarters with any information about fortifications along the coast of Singapore.

He risked a spoken command although the distant noise of mortars and artillery had died down. He needed to prevent his nervous men from jumping the gun.

He said softly but not sibilantly, it had been mentioned in a lecture at the training school that whispers carried much further than lowered voices, 'Stand your ground. Do not engage until I give the signal. Then take out as many Japanese as you can and retreat.'

He hoped rather than knew he had been heard and understood.

The first craft reached the shoreline. The soldiers leapt out and dragged their dinghy on to the beach. The others followed suit. They were completely quiet. Chan, his chin wedged into the dirt, watched their silent discipline with admiration. He waited until all the boats had landed. The soldiers made their way up the steep incline of the beach, their feet sinking in the soft sand.

He shouted, 'Fire!' and started shooting.

His first shot caught a soldier in the stomach. Chan watched him drop his gun and clutch his belly, eyes wide with shock, before toppling forward on his knees and then face down in the sand. The second bullet – he was on his feet now – caught a soldier lagging behind. His head exploded in the twilight. Then the evening was torn apart by the whine of bullets and screams of dying men. It was impossible to tell whether he was hitting anything or wasting precious ammunition. In what seemed like mere seconds, Chan screamed the retreat. The men fell in behind him, turning to fire randomly as they struggled to follow him under cover of the trees. Chan heard a bullet whistle past his ear. He felt a searing pain in his shoulder. He guessed he had been hit but did not dare stop. Next to him, a young Chinese boy, he could not have been more than eighteen, keeled over. Chan fell down on his knees next to him, turning the boy over. The bullet had pierced an artery in his neck. The blood was black against the sand. The boy's eyes were glazed. He would be dead in minutes. Turning the boy over had aggravated his own shoulder injury. Pain flooded his brain. Chan got to his feet with difficulty, picked up his rifle and ran. His steps grew heavy and his direction erratic. He made it into the trees, stumbled forward another fifty yards and then collapsed to the ground. He crawled behind the trunk of a sturdy rubber tree and leaned against it. There were no sounds of pursuit. The guns had fallen silent. He wondered why. He had seen numerous Japanese soldiers killed and wounded. His men had maximised the element of surprise and many of the enemy had fallen in the first hail of bullets. But surely enough had been left to take the fight to the amateurs of the Singapore volunteer force?

There was a crashing in the undergrowth and a man rushed past. Chan stuck out a leg and tripped him up. His fellow volunteer came crashing to the ground. It was Ho, one of the older men.

'Why did you do that?' asked Lim in an angry whisper.

'Had to stop you!'

Lim nodded, mollified. 'You are hurt!' he said, sharp concern in his voice.

Chan shrugged and then grimaced because the movement had caused the dull throb in his shoulder to sharpen into acute pain. He suspected the bullet was lodged against the bone. He could not find any exit hole. The piece of metal that had been fired at him to kill him was now lodged in his body.

'That is not important,' he muttered.

It sounded like foolish bravado but Chan meant it. His fate was the least significant thing on the beach that day. 'Get back to HQ. Tell them what happened,' he continued. 'Explain that we ambushed a small Japanese force trying to land east of Jurong. It might mean that the big landing is imminent. Tell them,' he paused and then grinned at his fellow soldier, his sweat drenched face crinkling with amusement in the darkness, 'tell them that the Singapore volunteers were victorious in their first encounter with the Japanese army.'

'What about you?'

'I'll rest for a while here and then make my way back.'

Lim nodded. He was sympathetic but not sentimental. He knelt down by Chan, ripped off his uniform shirt and tore it into strips. He tied it around Chan's shoulder and said, 'This will help stop the bleeding.' He gripped Chan's left hand and said, 'Good luck.' He got to his feet, glanced around furtively and made off into the rubber trees. He was soon lost from sight.

Chan sat back again, ashen and exhausted from the effort

of talking to Lim as well as his crude attempt to staunch the bleeding. He thought of his family, especially his beautiful daughter Mei Ling. He hoped she was all right.

***

'They're here!'

'What do you mean? Who's here?'

'The Japs! The Japs are on the estate.'

Mei Ling gripped his arm, her face pale. Even in his alarm, Rajan found time to think that she looked like a porcelain vase, her face drained of its usual healthy tint.

'They are here already? What are they doing?'

'They're with my father. They have gone to look at the manager's bungalow.'

'They won't like what they find there.'

'What do you mean?'

'I told the communist party chief in town that it was deserted. He said that he would arrange for anything valuable to be removed and sold to fund the war against the Japanese.'

'Have you gone mad? This is not some sort of game. These people are barbaric. We cannot risk crossing them!'

'I did not think you were such a coward.'

Rajan flinched but stood his ground. 'It is not cowardice to pick your battles. These soldiers are cruel. Their colonel – his name is Hidojo – kicked my father to the ground because he did not bow to them. Pappa didn't even know that's what they wanted him to do. He didn't understand.' Rajan's voice cracked a little on this last statement as he remembered his father's humiliation and his own foolish intervention.

Mei Ling led him into the shop. She looked at him under the light of the single low watt bulb and exclaimed, 'What happened to your face?'

Rajan put a hand to his jaw. It was throbbing. He could taste the sharp iron of blood in his mouth. He ran a tongue over his teeth. One of his molars was loose. He grinned and winced.

'I tried to help my father. The colonel doesn't agree with you about my being a coward. He said I was very brave. He hit me to encourage more respect the next time.'

Mei Ling's eyes were wide with shock. She wet a towel and held it to Rajan's face. It hurt at first but also worked to numb the pain.

'Thanks,' he whispered, wishing that he could feel the soft skin of her hand rather than the cool cloth.

'What do you think I should do?' she asked in a small voice.

'I've heard such terrible things about the Japanese, and now ... now I believe that all those stories are true. I'm terrified for you ... for us all, but especially for you.'

He did not finish. Neither of them needed to have the behaviour of the Japanese towards Chinese women spelt out. They had heard about the atrocities in Nanking. Mei Ling's race, her sex, her youth and her father's activities all made her vulnerable.

Mei Ling touched Rajan's jaw with cool fingers as he had hoped she would do just seconds before.

'If only your father was here,' said Rajan, betraying his youth.

'I wish that too. But he had to do what he thought was right. I just hope he has not been hurt ... or worse.'

Rajan said diffidently, 'I have heard that some girls have dressed as boys, cutting their hair and wearing loose clothes.'

'I could try that, I suppose.' She looked doubtful and Rajan did not blame her. Although her features were strong, with high cheekbones, a firm chin and eyes like horizontal teardrops, they were also distinctly feminine.

They fell silent.

'Can you hide?' asked Rajan.

'For how long?'

'Until the British come back?'

Mei Ling started to giggle. 'That could be a very long wait,' she said.

***

Murray the policeman was burning documents. He carried huge piles of paperwork to the fire raging on the lawn in front of the police station. He watched the papers curl and blacken, little pieces taking to the air in a merry dance. His sergeant came out with another armful and dumped them on the blaze. For a moment, it looked as if the conflagration had been defeated by the volume of paper but then tendrils of fire, like long fingers, appeared around the edges and engulfed the documents in a fiery embrace.

The Scotsman, his face the same shade of red as his

hair from the heat, grinned at his junior, 'At least we're not leaving the Japs anything useful!'

His sergeant nodded. 'We have destroyed almost all the documents on suspected communists in the area.'

'Well, we're on the same side now – the commie bastards are all that's left of the fight for Malaya. No point in leaving a file on every one of them for the Japs.'

The sergeant pushed his hat back and scratched his head. He had spent the last few years working with the Scot to track down members of the Malayan Communist Party to jail them or deport them. Now he was being called upon to protect them. He wondered what other u-turns this war would require of him.

'What about you, sir? Why haven't you tried to get to Singapore?' he asked.

Murray rubbed his eyes with grimy knuckles. They were smarting from the soot. 'Left it too late, I'm afraid. The Causeway's been blown. There's no escape now.'

'What will you do when the Japanese arrive?'

Murray smiled, exposing the wide gap between his front teeth. 'Sergeant Hashim, I have no bloody idea.'

The sergeant picked up a stick and poked the fire, causing the embers to glow red and orange. He could not believe that the war was lost. The invincible British had been beaten – not just beaten but humiliated. He glanced up at the man who had been his superior officer for five years. Murray was a decent fellow. His colourful language and rough and ready methods had surprised the young policeman at first but he'd got used to it. He had learnt to admire the hardworking, dogmatic policeman who had been one of the first to realise that the British were not infallible.

'Why were you so sure that Malaya was in danger from the Japanese?' he asked.

Murray laughed. 'Maybe because I'm a Scot – less likely to believe Westminster half-truths about our wonderful fighting machine in Asia.'

Hashim's attention was drawn to the road leading to the station. A phalanx of bicycles had turned the corner. He said, his voice grim, 'They're here, sir.'

Murray spun around and watched the approaching Japanese, riding their bicycles with the same attention to formation as bombers on a sortie.

'Is there anything left to burn?'

'One more bundle, sir.'

'Get it!'

Sergeant Hashim ran up the slope into the building, a wooden structure painted white and blue. The last stack was on Murray's table. He grabbed it and hurried out, his arms full.

The Japanese dismounted from their bicycles and walked through the front gates. The big scarlet flowers on the hibiscus bushes nodded a welcome.

The soldiers carried their weapons in their hands. Their loose grip suggested to Hashim that they were not expecting trouble. The war was over. They did not expect that many would fancy martyrdom for a lost cause.

Murray stood waiting, his hands by his side. He had a gun in his belt but he made no attempt to get it.

'Who is in charge here?' The interpreter barked out the translation, copying even the inflexion in his superior's voice.

'I am,' said Murray.

The soldier beckoned to Hashim who was still standing by the station, uncertain what to do.

Hashim marched over. He tried to look unthreatening. He had never had so many rifles pointed at him before in his life.

'Who is this?'

'My number two, Sergeant Hashim,' explained Murray.

Hashim was glad he had not been required to speak. His throat was tight with fear.

'What are you doing here?'

'Burning documents,' he said.

'Sergeant Hashim,' said the colonel, 'you're now in charge of the Bukit Pagoh police station. The Japanese Imperial Army has liberated you from the British.' He pointed at Murray. 'Now, arrest this man.'

Hashim's face drained of colour like a newly painted wall in the rain. His hands were still full of paper.

'Chuck that on the fire. Let's finish the job.' Murray spoke with authority.

The senior policeman was on the opposite side of the fire. The air between them shimmered with heat. The big Scot looked like an apparition, thought Hashim. By contrast, the Japanese soldiers with their guns trained on him seemed very real indeed.

The young policeman laid the papers on the ground at his feet. He walked around the fire like an ancient performing a ritual. He pulled out his revolver. He said, 'Commander Murray, you're under arrest.'

***

Andrew Coleman tied a handkerchief around his nose and mouth. The stench of rotting flesh mingled with bombed sewage was unbearable. He swallowed the bile in his mouth, tried to avoid throwing up. He couldn't believe this was Singapore. He'd spent so many holidays here, watching the dancing at the Raffles Hotel, squeezing in dinners, film premieres, regattas and endless parties. Even Sarah would perk up when it was time for one of their forays to Singapore.

A huge black pall of smoke hung over the whole city. It began to drizzle and he noted that the raindrops turned black before they hit the ground. There were fires blazing everywhere. The fire brigade had abandoned any hope of putting out the conflagration. The continuous bombing raids made that impossible. Their efforts were focused on key buildings like hospitals, military headquarters and barracks.

Coleman marched towards the docks. He hoped to get on a ship leaving Singapore. It had been his routine for three days now, this walk from the house he shared with a number of other British lost souls. The others dared not venture out. Coleman couldn't bear to stay put and listen to the whistling sounds of bombs falling through the air. As he picked his way through the streets, he heard the big guns on Pulau Belakang Mati, south of the island. These had been turned and were now firing across the breadth of the island towards Johore and the Japanese.

'A complete waste of time,' muttered a soldier. 'The ammo was designed to be armour-piercing – for ship hulls. They're useless against ground troops.'

'Why use them then?' asked Coleman.

'Keeps up morale in Singapore, I suppose.'

Coleman walked past more bewildered military personnel wandering around aimlessly. Corpses littered the streets. He grimaced. It was a bit too late for morale boosting exercises.

When he got to the docks he had to fight his way past soldiers competing for a way out on anything that would float. Coleman was turned away at the dock gates as had happened the three previous days.

'We're giving the women and children priority, sir,' said one of the tired-looking sentries given the unenviable job of ushering his countrymen away.

Coleman wiped the sweat away from his forehead with his sleeve and watched it come away streaked with dirt. He was covered in grime from head to toe. His moustache, that he had groomed every day with such pride, was long and straggly, hanging over his top lip like a fringe. There was no clean water. The Japanese had bombed the water mains and shortages were becoming acute.

He spotted a fleet of Japanese planes on the horizon. He counted the planes, twenty-seven flying in a diamond-shaped formation. There was a huge crush of women and children standing exposed on Clifford Pier. They were mostly dressed in white, like lambs to a slaughter. There was nothing he could do. He ran to an air-raid shelter and was taken aback to see it was built of corned beef tins.

Seeing his bemused expression, one of the soldiers hiding in the shelter said, 'The shrapnel from the bombs – it can pierce the side of a ship but not corned beef, I've been told.'

'I hope you're right,' said Coleman.

It felt like hours as the shelter juddered with the impact of ear-splitting explosions but could not have been more than a few minutes. His ears were ringing as he clambered out of his temporary but effective refuge. His gaze was drawn to the pier. To his amazement he saw that the women and children were still standing there, unharmed. The Japanese pilots had been merciful. The bombers were just specks on the horizon now. Their work was done. They could return to one of the airfields in Malaya captured from the British to refuel, re-arm and carry out another devastating attack.

Coleman made his way to the Raffles hoping to get some news. Or perhaps it was just that old habits died hard, he thought, remembering how he and his wife had made a beeline for the elegant building whenever they came to Singapore. He was amazed to see that a social programme was still running despite the bombs falling all around. He listened to the conversations of the patrons almost in awe.

'We need to set the right example and show the right spirit,' a gentleman he vaguely remembered from his early days on the estates proclaimed.

'Well, I wouldn't worry too much. Our boys will soon have those Nips on the run,' responded another.

'But the Causeway has been destroyed,' Coleman interjected. 'Malaya is lost!'

There were a few pitying glances in his direction and he realised for the first time that the other diners were still well turned out, not covered in blood, dust and grime like he was.

He insisted, determined to be indifferent to their pity and disgust, 'Singapore will not hold out for long.'

'Just a temporary setback, old fellow,' said one of the men. 'Perhaps you should get cleaned up and then have a lie-down.'

Coleman felt like screaming for a moment, smashing the crockery, doing something – anything – to get through to these men. This was not so much a stiff upper lip as a terrifying reluctance to face the facts. Instead, he left, unable to cope with the smart clothes and dance music. He didn't belong amongst the brittle smiles and finery.

He sat down on a kerb outside, his back to the graceful landmark of colonial Singapore. Coleman buried his face in his hands but he was unable to shut out the sounds of war accompanied in this instance by the faint music of the band playing elegiacally at the Raffles.

CHAPTER 8

There is a photo – taken on the day that General Percival surrendered Singapore to General Yamashita at the Old Ford Factory on Bukit Timah Road – that sums up the British capitulation. General Percival, so thin as to be almost emaciated, marches forward, his spindly legs protruding like sticks from baggy shorts. He is ahead of the shorter, scruffier Japanese soldier who is his escort, as if Percival is going to accept the surrender of the Japanese and not the other way round. But around him are other officers carrying the Union Jack and a big white flag (a bedsheet? presumably they didn't have a stock of white flags around in case they felt like surrendering.)

The battle for Singapore was over … but in a sense, for you and me – and Mei Ling – it had just begun.

It had not been an easy decision. Mei Ling's mother had been reluctant.

'What if your father comes back?' she asked. 'How will he find us?'

'You know he is more likely to disappear into the jungles

to fight than come back to us. And that's why we're not safe.'

'The Japanese will not know about your father's activities. We will just keep quiet and stay out of the way.'

Mei Ling smiled at her mother in genuine amusement. She had never understood her parents. Their personalities were so different. Her father was an active, determined, stubborn man who sought out trouble on the rare occasion it did not find him first. Her mother's entire attitude was summed up by those words, 'keep quiet and stay out of the way'. Her only vice was to rattle the bone tiles at the *mah jong* table.

'I wish your father had not gone away,' repeated her mother.

'We must respect him because he is sacrificing himself for what he believes in – otherwise what is the use of having ideals in the first place?'

'You are your father's daughter, Mei Ling. He would be proud of your courage and decisiveness. I do not have your strength.'

Mei Ling put her arms around her mother and hugged her tight, marvelling at how frail and thin she was. Worry over her husband and the war had cost her her appetite. Mei Ling felt guilty that she hadn't noticed. She had been too preoccupied with her own anxieties.

Mei Ling was shorter than her mother, but the older woman was stooping slightly, as if the weight of recent events was physically bearing down on her. Mei Ling knew that, in the absence of her father, she would have to make the decisions for the family.

'We cannot remain here, mother. Too many people know

of father's communist activities. If the Japanese find out, I am afraid that they will take their anger out on you and me.'

'Surely the people who know are our friends?'

'You might be right, mother. But this is a time of war. It is better that we have faith in each other and no one else.'

Mrs. Chan looked doubtful.

'We place our friends in danger too by our presence. If the Japanese find out about father – they might harm them for having been silent about his role. Or they may try to find out more through torture. Father has told us stories of the cruelty of the Kempetai.'

'Very well, I agree,' said her mother at last. 'We will flee into the jungles.'

***

Das, forewarned by Thomas, bowed the moment the Japanese put in an appearance. He shouted in Tamil for the tappers to do the same. There was some confusion and a few unconvincing efforts but on the whole it made a reasonable spectacle of obeisance to the Japanese troops. The soldiers stood to attention before their fluttering flag, its red rays spreading out to all four corners of the cloth just as their empire was spreading bloodily across the Pacific.

The colonel was dressed with precision in khaki jodhpurs, a white shirt of which only the snowy collar showed, a dark blue coat buttoned up to his throat and knee-high riding boots. Thomas noted that the tips of his large ears were red and peeling – too much exposure to the sun.

'Colonel Hidojo welcomes you to a new dawn as subjects of the Emperor,' said the interpreter.

There was no response except for blank stares from the tappers. None of them spoke English well enough to understand the Japanese-accented translation.

Das stepped forward. 'It would be a privilege to translate for the workers, sir,' he said. 'I am afraid their English is not very good.'

Colonel Hidojo nodded once.

Das translated the first remarks into Tamil. To Thomas's amazement he then continued in Tamil to tell the workers how to react.

'Colonel Hidojo – who is the leader of the Japanese here, the one wearing the blue coat – says that we are welcome to be the subjects of the Japanese Emperor. When I count to three we should all break into a loud cheer. One, two, three!'

Not all the workers realised what Das was getting at. A few of the sharper ones did and the others followed suit.

Thomas stole a glance at Colonel Hidojo. If he was puzzled that Tamil was such an unwieldy language, he did not say so. Instead, the colonel broke into a broad grin at the reaction to his first remarks.

He clapped his hands together and said, 'We will celebrate the liberation of Malaya from the British together!'

The cheers that greeted this remark, prompted by Das, were even louder.

***

Rajan was acutely aware that Mei Ling was not at the gathering. Her mother was not present either. He wondered where they were. Their failure to attend the first meeting on the front lawn of the manager's bungalow could be viewed as disrespectful.

The tappers were dismissed. He saw Das and Thomas go over to the Japanese and bow. There was going to be a lot of bowing and scraping in the next few years, he supposed. Perhaps they would get used to it but he doubted it. The one occasion when he had been privileged to show obeisance before the invaders, it had only been the pressure of his father's hand on his shoulder that made him double over.

Rajan slipped like a shadow between the trees until he was within hearing distance. He ducked behind a *kapok* tree, his mother's favourite source of stuffing for pillows and mattresses. The skills he had honed growing up on the estate were turning out very useful. No one knew the land like he did. Not the manager, not Das, not the tappers, not even his own father. Matthew had run him a close second. But the English youth had not yet achieved his encyclopaedic knowledge of the hundreds of acres. After all, the plantation had been Rajan's playground his whole life. He spared a thought for his friend, almost wishing he was there with him, crouching in the shrubs, eavesdropping on the adults, as they had done so many times in the past.

'The workers should continue to bring in the latex. There must be someone found to repair the machinery in the factory.'

Thomas agreed at once.

It was Das who asked in a nervous voice, 'Sir, will the workers be paid?'

'Of course they will be paid!' snapped the Colonel. 'We, the Imperial Japanese Army have liberated you from the colonial oppressors. We do not ask you to be slaves.'

Rajan doubted this promise of payment. His father and Das appeared relieved. Perhaps they were choosing to look on the bright side. It was almost impossible to contemplate conditions if the Japanese put people to work without payment. Thinking about essential goods made him think of Mei Ling and her mother again. Where had they gone? The sundry shop was closed. The front of the building had been shuttered when he went by that morning. He'd assumed they had gone ahead to the meeting summoned by the colonel. Had they fled instead? But where in the world could they go? There were not many people who would aid the wife and daughter of a communist fighting the Japanese. The risks were just too great. Everyone had something precious to protect. Something that was too valuable to risk. Even if they had a safe haven, how would they get there, a woman and a girl travelling alone?

'The British manager did not pay us before leaving,' said Das, 'so all the tappers are struggling. He was furious because we refused to slash the trees. Would it be possible to advance some wages?'

Rajan was forced to admire Das's sly cunning. He had managed to slip in their refusal to damage the rubber plants.

'Yes, we will give you half your wages in advance,' said

Colonel Hidojo. He turned to one of his men and issued an instruction in curt Japanese.

The language sounded to Rajan like the sharp staccato of a small dog barking at night. There was no softness or rhythm to the speech. Perhaps it was just the way they communicated in the army, he thought. Maybe in a non-military context it was possible to converse in Japanese in a way that was less uncouth to the ears of a non-speaker.

The soldier opened the leather bag he had slung around his neck. He took out a sheaf of notes tied up in a rubber band. He handed it to the Colonel who counted the money and then initialled the journal he was handed. Rajan guessed that the bookkeeper in his father would approve of this careful attention to records.

The Colonel handed the wad of cash to Das who bowed with a flourish, followed by Thomas when he noticed the interpreter's eye on him.

The Colonel growled an instruction in guttural Japanese and his men hopped on their bicycles. The Colonel followed suit more slowly, still using Thomas's motorbike.

Das looked down at the bundle of money and then at Thomas in disbelief.

'What is it? What's the matter?'

Das stretched out his hand and Rajan, emerging from the bushes to join them, heard him say, 'Japanese money!'

They looked down at the paper money in Das's hand. The notes had an assortment of languages, Japanese, English, the Jawi script and various designs on the front.

Rajan took a note from his father's hand. It was a ten-dollar note with a drooping banana tree on the front.

He snorted. 'I wonder whether this "banana" money is worth anything?'

Thomas and Das looked worried, their faces creased with dark lines. 'Let's hope so,' said Das. 'Otherwise, we're all in big trouble.'

***

It was easier than Mei Ling could have imagined to march away from a previous life. She felt a pang of regret that she couldn't tell Rajan where she was going. She knew he would worry when he discovered their absence. But to tell him of their plan to hide out in the jungle with the anti-Japanese communist elements would endanger him. As her father had explained so recently – and yet it seemed so long ago she looked on the person she had been as an inexperienced child – not all the people of Malaya would react the same way to, or be treated the same way by, the Japanese. Rajan was in no particular danger. His father might even get some kudos for not implementing the British plan to ruin the rubber trees. Her comfort would have to be the knowledge that she had not placed him in harm's way.

Mei Ling closed the shop and shuttered the front. It was sad to leave the place but someone would take over. Even a Japanese-run estate needed a sundry shop for the simple necessities like mosquito coils and bread. She went home and hurriedly went from room to room, opening and closing cupboards and drawers. She found what she was looking for, a sheaf of letters between her father and the communist leadership in Singapore. She didn't want to leave any clues for the Japanese that there had been anything untoward about the family living in this small house.

Mei Ling had a brainwave. She picked up a piece of paper and a pen and wrote a neat note marked to the attention of 'Mr. Thomas, Estate Clerk.' She explained that the family were leaving town to go to Cameron Highlands because they had received news that her grandmother was seriously ill. Word had been brought by a relative and they were going back with him. She intentionally used the word 'family' hoping that it would be interpreted by the Japanese to include her father so that his whereabouts would not be queried. But she did not dare say so expressly for fear that it would put too much pressure on Thomas and the others to keep the secret.

The women hitched a ride into town with one of the contractors who knew them by reputation but had no idea that he was assisting an escape. He dropped them outside a tyre shop and the two of them ducked indoors. The place was piled high with tyres and smelt of new rubber. They were greeted by the owner, Mr. Lim, with great courtesy. He was a member of the communist cadre in the town, and Mei Ling knew that her father trusted him. She explained her fears to him – that they would be singled out by the Japanese for terrible retribution if word got out of her father's activities. He agreed that there was great danger but when Mei Ling told him her plan to hide out in the jungle he looked genuinely shocked.

'The life will be very difficult for the anti-Japanese army hidden in the jungles,' he said. 'The enemy will always be looking for them. They will have to depend on people for food. There is great risk of betrayal. There are jungle diseases like malaria and beri-beri ...'

'We know we might not survive, dear friend,' said Mei Ling's mother. 'But I know we have no chance on the estate. If we try and run away to family, we will put their lives in danger. Let us throw in our lot with those who have already taken the risk of death and discovery and chosen to fight the Japanese. At least we cannot endanger them any further.'

Although it was her mother who had spoken, it was Mei Ling whose expression persuaded the communist that they were serious. She had clenched her jaw and her firm chin was thrust forward. Her eyes were trained on him as if she wished to gauge his mood and guess his response even before he spoke. She looked scared but determined.

'Very well', he said. 'I will arrange for an escort to the camp in the jungle. I'll be back in ten minutes.'

He was as good as his word. He came back with a large Chinese youth with a round boyish face who said his name was Siow. He agreed at once to escort the women into the jungle. He was going back that evening anyway. He'd only stayed long enough to collect food hampers from sympathetic townsfolk. In future, he explained, they would not risk coming to the city centres. The communists would depend on farmers on the fringes of the forest to provide their needs. The rest they would have to grow themselves.

Mei Ling's mother brightened up at this. She was a keen

gardener. She might be able to do something to occupy herself in the long months ahead in a way that would also benefit the cause that was her husband's passion.

Mr. Lim offered to drive them to the outskirts of town and they accepted gratefully. He led them out and they all clambered into his Morris 8, a small battered car but with brand new tyres. He drove quickly and well, keeping a sharp eye out for any signs of troops or trouble.

'The Japanese are garrisoned south of the town,' he said. 'They have not come in yet but it will not be too long. Fortunately, not many people know of my role with the anti-Japanese army so I think I should be quite safe. It is important for us to have spies in town to keep an eye on things.'

'Do you have any family?' asked Mei Ling.

'Five children. They are at home with my wife. The oldest boy is twelve and the youngest is two.'

'Why do you help us when you have so much to lose?'

Mr. Lim appeared to give the question great thought, both hands on the steering wheel, his eyes focused on the dark road ahead.

'Your father,' he said in an undertone, 'is a friend of mine and a loyal comrade. I cannot do less for him than he tries to do for all of us. Besides, I hope if my wife and children need assistance, others will help them. I could not ask or expect it of my neighbours if I were not prepared to do it myself.'

He drew to a halt. The only light was from the car headlights. When he switched them off, the darkness, like a black velvet curtain, was absolute.

***

Chan made his way through the secondary forest, holding his injured arm stiff by his side. He felt feverish – an infection had set in. In the heat and the humidity it wouldn't take long for his wound to turn gangrenous. Chan needed someone to remove the bullet if he was to survive his first encounter with the enemy.

He stumbled across some Australian soldiers.

'Well, mate. You caught a bullet as well!'

One of the young Aussie soldiers grinned at him although his smile turned into a grimace of pain. Chan could see that his upper arm was bound up with a makeshift bandage. In fact, most of the Aussies were carrying injuries.

'What happened?' he asked.

'We were over-run. Held out as long as we could but they've landed and established a beachhead. It won't be long before their tanks and bicycles spread out across Singapore.'

Chan closed his eyes.

The Aussie asked with rough sympathy, 'Your shoulder hurting you?'

Chan did not tell him that it was more than his shoulder. His heart ached for the people of Singapore.

'Can we push them back, do you think?' he asked.

'I doubt it. Without air cover ... every time we look like we're holding them, they just send in those bloody planes.' He looked at his men. 'Most of our injuries are from bomb shrapnel. We were doing all right against their ground troops.'

'What are you going to do now?' Chan's question had a

rhetorical feel. What exactly did defeated troops do?

'We've been told to regroup further inland and join up with an Aussie brigade there ... do you want to come with us?'

'I need this shoulder fixed first,' said Chan. Beads of sweat popped out on his forehead as he grew hot with fever again.

'Here, let me bind it up for you. You're going to have to find a hospital to dig the bullet out.'

The next few hours passed in a blur. Chan stumbled forward, unable to keep low or keep quiet, just concentrating on putting one foot ahead of the other. He reached a large house and looked in the kitchen window. It seemed abandoned. The cupboards were open and their contents strewn on the dining table and kitchen counters. He tottered in the door and turned on a tap. A trickle of water came out. He drank like a dying man who had found the fountain of youth. The cool water trickled down the back of his throat. He felt his cracked lips sting but it was a sharp refreshing pain compared to the dull agonising throb in his shoulder. He found a bottle of whisky in the cabinet under the kitchen sink. He took a long swig and grimaced as the fiery liquid hit his empty stomach. Fortified with liquid courage, he poured the rest of the bottle on his wound. Chan passed out from the pain.

When he came to he was lying on the kitchen floor with the whisky bottle next to him. He could hear that a storm had blown up outside. He was glad to have found shelter and the weather might slow the Japanese advance. Looking out of the window, he could see the house was isolated and palatial. It must have belonged to a Chinese *towkay* who had abandoned it to move to the city for whatever last-ditch protection was available.

Chan climbed upstairs, supporting himself on the carved balustrades. He found a bedroom with a large neatly-made double bed. He lay down on top of the covers, feeling guilty about soiling the crisp white cotton sheets, and fell asleep in an instant.

He woke as the early morning sun streamed in a window like a benediction. He was stiff from the exertions of the past few days but his arm hurt less. He did not feel feverish. It had been twenty-four hours since he had eaten. His stomach was cramped from hunger, gastric juices churning within. Chan hurried down to the kitchen and opened the cupboards. He found a loaf of white bread, ripped off anything that was green and stuffed the rest into his mouth. The bread was moist and tasted as delicious as the freshly baked bread slathered in butter and *kaya* that his wife made him for breakfast every morning.

He had another long swig from the tap. He found an empty bottle and filled it with precious water. His own leather water carrier had disappeared in his flight from the beach. He looked down at his bedraggled blue uniform. His rifle was leaning against the kitchen wall but he was out of bullets. Chan went upstairs and ransacked the cupboards. He found a pair of black cotton trousers and a white shirt that he slipped on. The clothes were too loose. The *towkay* whose things he was stealing had been a well-fed man. He hunted for a belt but there wasn't one. He found some pink raffia twine in the kitchen and slipped it through the belt loops, tying it around his waist. His boots were not army issue so he decided to keep them. He would have looked more natural in a pair of slippers but he had a long trek ahead of him and needed comfortable footwear.

Chan took a deep breath and stepped out of the house. He felt as if he was leaving his last safe refuge to venture into an unknown and dangerous world. He knew that the feeling of security was illusory. It was only a matter of time before the Japanese commandeered the building as a luxury dwelling for one of their officers. Well, they would be short a mouldy loaf of bread, a pair of trousers and a white shirt, he thought.

It was not difficult to decide which way to go. The city of Singapore was burning and the thick smoke served as a beacon.

He walked along the main road. Tall shady *angsana* trees lined the roads, their trunks covered in luminescent orange lichen. Chan passed Tengah Airfield. It was deserted. The smoking ruins of Buffaloes and Hurricanes littered the runway and airfields. The watchtower had taken a direct hit and was lying on its side. It was no wonder the Japanese had control over the skies. Chan continued on his way, keeping a sharp eye and ear out for any traffic. The road was peculiarly empty. He felt extremely nervous about what it signified. Had all the troops been driven back? Had the north shore of Singapore been abandoned by the Allies? And if so, where were the Japanese? What had happened to those long columns of refugees streaming towards the city like a procession of worker ants?

Needing a break, Chan stepped off the road and wandered into the forest. Immediately, he was in another world. It was cool under the shade of the trees and the sun was dappling through the leaves, creating light and dark shadows that were restful on the eyes. Huge epiphytes balanced precariously in forks in the branches, their roots hanging down like unkempt beards. Chan tried to untie the raffia he had tied around his waist. It took him a few minutes of unpicking with dirty, clumsy fingers before he could relieve himself in the undergrowth. He watched an arc of urine puddle on the ground. Bugs and ants rushed over, looking for a new source of food. Chan knew the jungle would be just as quick to devour him. It didn't bother him. He appreciated that nature did not squander resources.

It was pleasant in his little spot. Even the sounds of distant warfare were muffled. He sat down on a rock, had a swig of water from his bottle and considered his options. His immediate plan was to get to the city, have the bullet taken out of his shoulder and perhaps have one more tilt at the Japanese. Right at that moment, though, he just felt like sitting in this tranquil place – imagining a time and place before this war had come to Malaya.

His reverie was interrupted by the sound of hoarse voices and the clanking of chains. Surprised and nervous, he parted the fronds of the big palms and peered down the road.

It was his first sight of the Imperial Japanese Army in daylight. It was a force of infantry in their light coats, trousers tucked into boots. They pedalled along energetically on black bicycles. The bicycle chains rattled. The troops were tanned a nut brown, leather helmets lending them a robotic uniformity. Their rifles were slung across their backs, muzzles pointing up. The fixed bayonets caught the light and glinted in the sun. The soldiers cycled in neat rows, three abreast, five feet between bicycles. If he had witnessed this advance the day before, Chan would not have had the courage to attack with his enthusiastic but untrained and ill-equipped volunteers. The Japanese hordes looked formidable.

He waited for half an hour after the soldiers had passed and then made his way towards the city again. He hugged the side of the road and kept a sharp ear out for more enemy troops. When he heard the chugging of a motorbike he ducked back into the bushes. It was a civilian – a Malay man in a sarong and *songkok,* a black stiff brimless hat. He had a basket of chickens on the back of his bike. Chan took his life in his hands and emerged from his hiding place.

'Will you give me lift?' he asked politely in Malay.

The man stopped his bike and looked at Chan. He nodded brusquely.

'But if we see any Japanese, you must go away,' he said. 'Because I think you are one of Singapore volunteers and they will kill you … and me.'

The man dropped Chan on the outskirts, waved off his thanks and dashed away. It was like that in war, supposed Chan. He was reliant on the help of strangers and at their mercy. But there were many who were willing to help at great personal risk.

***

'There should be a moon tonight,' said Lim, gazing at the blackness outside.

'Must be behind a cloud,' said Siow. Everyone in the car jumped a little. It was a night for hushed tones and nervous gestures. Siow's indifference to the atmosphere was disconcerting to the rest of them. He continued on a more practical note, 'Not to worry, I have a torch.'

Lim said, 'Go through the rubber trees. You will come to the edge of the forest. There is a path. Siow knows where it is. It does not go all the way and there are streams to cross, but I think you will make it.'

'I am not worried,' said Mei Ling. She was not quite sure whether she was trying to reassure her mother or herself. The night was like a wall, impenetrable.

They clambered out of the car. Lim got out too and shook hands with the two women. 'Good luck,' he said. Mei Ling felt bereft to be left there by the side of the road.

'Follow me,' said Siow. 'Put your feet where I put mine.'

He switched on his torch. The flickering beam accentuated the darkness around them. They hitched their bags on their shoulders and stepped off the road. Siow walked briskly. Mei Ling knew that her mother would soon flag at the pace. She assumed that he was anxious to get them away from the rubber trees into the jungle. If he did not slow down then she would have to say something. Right now, escape was the priority. After half an hour of trekking, she could hear her mother's laboured breathing. They marched between the rows of trees. The undergrowth was knee high. Mei Ling was terrified that one of them would step on a cobra. The cicadas screeched constantly. The long mellow hoot of an owl made her jump with fright. Bats flitted past chasing after insects, brushing her cheeks with their soft wings.

They reached the end of the seemingly relentless rubber trees. The hills of secondary forest were ahead of them. The moon had appeared from behind the clouds. Mei Ling heard the distant rumble of thunder.

'We will stop here for ten minutes to have a drink and a short rest,' said Siow, his voice loud and alien in that environment.

The two women did not answer. They had no spare breath for courtesy. Mei Ling helped her mother sit down on a fallen log and handed her the water bottle. She took a long slow drink and returned it to Mei Ling who gulped the water. It was the simple things that provided all the pleasure in difficult times, she thought. Never before had a mere sip of water turned her mood from depression to light heartedness. It was as if the water had turned into wine or the purest malt whisky. She felt ready to tackle the toughest part of the journey.

Half an hour later, her burst of optimism had evaporated. It was a tortuous uphill climb. She was drenched with sweat. Her thigh muscles were protesting every step forward. Her bag was like a dead weight on her shoulder. She did a mental inventory of the things she had packed and wondered how she had decided that they were essential. She would willingly have thrown the bag down the nearest ravine.

They were following some sort of path. The route was not completely overgrown. She had no idea who had created the track – it was the product of use rather than intentionally cleared. It could be the way to a fishing hole. Perhaps the Sakai, a tribe of nomadic hunters, used it. Mei Ling considered the possibility that it was created by wildlife, wild boar perhaps or tigers. She dismissed the thought from her head.

Dawn was breaking as they reached a swift moving river, milky brown from the churning mud. It did not look deep. Rocks were visible right across the water.

'The path ends here,' said Siow. 'We will make our way along the river for a while. It is better to walk in the water to hide all tracks.'

He sat down on the ground and took off his shoes and socks. The women followed suit. Mei Ling's mother leaned back against a boulder with her eyes closed. Even in the half light of the early morning the blue shadows under her eyes were visible. Her arms were covered in shallow cuts from the long grass. The *lallang* had edges like sharp knives. Mei Ling noticed that her arms were in the same shape, bleeding and stinging from numerous cuts and scratches.

Siow, in a long sleeve shirt, was less affected. Lesson number one, thought Mei Ling, wear long sleeves in the rainforest. She hoped that every lesson was not going to be learnt through painful experience.

'Can we rest here for a while?' asked Mei Ling.

Siow looked uncertainly at the sky. The clouds were building up, puffs of grey-black cotton candy. 'Yes, but I am worried that there is a storm coming.' He sniffed like a dog discovering the scent of something rotten. 'I can smell rain,' he added.

They took turns to sip from the water bottle and ate a sandwich and a squashy blackened banana each. Mei Ling wrinkled her nose. All she could smell was rotting vegetation and her own body odour, a sharp tangy combination of blood and sweat.

She felt a pang for her life so abruptly left behind. She wondered whether Rajan had noticed her absence. She did not know when, if ever, she would see him again. Her eyes were hot with unbidden, unexpected tears. The strength of her sudden longing for Rajan took her by surprise. Mei Ling brushed the tears and the thoughts away as best she could. She didn't want to communicate anything except optimism and resilience to her mother and she didn't want to succumb to regret at her choice to leave the estate and take to the jungles.

She hauled herself to her feet, stuck out a helping hand to her mother and said, 'Let's be on our way.'

Siow, perhaps startled by her sudden energy, scrambled to his feet and waded into the river. They all followed suit. The water was cool against their legs but it was hard work making their way against the flow. Mei Ling was constantly slipping on the wet rocks, sinking in the wet mud or stubbing her toes against unidentified solid objects. Despite the hard going, Mei Ling found the experience of battling the swirling waters liberating. This was the point where it ceased to be an escape and became the first step in her new life, she decided. Amongst the rubber trees and on the path in the jungle, there had been the sense of potential pursuit. She could not escape the knowledge that the choice to hide out in the forest had been forced upon them. Now she was exercising the free will that her father had taught her to value.

Suddenly, the older woman slipped on the rocks and fell. Mei Ling's mother struggled to get up, thrashing about in the water. She was weighed down by sodden clothes and exhausted from their journey. Siow and Mei Ling struggled to her. They grabbed an arm each, hauling her out of the river. Her hair was dripping and plastered to her face.

'My legs, my legs!' she screamed.

They helped her out and rolled up her trousers.

Leeches. Dozens of the bloodsucking creatures were attached to her mother's calves. Mei Ling looked down and realised that she had suffered the same fate. Her mother was crying. Salty tears mixed with muddy water. She shook her legs violently, trying to dislodge the creatures, too afraid or disgusted to use her hands.

Siow took a packet of cigarettes out of his breast pocket and lit one with a match, his hand cupped around the flame to protect it. Mei Ling wanted to scream at him for his nonchalance. He took the cigarette out of his mouth and held it to a leech. It shrivelled and fell off. He painstakingly repeated the process until all the leeches were gone and then repeated the trick with Mei Ling. Her mother was still sobbing under her breath.

'Better to walk where the water is running faster. Leeches

– they don't like it when water flows fast.'

Mei Ling remembered that Siow had been wading close to the centre of the stream. She and her mother had hugged the sides where the going was less tough. Mei Ling had assumed that Siow was behaving foolishly – trying to impress her. Well, now she knew. He had a purpose, but it was nothing to do with her.

She looked at her mother with great worry. She looked older. The lines on her face from her nose to mouth were etched so deeply they looked like scars. As Mei Ling watched, she crossed her arms along her raised knees and pillowed her head on them. Mei Ling could no longer see her face, only the rivulets of red blood trickling down her legs from where the leeches had been removed. She looked up at Siow and he smiled at her a little uncertainly. She guessed he was as dubious as she was about this relocation plan of theirs. It was too late though. The die was cast. The jungle was their home for the foreseeable future. They would have to make the best of it.

***

There was an eerie silence in the town. The guns had fallen silent. Chan had become accustomed to the mortars and artillery fire as well as the screams of anguish as loved ones were killed and property destroyed. Overhead there had been the constant drone of enemy aircraft punctuated by the whistling of bombs. Now, only crackling fires and hushed conversation on street corners could be heard. The residents of Singapore, many of them bloodied and filthy, gathered to discuss rumours of surrender. Chan refused to believe it at first. It was only that evening, when he saw an enormous Japanese flag draped across the parapet of the Cathay Building, that he finally accepted that the British had capitulated.

CHAPTER 9

I left so suddenly, with hardly any opportunity to say goodbye. I didn't see Mei Ling at all. I know that one of the last things I said to you was that I regretted her coming to the estate and how it had affected our friendship. I felt guilty about that. It was an exaggeration. She was my friend too and, huddled on the deck of the ship sailing into the unknown, I found I could picture her face as clearly as I did yours.

I assumed somehow – how naïve I was – that life for you both was continuing as 'normal' and I was envious, wishing that I could have stayed in Malaya too.

Under the low roof of black smoke that clogged the nose with soot and made breathing difficult, Chan saw British soldiers emptying whisky bottles into the drains. Every now and then they would have a swig. Their task of ensuring that the precious liquid did not fuel a rampage by the Japanese soldiers was fast becoming a riotous exercise. On Clifford Pier, civilian cars were being pushed into the sea for fear they might prove useful to the invading forces. He watched as Austins, Hillmans and a small Morris were run off the edge into water that was already swirling with oil and grease from the burning fuel depots. They would have been better off throwing some of the bicycles into the sea as the Japanese advanced, thought Chan bitterly.

He needed a hospital but didn't dare approach one. He spent the night in the open, sitting on a kerb across from Robinsons, the big department store. The furniture department was being used as a comfortable place for a kip by Allied soldiers and Chan considered joining them. It might be his last chance for a while to get some sleep. But he didn't think he would be able to shut his eyes. His fear for his wife and daughter and his shoulder wound would conspire to keep him up.

The next morning he saw his first Japanese soldiers at close quarters. They wore scruffy uniforms. Pencil moustaches adorned thin lips. They surveyed the city that they had captured with such brutal efficiency without any noticeable pleasure. There were fewer Japanese around than Chan had expected. An Australian soldier told him that only the Kempetai, the Japanese military police, had been allowed in. The bulk of the Japanese forces were outside the city. Yamashita was trying to moderate the behaviour of his troops by keeping them out of town and out of mischief. A few Australian soldiers went up to the Japanese with their hands in the air. The Japanese soldiers waved them away.

Later, loudspeakers announced that civilian members of the population should line up along Bras Basah road to welcome the Japanese troops on their victory parade.

Chan stood by the road with the other anxious residents of Singapore, not knowing how to react to the sight of thousands of Japanese troops, infantry men, combat troops in trucks, officers grinning broadly in open cars and more than a hundred tanks. Malays and Indians were waving Japanese flags and he wondered where they had got them. The Japanese were pleased with their welcome and shouted 'Long live the Emperor!'

Chan ate some canned pineapple he found in an abandoned, bombed shop for dinner and lay down in a small room in the back. After a night of tossing and turning, he woke to a beautiful day. The smoke had cleared and the sun shone on the war-ravaged city.

The first thing he heard when he stepped out was that the Japanese were ordering members of the Chinese community, old, young, healthy and wounded, to assemble at various points in Singapore for screening. Those who had been vetted were given a small piece of paper with the word 'Examined' stamped on it. Unless he got himself that ticket he would have no freedom of movement and would never make it back to Malaya and to Mei Ling and her mother. Checkpoints were springing up all over the island, manned by Japanese troops. Already, he had seen a few decapitated heads impaled on spikes along the Singapore river. A notice underneath read that they had been caught looting.

He went to the screening point beside Tanjung Pagar police station. The sun overhead was scorching, the sky a single shade of eye-watering blue. He could smell the tar from the road, it had a medicinal scent. The place was

149

crowded with thousands of Chinese residents. They sat on the pavements, formed queues or milled around. The people waiting looked uncannily similar. Chan realised that it was the operatic masks of fear they wore that made them look like kin.

The Japanese had erected barbed wire enclosures on the roads. The attendees were divided up and then interviewed by Japanese soldiers. They had all sorts of ways to identify trouble-makers or anyone they thought harboured anti-Japanese sentiments. Those wearing the blue of the Singapore volunteer force were separated from the main group. Chan was glad he had removed his uniform. Anyone with a tattoo was viewed as an unsavoury element, a member of a Chinese clan, and detached from those assembled. As he got closer, he realised that those who confessed to working for the British or being able to speak English were penned separately. Despite observing as carefully as he could, Chan could not identify all the possible reasons for being singled out. There were men and boys and even a few women who were told to stand aside for no discernible reason.

He guessed that those who were removed from the group and packed into trucks like sardines would end up in some sort of prisoner of war camp. He didn't want that. He wanted to get home to his family. He was worn out by his wartime adventures.

His turn would come soon. Chan felt his hands grow moist. He wiped them on his trousers. His throat felt as if he was wearing a too-tight collar to a family wedding. It was so much worse than waiting on the beach for the first wave of Japanese attackers. On that occasion there had been the hope of victory and the reality of comradeship. Here, there was no outcome that was acceptable. Even if he made it through all around were those who would not – fellow Chinese, fellow Malayans and Singaporeans, fellow haters of the Japanese, all at their mercy.

He noticed that there were a couple of men in hoods at the front with the Japanese soldiers. Grown men in fancy dress. Instead of being ridiculous, they were terrifying. Chan realised that they were informers. They leaned forward and whispered in the ears of the interrogators from time to time. Whenever they did so, the interviewee ended up in the trucks.

Chan was directly behind a woman. She was tall for a Chinese with short hair in a modern bob. She wore a loose *cheong sam*-styled blouse over a pair of black pyjama-like trousers and open sandals. Although she bowed her head when she reached the front, Chan could sense her reluctance. There was pride and courage in the stiff back.

The soldier snarled in heavily accented English. 'What is your job?'

Chan knew that this was one of their traps. If she answered in English she was bound for the trucks.

'I am a teacher,' she replied in Cantonese.

'What do you teach?'

'English literature.'

The Kempetai officer, a tall, thin man with elongated arms and legs and bulbous eyes – Chan thought, he looked liked a praying mantis – smiled widely.

'There is no such thing as English literature – all the great works of writing and learning are from the land of the Emperor.'

Chan willed the woman to agree. She kept silent.

The man stood up and sauntered around the table. He said, 'You are responsible for polluting young minds with British propaganda!'

The woman raised her head and looked the officer in the eye.

This assertiveness incensed the man. He screamed at her in Japanese. Chan had no idea what he was saying. He brought his long arm down and slapped the woman hard across the cheek. It was a massive blow and she fell to the ground. Chan flinched and took an involuntary step forward.

The Kempetai officer wore boots. He kicked the woman once, and then, when she curled up into a foetal position to avoid further blows, again. Chan heard the snap of a bone. The woman was whimpering. This delighted the man because he turned to the crowd and said, 'This is what happens to people who defy the Emperor.'

He looked up at Chan who was next in line. 'You – you wish to show your loyalty to the new order?'

Chan hesitated, nails digging into his palms, and then nodded.

'Then you must help me teach this woman a lesson.'

He kicked her again as she lay prone. With a flourish, he took off his hat and waved Chan forward, urging him with a little mimed kick to join him.

Chan did not know what to do. He bowed to the Japanese soldier but shook his head, as if he did not understand what was being asked of him.

'You help me teach this woman a lesson,' shouted the Japanese, his face growing red with anger, white lines around his mouth indicating that his teeth were clenched.

Chan looked at the woman on the ground. Her eyes were shut. She was not making any sound although her chest was still rising and falling, rising and falling. She had passed out from pain and shock.

'She is finished,' said the soldier. 'The question is – are you going to show your loyalty to the Emperor or to this traitor?' He kicked the woman again, this time catching her on the side of the head. She started to bleed from the impact. Chan could see her blood pooling on the road, running between the cracks on the uneven surface.

Chan stepped forward, willing himself to do it. He knew if he did not his fate was sealed. He would end up on the trucks – quite probably after a beating. He might not survive antagonising this mad Kempetai officer. The man was revelling in his own absolute power. Chan looked down at the woman. Her head was on its side. He could see the redness on her cheek from the first blow she had suffered. Why had she been so stubborn? Chan felt a wave of rage at the creature lying on the floor. This was her fault, not his. It was perfectly understandable and sensible for him to do what the officer wanted. She deserved it for her stupidity. Besides, she was unconscious now, she wouldn't even feel it.

Chan stole a glance at the Japanese. He was grinning

from ear to ear, his mouth wide, his plump lips red and moist as if he had just licked them. He was enjoying watching Chan wrestle with his conscience. Chan thought of his wife and Mei Ling. What was going to happen to them if he did not make it back?

Chan looked up at the soldier and bowed deeply. 'I am sorry,' he said, 'but I cannot harm this woman. She has done nothing to me. She is an innocent.'

A whisper ran though the crowd who had been watching with fear but also with the piqued interest of spectators at an execution.

The officer was apoplectic with rage. He grabbed a rifle from a soldier and with one swift action, twirled it around and hit Chan with the butt. The blow caught Chan on his wounded shoulder and he fell to his knees. The shock of pain made him light-headed. Slowly, he got back up to his feet, swaying slightly.

'This is your last chance.'

Chan shook his head. He did not bother to bow. He uttered a single word, 'No.'

The next blow from the rifle caught him on the jaw and he passed out.

***

Rajan was frantic. He had looked everywhere for Mei Ling. She and her mother had left. He had taken her short note about going to visit a sick relative to his father. Thomas had been ready and willing to take its contents at face value. Not so Rajan. As far as he was aware, Mei Ling's mother's parents had died some time back and her other grandparents were in China. It was some sort of ruse. But to what end? At first, he thought that perhaps her father had returned and they had all fled because he was a wanted man. But how would Chan have got back through enemy lines? The Causeway had been blown up by the retreating Allies. It was unlikely that Chan had made it back. Mei Ling and her mother were on the run on their own.

Rajan could not imagine where they might have gone. It was true that the family might have been targeted on the estate. But at least it was an environment Mei Ling knew. And she had people around with her interests at heart – like him. If they were on the road, two women on their own, they would just draw attention. Who could they depend on to feed and house them in this time of war? Very few people would be willing to take in a dissident's family.

And why had she not told him where she was going? Surely she trusted him? Whatever his unarticulated feelings, was he not her best friend? They had spent so many hours together, chatting, laughing and exchanging ideas. He didn't share her views but he admired her principles and her determination to make a mark on the world – to leave it a better place than she found it. Rajan was quite happy to support her and protect her while she tried to do what was right. But she hadn't turned to him. She had fled into the night, not just from the Japanese but also from her past life and from him. It hurt.

Rajan sat under the flame of the forest tree that grew

just outside the offices. The spreading canopy was covered in scarlet blossoms like flames leaping into the sky. He remembered that he had drawn Mei Ling's attention to it once and she had glanced up, nodded her head and said absently, 'Yes, it's very nice.'

He had laughed and told her that she had no appreciation for beauty. He knew that was not true. They just found beauty in different things. He was captivated by nature showing her true colours to man. He was fascinated by the feather wings of the Rajah Brooke butterfly, luminous emerald and velvety black. He loved the flash of a blue kingfisher and the rhythmic tapping of a goldenback woodpecker on the hard trunk of the ironwood tree. Unlike many of the residents of the estates who would kill an iguana on sight and sell it to a contractor for his dinner, Rajan would watch the lumbering prehistoric beast with affection and shepherd it back into the undergrowth so that no one else would turn it into a meal.

Mei Ling, nurtured by her father, found beauty in the written word, in the heroic behaviour of individuals, in the triumph of ideas – she was quite different from him and perhaps for that reason she had not trusted him enough to tell him where she was going.

Rajan got to his feet and went to find his father. He was in the office, at his usual desk. His nose was buried in a stack of papers. The scene seemed so normal that Rajan felt a terrifying sense of dislocation – as if he alone was aware of a future in which the Japanese invaded and Mei Ling ran away. His father looked up and the fatigue in his bloodshot eyes indicated that the last few days had not been as ordinary as the scene suggested.

'What is it, son? It had better be important. I don't think you can just stroll in here. The Japanese are hard taskmasters and very quick to take offence.'

'Where are they now?'

'Das is taking them around the estate.'

"Oh ..."

'So what is it?'

'Mei Ling and her mother.'

'What about them?'

'I don't believe their letter. I think they've gone into hiding.'

'There's nothing we can do,' said Thomas, looking his son directly in the eye as if to compel him to agree.

'But what if they're in trouble? '

'They were not safe here either.'

Thomas paused and looked down at his ink-stained fingers. For all the years that Rajan had been coming to the office, his father had had ink stains on his fingers. It was the only blemish on his otherwise pristine appearance. Thomas wore it like a badge of honour. It indicated that, unlike so many other Indians in Malaya, he had a desk job. He was literate. He was quite different from the rest.

'But we should look for them – help them!'

Thomas shook his head. 'No! We should stay out of trouble. In many ways it is a good thing they have gone.'

'What do you mean?' demanded Rajan.

'It is quite likely that the Japanese would have found out

about Chan's activities. We might all have been suspected of similar attitudes – it would have made it very tough if the Japanese were uneasy about our loyalties because we had been known to associate with anti-Japanese elements.'

'*Known to associate*? Pappa, Mr. Chan was your friend.'

'And I wish him well. But he acted irresponsibly and put his family in danger. I don't intend to do the same with you.'

Rajan felt as if Mei Ling was putting words in his mouth. 'Pappa, sometimes the principle has to be more important than just safety. We cannot sacrifice our friends just to keep out of trouble!'

Thomas looked at his son and sighed. He stood up slowly. Rajan realised that his father was getting older. He seemed fragile in his well-ironed trousers and crisp, starched white shirt – as if his clothes kept him upright instead of the reverse. The skin on his throat was loose and hung in folds. Thomas walked around the table and put his hands on his son's shoulders. Rajan, with the lankiness of a teenager, was taller than his father now, an elongated youth, not yet filled in with an adult's bulk.

'You're right, son. But there is nothing we can do for them. They have gone. I would not be human if I wasn't relieved that we have not had to choose between *their* safety and ours. I know you're fond of the girl. But forget it. There is no future there. She is Chinese, she is the daughter of a communist and she is on the run. It is not our responsibility any more.'

***

Chan recovered consciousness. He was reeling from the pain in his jaw and shoulder. He shut his eyes, hoping for oblivion again. There was to be no further respite. Fear and curiosity got the better of him. He opened his eyes a crack. He was on an open truck. His hands were tied behind his back with a thin cable, a telephone wire that cut into his wrists. The same cable was tied to the other prisoners so that they formed a human chain.

A couple of Japanese guards sat at one end. They were separated from the prisoners by a couple of feet. The prisoners themselves were a mixed bag of men and older boys. There were a couple of old men in wire-rimmed glasses. No doubt the Japanese had assumed they were Chinese intellectuals. The woman who had earned him his place on the truck sat opposite him. He had almost failed to recognise her. Gone was the tall defiant woman. In her place was a hunched, tortured creature, her eyes swollen shut, the blood from her head wound soaking into her clothes. She had been subject to a further beating. There were injuries he did not remember seeing inflicted.

No one on the truck was going to risk attracting the notice of the guards by telling him, but the Kempetai officer had ordered that Chan be put on the truck. The Japanese were embarrassed by the courage he had shown. They were anxious to get him away in case his example provoked a wider rebellion. The Kempetai knew better than most that control of a civilian population in wartime required that they be browbeaten and terrified, unable to trust even their kith and kin, and subject to violent and arbitrary punishment. The social bonds that held communities together had to be severed so that neighbours were suspicious of each other and every stranger was presumed to be an enemy. Any act of courage that defied this paradigm was insidious. So Chan was removed from the people and put on a truck, his act and his person to be forgotten as soon as possible.

To consolidate his hold over the population, the long-limbed Kempetai officer had strolled along the line, selected a man with furtive eyes and led him to the front. This man did not hesitate to earn his freedom by kicking the young woman on the floor with his dirty slippered feet. Those in the crowd who were inspired by Chan's courage now watched another buy his escape by turning on his own kind. They did not protest or argue. They looked down at their feet and covered their children's eyes and longed for a time before the Japanese had come to Singapore.

Chan wondered where they were being taken. He had seen the rows of white POWs being marched towards Changi prison in straggly lines. He doubted that the Japanese would house local prisoners and foreigners together. But the route they were taking was in the direction of Changi. He hoped there would be some rudimentary medical care. His jaw needed looking at and the woman across would not survive without careful nursing. He feared that she was doomed. His refusal to carry out the Kempetai officer's instructions had cost him his liberty for nothing. Chan was still glad that he had behaved as he did. He was ashamed that he had been tempted to do as he'd been asked.

The truck slowed down. Chan badly needed a drink. His mouth was parched. His tongue was sticking to the roof of his mouth. His lips cracked painfully. The blood tasted salty. It had been a long hot slow drive after a day spent queuing along main roads under the blazing sun.

Chan could see a looming concrete tower of cement grey – the watchtower at Changi prison. To his surprise, they drove right past the jail. When the truck came to a stop it was on the yellow sands of Changi beach, beyond the ominous structure of the prison. They were ordered out of the truck. As the prisoners were tied together, it was difficult to disembark. Those who were too weak to stand had to be supported by those on either side. The young literature teacher was like a rag doll. Her knees had buckled and her head was lolling.

The Japanese soldiers did not speak any English or Malay. They made their demands known with loud shouts and gesticulations. The men and the few women prisoners understood that they were to walk towards the sea. Chan was puzzled. Was it some new way to torture the exhausted prisoners – most of whom had been wrenched away from loved ones just that morning?

The man tied next in line to Chan, a middle-aged, pot-bellied, balding desperately ordinary man who in a past life would have been a shopkeeper or a restaurateur, began to cry.

The soldiers were pointing at the beach. The first in line, shoved in the direction of the sea, started moving. The pace of each person was dictated by the prisoner tied to him. It was a slow erratic line but they made steady progress towards the water. Chan's eyes watered from the reflection of light on sand. The sea was a deep turquoise, the waves tipped with white foam. A steady breeze was blowing in from the water and it made the going cooler. The prisoners took heavy steps, feet sinking deep into the coarse sand, until they were ankle deep in water.

A hoarse shout caused them to stop. They stood facing out to sea. From somewhere further up the beach, there came the rapid staccato of machine gun fire. It was such a familiar sound that Chan didn't grasp its significance. Vaguely, he wondered who was fighting after the surrender and ceasefire. Perhaps a band of diehards had refused to turn in their arms.

The waters around his ankles turned red. The fat Chinese man next to him exploded in a hail of bullets, collapsing face first into the waters, his back riddled with bullet holes. Tied to him with the telephone cable, Chan was dragged down by his dead weight. He felt an explosion of pain in his back. He had been hit too. He fell in the water. Chan turned his head in time to see the other victims fall like a row of dominoes.

His back was almost beyond pain. It was a sensation he had never known before, an out of body experience where his nerve ends recognised that he was in agony but his mind refused to process the pain.

The gunfire ceased. There was silence except for the wind and the waves and the whimpering of those who were alive. Out of the corner of his eye, Chan saw Japanese soldiers wade in amongst the dead and injured. They were holding their rifles, bayonets on the end. He shut his eyes and lay still. He rode the shallow waves, his head turned sideways so that he could breathe. Sand and salt water went up his nostrils. From time to time he heard a scream or a gurgle as the soldiers made their way methodically down the line. He turned so he was face down in the water. He held his breath. He could hear the sounds of heavy boots splashing in the water around him. He floated limp in the water, willing the soldiers to ignore him. One of them kicked him in the side. He did not respond. It did not require an act of will; Chan was so focused on holding his breath that he barely felt it. His lungs were burning, the desire to take a breath obscuring every other thought. He sensed rather than heard the soldiers move on. He estimated that he was close to the end of the line. He counted another ten seconds, and then let his head drift sideways in the swirling waters. He sucked in air between waves but did not open his eyes. A soldier might glance his way and come back to stick a bloodied bayonet into him. Chan lay still and prayed to a God he did not believe in.

Silence fell. Even the guttural-voiced Japanese soldiers were quiet. Chan thought that he could smell cigarette smoke mixing with the rusty metal smell of blood. The soldiers were having a rest after their bloody afternoon's work. Chan was dimly aware that if he had been in deeper water, even a foot further in, he would have drowned. But where he was, it was possible to breathe as his body scraped against the sandy bottom. The salt water stung his wounds and the sun beat down on his back and neck.

Chan heard voices speaking English, Australian he thought from the accents, raised in shock. Chan guessed they must have spotted the carnage on the beach.

'My God! What have you done?' exclaimed a man.

There were snarled Japanese instructions. Chan heard clanking sounds. 'We are not going to help you bury the evidence of your crimes. It's not something we're required to do as prisoners of war,' said an Australian in a clipped angry voice.

This time the Japanese officer spoke in English. 'You will do what you are told. Here are the shovels. Or you can join them.'

It was not difficult to guess who 'them' was. Nor was it surprising that the Australians complied. It was pointless to be killed for refusing to bury the dead. Bravado and defiance had a time and place, and this was not it.

Again, Chan heard splashing in the water. This time it was Australian soldiers dragging the executed out of the water. There were more exclamations of revulsion when it was discovered that the victims were all tied together and had been shot in the back.

'You've just *murdered* them,' said one of the men. 'You deserve hanging for this.'

The Japanese officer laughed and said something in Japanese. All the soldiers broke into loud guffaws. They did not anticipate a day when the war would be lost or their army held to account for their deeds.

Chan felt his arm gripped by a strong hand. He was turned over. The cord binding him to the next man had been cut. A sudden stab of pain in his shoulder caused his eyes to flicker open. He made out the dim outline of a man against the sun.

The shout that he had been dreading came.

'Hey! This one's alive. This man is alive!'

Chan opened his eyes. It was too late to pretend that he was dead. He was being held out of the water by a soldier. He looked at the man and saw his face, thin and long and marked with grief. Another shadow loomed. Chan could see the khaki uniform and the high boots of a Japanese soldier. He was kicked once and then again. His face twisted in pain. Unlike earlier, he could feel every nerve screaming with agony.

The Japanese man waved his hands in the air, miming his orders. It was not difficult to see what he wanted – the Australian soldier to hold Chan's head under the water.

'No way!' said the Australian. 'You can do your own bloody dirty work.'

A gun was raised and pointed at the soldier's head.

'Please don't make me do it.'

There was complete silence on the beach. The rest of the men watched the unfolding drama, the Australians afraid to intervene with a dozen guns trained on them, the Japanese amused but watchful.

The Japanese officer's finger tightened on the trigger.

The soldier looked down at the man cradled on his lap in the shallow waters and mouthed, 'I'm sorry.'

'Please don't. I have a family,' whispered Chan.

'So've I, mate,' the soldier said, his voice a murmur

carried away on the sea breeze. 'So've I.'

He slid Chan from his knees and held him down. There was no fight left in the man who had made his way to Singapore to take the war to the Japanese.

Chan thought of his loyal wife briefly. And then, although it caused a pain beyond anything else he had experienced, he thought of Mei Ling. The last thing he saw were tears running down the face of a good man who had no choice.

As he opened his mouth and let the seawater take him, he never heard the whispered, 'God bless you, mate. And God forgive me.'

CHAPTER 10

It was difficult to adjust to our new circumstances as refugees aboard a troop ship sailing into the unknown. My time was spent hoping and praying that we weren't spotted by a Japanese air patrol. I wanted to survive, to live, to see you and Mei Ling again. I wanted to grow old.

As I sit here writing to you, I realise that I've got at least part of my wish. I have a blanket across my knees. Checked. Why are they always checked? Like airport carpets, I suppose, with their vivid patterns – they hope that the food stains and blood and drool won't show. I've lost most of my hair. All that is left is a band that runs from ear to ear, lank, grey and flecked with dandruff, hanging down like the red skirting they used to thumbtack to Formica tables when the Chinese contractors held those grand dinners for the planters.

Well, I've grown old with the memories ever present. My wish has been my punishment.

Rajan marched out of the room and went in search of Das. He had been close to the Chans. He might know something that his father did not or wasn't telling. And he was a sympathetic man – he would understand that Rajan needed to know what had happened to Mei Ling. He tracked Das down to the estate factory where the rubber was cured, rolled and stacked into sheets for export. Das was with the Japanese colonel, so Rajan kept his distance. This was not the time to get into further trouble or give away his concerns about the Chans. The less said in front of the Japanese the better.

He waited outside, hiding his bicycle in the undergrowth. The Japanese were now well ensconced in the big bungalow. He had heard them the previous night. They had raided the manager's liquor stocks, if the loud singing and raucous laughter was anything to go by. He'd been tempted to peer in the window but had decided on prudence. He was looking for traces of Mei Ling. He didn't want to draw attention to himself.

At last, the Japanese officer came out, nodded to Das, leapt into a Land Rover and raced off in a big cloud of red dirt. Das dusted himself and walked back into the factory. It was not yet operational. The place had been quiet since Coleman and Murray had damaged the equipment with a few hammers and a lot of sweat.

'Mr. Das!'

Das turned a startled face around and smiled when he saw Rajan. He beckoned to the boy to follow him into the factory. The smell of the processed rubber was strong and Rajan wrinkled his long nose. He'd always avoided the factory because of the stench. Rajan ran a hand over the damaged equipment. The metal was cold to the touch. 'Can this be fixed?'

'I hope so,' said Das. 'The Japanese have given me twenty-four hours.'

'What will they do if you can't manage it?'

Das grimaced. 'I really want to avoid finding out. The person I need right now is Chan. He would know how to get this sorted out. But I have no idea where he might be.'

'Or Mei Ling and her mother.'

Das looked at the boy sympathetically, 'I heard from your father that they had left.'

'Yes, the note said they went to see some sick relative but I don't believe it.'

'I'm not sure I do either.'

'Where do you think they've gone?'

Unlike his father who had been determined to show no interest, Das's brow was furrowed, like a smallholder's vegetable plot. He too had tired eyes as if the Japanese had banned sleep. 'I don't know. I've been thinking about it. I can't imagine where they would feel safe – or even safer than here.'

'I'm so worried,' admitted Rajan.

Das put an arm around the boy's shoulders. 'Me too.'

He said at last, 'There is one place where they could hide out from the Japanese until this war is over ...'

'Where? Where do you think they might have gone?'

'Into the jungle.'

'What?'

'Chan told me before he went that the 'left behind' force

that he was joining would launch a guerrilla war against the Japanese if the British were defeated – from the jungles. I have heard that a lot of Chinese and a few Indians and Malays have abandoned their homes to move into camps deep in the rainforest.'

Rajan sank down on a latex-stained stool. He felt as if he'd been punched in the gut. He was winded, struggling for breath to speak. In his wildest imaginings, he had not thought that Mei Ling, she who did not know the difference between an owl and an oriole, would try and survive in the jungle. And yet, it was a logical step in so many ways. It would appeal to Mei Ling, the idea of hiding away with people who believed in her cause. It would be a safe hideout for her father if he should return from Singapore. It made a lot of sense. Except that when he thought of the threats she would face, from the Japanese to malaria, he did not think she would survive.

***

The guerrilla camp consisted of a collection of bamboo huts on stilts in a clearing halfway up the side of a low hill. The roofs were *attap,* carefully thatched palm leaves. The terrain was covered in dense jungle. Light hardly penetrated the canopy. When it did, it had a greenish tinge. The ground was damp and fetid and stank of rotting vegetation. It was about an hour away from the nearest dirt track on foot with another hour on bicycle to the main trunk road that meandered through Johore.

The commander, political commissar and a couple of senior men shared accommodation. The men, about fifty of them, were divided between two longhouses. There was a separate hut for women. When Mei Ling and her mother trudged into the camp, trailing after Siow, they were the only women there. They were told that a couple of trainee nurses, the daughters of tin mine workers, would join them soon. There was a stream close by so fresh water for washing and drinking was not a problem. Mei Ling looked at the toilet facilities, holes dug in the ground with wooden rails running across them, some way downstream. She knew as a matter of intellectual certainty that a human being could survive all manner of tribulations and indignities. But it was still disconcerting to be confronted with the reality of jungle living.

Her mother was troubled by their throwing in their lot with the newly formed Malayan People's Anti-Japanese Army. Mei Ling, on the other hand, was excited. These were communists who, having spent a good part of the previous ten years harassing the British, had decided that they had a common enemy, the Japanese, and it was time to join forces. The first concrete example of the détente was the small cadre of communists, including her father, who had been trained by the British. Mei Ling's safe haven was one of the fledgling guerrilla groups that had been organised in Johore.

'Does anyone know you are here?' demanded the camp commander, Chung.

'No, sir.'

'The Kempetai has made intelligence inroads into civilian populations.'

Mei Ling already knew this – through a combination of torture and bribery the Japanese were having some success in getting neighbour to tell on neighbour and brother to view brother with suspicion.

'Anyone who reports to the Kempetai that a family has a son or a daughter in the jungles with the MPAJA is well rewarded. Are you sure you have left no trail?'

'No one knows we are here. Our past is erased.'

'I hope so – the Kempetai has ways to make those we love betray us.'

Siow had winked at her, a reassuring gesture as she was subjected to the commander's hostile questioning. Later, he told Mei Ling about his worries for his own family. His parents were old and he had two young sisters. She asked him why he had risked joining the MPAJA. He opened his mouth, exposing crowded overlapping teeth, and then shut it again – a big, friendly creature filled with an undisguised admiration for his new compatriot. But while she was polite and did not discourage Siow from hanging around her, Mei Ling did not hint that her affections were available. The memory of Rajan's smiling eyes would encroach on her conversations with Siow and the other guerrillas. She wondered at this, at herself. She had known that Rajan was fond of her, had read in his brown eyes all that he had been too inarticulate to say. But she had not suspected for a moment that she reciprocated Rajan's feelings, instead treating him as a friend, even a brother. Well, she should be grateful, she decided. Leaving the estate had been difficult enough – she might not have found the strength to do so if she had known how much she would miss the skinny youth who was sceptical of communist teachings but who knew where to find fireflies. She decided to put Rajan out of her head until such time as they were together again, and then spent the next fifteen minutes thinking of nothing else until she was summoned to help with the food preparation.

Food was not the huge problem she had feared. It was, however, a complicated logistical exercise. It involved guerrillas making forays into town to receive food parcels from the villagers and townsfolk, mostly Chinese, who supported their anti-Japanese activities. Sometimes, the Chinese *towkays* donated cash and the fighters would purchase what was needed. They collected tropical fruit like mangoes and durians from orchards on the jungle fringes. Meat and fish were very scarce, almost impossible to obtain in the villages. There was more money to be made selling them on the black market than at reasonable prices to townsfolk. Further, because the guerrillas who were sent into the villages were sometimes delayed from returning by Japanese patrols, bad weather or the necessity of waiting for news at one of the letter drops, the precious meat or fish would spoil before they made it back to the camp. Very occasionally the men would trap a wild boar or catch some small freshwater fish in the stream. The whole camp would be filled with excitement when this happened. There would be a spring in every step at the thought of real wholesome food.

Mei Ling's mother planted food crops in the clearing next to their hut. Their diet was soon enhanced by a daily stew of tapioca and tapioca leaves although Mei Ling was dubious about their nutritional value. She soon found herself in sole charge of the makeshift camp kitchen. She cooked rice and tapioca, served the men and then went to Chung and made it clear that, while she did not object to doing women's work once in a while, she had thought that communist ideals included equality of the sexes. Chung, a grizzled veteran of the war in China, had known Chan for many years and was prepared to humour the daughter out of respect for the father. He agreed that she should have weapons training.

Mei Ling soon learnt how to fire rifles, handguns and even the Tommy gun although this last was unwieldy and heavy, not only in her hands but also in the hands of the slightly built Malayan Chinese guerrillas. The Bren machine guns were too big for her to lug about – two guerrillas were deployed to carry the gun, one in charge of the actual gun and the other the ammunition and a spare barrel. Mei Ling practiced firing the Bren, lying prone and resting the weapon on its specially designed bipod. Chung showed her how to camouflage the distinctive curved magazine when preparing an ambush. She was also instructed in the art of preparing bombs. The MPAJA seemed to have a very ready supply of gelignite and TNT.

In a strange way, Mei Ling was happy. The life was hard but it was punctuated with interesting experiences like learning weaponry and jungle warfare. She enjoyed the lectures by senior cadres on communist philosophy and principles every morning. She was bored by the task of cooking rice but at least it kept her occupied, as did weeding her mother's vegetable patch. She missed Rajan but took comfort from the fact that her absence from the plantation was keeping him safe. There was still no news of her father. Chung had sent word for information to be sought about his fate but none had been available.

Mei Ling feared the worst but was determined to keep hope alive.

***

The word went out that all Caucasians were to assemble on the Changi Peninsula, civilians and military personnel both. Andrew Coleman heard the instructions with relief. He could not have carried on much longer. He was tired in body and soul. His frantic dash to Singapore had been the last fling of the dice. Now that the island had fallen into enemy hands, there was nothing more he could do to escape. He thought of all those soldiers who had died. Their young lives snuffed out in a vain sacrifice. Seventy days from end to end, that was how long it had taken the Japanese to defeat an empire.

He joined a long line of people walking towards Changi. There were women and children, old and young, soldiers and civilians. The only thing they had in common was that they were white and they were prisoners of war. Coleman found it difficult to watch his countrymen so reduced. Just a few weeks earlier, they'd been the pinnacle of power in this tropical kingdom. Now they dragged their feet and hauled the small bags that contained their most private and valuable possessions. Every other trapping of wealth and prestige had been abandoned somewhere between Kota Bahru and Singapore.

Coleman recognised some of the men and women in the column. There were planters he had known from other estates and members of the Malayan civil service whom he had met at the 'whites only' clubs, the cocktail receptions and the dinner dances at the Raffles Hotel.

Coleman didn't make eye contact with his acquaintances. They did not seek him out either. Each was trapped in a personal cocoon of misery. The Japanese discouraged conversation with a kick or a rifle butt. They were not provided any water or food and the slow trudge took on a nightmarish, never ending quality. Houses en route had small Japanese flags flying from the front gates. Coleman could not believe that the civilian population had turned on their colonial rulers so rapidly, especially after the hammering the city had taken from the Japanese bombers. He hoped it was a Japanese-organised propaganda exercise.

Local people had come out of their homes and shops to watch the sorry spectacle of their erstwhile rulers being led away like thieves. Coleman's conviction that the flags were Japanese propaganda suffered a blow when some of the bystanders began to boo and jeer. One Indian man, who had the neatness of a middle ranking civil servant in the British administration, spat at him, his face contorted with a hatred that he must have bottled up for years. Coleman was too shocked to protest. He sidestepped the bubbly gob of saliva on the road more by instinct than intention. The man reminded Coleman of Thomas, his estate clerk. He felt a moment of regret for the subservience he had demanded and obtained from his underlings on the estate. Perhaps, somewhere in Malaya, Thomas was spitting at white prisoners of war too.

They passed through a Chinese neighbourhood. The mood changed. Women and girls were in tears. Some darted up to them bearing flowers, and more usefully, bottles of water and sandwiches. The prisoners hung back at first, nervous of drawing the attention of the Japanese guards. They watched but did not seem in the mood to interfere. Coleman gulped down clean, fresh water from a bottle thrown to him with real gratitude. He was touched to be at the receiving end of kindness after the catcalls from the earlier watchers.

It took them hours to reach Changi. They were escorted into the barracks that had previously housed Allied soldiers. Coleman had assumed they were heading for Changi jail but it was actually the military base that was their destination. The compound was surrounded by barbed wire with Japanese sentries around the perimeter. Inside, they were left to their own devices. Military prisoners were taking steps to organise the hordes. Women and children were bivouacked together. Coleman was shown to the corner of a large dormitory and allocated a space about six feet by four feet on the cement floor. He lay down, placed his small rucksack under his head, and tried to sleep.

***

Her mother was her biggest concern. While Mei Ling's health was robust, her mother grew frail. She picked at her food, smiled at Mei Ling and insisted that old people did not need to eat as much as young people. Her worry about her husband was taking its toll. She was convinced he was alive and back at the estate waiting for them. In vain, Mei Ling assured her that one of the sympathisers would inform him of their whereabouts. Mrs. Chan was not persuaded. She was sure her husband was taking terrible risks to find them.

She succumbed to malaria. The jungle swarmed with mosquitoes. The communists had incense coils and rubbed their exposed parts with crushed lemon grass leaves; the citronella oil was a good repellent. But the mosquitoes were plentiful and aggressive. It was very rare to see anyone at the camp without big welts from scratched bites. Mei Ling's mother lay on a handwoven mat on the floor of their hut, feverish and delirious. Mei Ling did her best to control the temperature by wiping her down with cold, damp towels. Her mother suffered terrible chills and would moan about the pains in her joints and her head. Mei Ling was beside herself with worry. There was no medicine at the camp. Chung sent Siow to a sympathetic doctor in the nearest town who provided them with as much quinine as he could spare – the Kempetai was cracking down on doctors and monitoring their drug supplies to ensure that they were not treating ill or wounded anti-Japanese elements.

Her mother got worse. Her conviction that Chan was back on the estate and waiting for them was now an obsession.

It affected her recovery. All her energy was focused on the whereabouts of her husband. Finally, Mei Ling agreed to go down to the estate and look for her father. Chung was furious when she insisted that she had to go.

'It is an unnecessary risk – to you, to my men and to this camp.'

Mei Ling nodded. She could not deny it. 'I will be careful. I will not show myself. I will contact a friend on the estate and just ask him whether my father has returned.'

'How can you trust this friend?'

'I don't know – but I do.'

'You do not have to go. I will send Siow. He has more experience than you in avoiding the Japanese.'

'It has to be me. I do not want to risk the life of anyone else. Also my mother will not be reassured unless I have looked into this myself. She is too ill and upset. She will not believe Siow or anyone but me.'

Chung could see she was adamant. 'Very well, Siow will take you down to the estate and wait for you. But he will not risk himself by coming with you to find your friend.'

'Thank you.'

She rushed over to tell her mother. She was lying on a ground sheet and her face and hair were damp with sweat. Another bout of fever and shivering had just passed. Mei Ling held her mother's claw-like hand. The skin over the bones felt like paper. She explained what she was going to do. Her mother looked at her through eyes that would barely open, gummed together with perspiration. Her pupils did not focus and Mei Ling thought she had not understood, that it was too late to reassure her. But then some of the tension went out of her body. Mei Ling had to lean forward to hear her whisper, 'I am glad that you are going to find your father. He must be so worried about us.'

'Mother, he might not be there. You must be prepared for that.'

Her mother, eyes shut, smiled. It almost broke Mei Ling's heart to see the cracked lips curve into the first glimpse of pleasure her mother had shown in months. 'I understand. Don't worry. Just go and look for him.'

***

Food was the main concern – the only concern – of the prisoners of war. They were fed three times a day. Every meal consisted of broken grains of polished white rice. The women took over the cooking of it, and the original sludge improved in texture but the taste was the same. An intrepid prisoner decided that salt would make the rice more palatable. He rounded up some men, walked to the sea every day from the barracks and collected big buckets of salt water. This was now used for cooking. Coleman admired the ingenuity of his fellow prisoners but could not taste any difference.

Once in a while, there would be some fish, caught by a prisoner in a pool of water, tapioca leaves grown outside the camp or prawn paste or *belachan*, traded with one of the men who came to the camp to run errands for the Japanese. On the days where there was some supplement to rice, there would be good humour around the camp.

Usually, Coleman had to force himself to keep spooning the rice into his mouth. Every swallow was accompanied by a desire to retch. Despite this, the prisoners watched out for their share and inflicted swift and brutal punishment on anyone foolish enough to try and sneak an extra mouthful during serving time.

In desperation, because a large number of prisoners were falling ill with beri-beri from the lack of vitamin B in their diet, medical staff amongst the prisoners arranged for bundles of *lallang* grass to be boiled into a soup and drunk as a supplement. It tasted foul but Coleman drank his share. There was very little supervision from the Japanese. The guards who sat around the perimeter were frontline soldiers, uninterested in the job of babysitting prisoners.

'I'm thinking of making a break for it,' whispered a young soldier.

'Where will you go?' asked another.

'There's nowhere – you'd stick out like a sore thumb,' Coleman pointed out.

'Someone will give us shelter.'

Coleman remembered the spitting, hissing crowds that had lined the way to Changi and shook his head.

'I'm in,' insisted the other man.

Coleman heard later that the two had been captured by residents of Singapore and returned to the Japanese in exchange for cash. The men were beheaded after being tortured. There was no escape.

The Japanese guards were replaced with Sikh soldiers who had defected during the fighting. They, despised by the British for changing sides, insisted on the same outward respect as the Japanese.

It stuck in Coleman's craw to bow to the Sikhs. Despite this, he behaved with feigned subservience. He was not looking for trouble. The big man had lost a lot of weight. He walked stooped, as if he had suffered a spinal injury, and his skin hung off him. His salt-and-pepper beard was as thick as the moustache he had sported when he was manager of his plantation. Although he was acquainted with quite a number of the prisoners, he didn't fraternise with them. He developed a reputation as a loner. People referred to him as 'poor' Coleman and shook their heads about the likelihood of his surviving.

A few months into his incarceration, he was instructed to join a work crew and sent to build Changi airfield with other prisoners. This was exhausting work, in the blazing sun, without adequate shade or equipment. His only desire at the end of a long day was to lie down in his small space and do his best to sleep. The lassitude that gripped him was alleviated by the hard labour. He was conscious for the first time of a desire to survive his ordeal and be reunited with his family – or at least Matthew, his son.

As he laboured on the worksite, a Japanese officer called for attention.

'We are looking for proud volunteers to assist the Imperial Japanese Army build a railway line in Thailand.'

The scrawny prisoners leant on their hoes and stared at the ground.

'Those who show dedication to their new rulers by

volunteering will be rewarded with better rations,' continued the officer.

Coleman raised his hand. Afer all, his situation couldn't really get any worse.

CHAPTER 11

I knew that you had a fondness for Mei Ling, of course, even in the early days. She was a better friend of yours than of mine when we were on the estate together. Thinking back, I was often resentful that you preferred to hang around the sundry shop with her than come fishing with me.

I sometimes wondered why she preferred you to me. Was it because I was white, do you think? After all, her father was always filling her head with anti-British propaganda. I'm sure you will tell me that it was your dark good looks! Maybe she spotted a weakness in my character that was hidden from me at the time.

We were good friends, the three of us, but you were the glue that held us together.

Mei Ling set out early the next morning with Siow in tow, retracing the route they had taken to get to the jungle camp. The journey was much less exhausting than it had been on the way up. Mei Ling was sure it was due to the sheer physical toughness of her day-to-day life. Despite the poor diet of rice and tapioca that was taking such a toll on her mother's health, she was stronger. The unfair advantage of youth, she supposed.

When they got to the main road after a few hours of trekking, Siow told her to wait. He set off to a nearby village where he knew a few sympathetic residents. In a short while he was back with a motorbike and Mei Ling climbed on the back.

'This is much better than walking!'

'And also less likely to attract the attention of the Japs,' replied Siow over his shoulder as they raced along the road.

Mei Ling enjoyed the sensation of the warm sun on her back and the wind in her hair. In the jungle, it was always sultry and steamy. The wind could not penetrate the trees and the sun rarely peeked through the thick foliage. Despite living outdoors, she and her fellow communists were pale and anaemic, less tanned than when they resided in the estates and villages of Malaya. It marked them out. They wore long sleeves to make their sallow skin less obvious to sharp-eyed enemy soldiers.

They didn't come across any patrols as they made their way to the fringes of the rubber estate that Mei Ling had called home until six months earlier. Siow came to a halt. Glancing up and down the street, he motioned for Mei Ling to get off. He wheeled the motorbike into the thick brush on the border of the plantation. When he was deep enough, he laid the bike on its side and drew some palm fronds over it. Mei Ling signalled that it was invisible from the road.

'I know Major Chung said that you were to go on your

own,' said Siow. 'But if you need me to come along, I will.'

'You're a good friend, Siow. But we shouldn't contradict orders. I'm in enough trouble already for insisting on this trip. I will manage very well on my own.'

'I *know* that you can manage very well on your own.'

Mei Ling knew that Siow's wistful remark contained a hint of criticism. Siow wanted her to depend on him, to lean on him for support. But that was not her character.

'I will meet you back here,' she said.

Mei Ling turned her back on the mournful young man and marched through the trees. She was sure she knew the way but it was a big estate and she didn't want to get lost. She estimated that she was about an hour away from the staff compound. She hoped to spot Rajan and signal to him – get him to come and talk to her without letting anyone else know she was around.

Mei Ling was excited at the thought of seeing Rajan again. Her lips curved into an involuntary grin at the thought of her dear friend whom she had not seen in six long months. She remembered the smile lines around his eyes and his curious folded ear that made him look like an elvish creature in profile. Mei Ling did not understand the strength of her feelings and it made her uncomfortable. She realised that her determination to take this risk and return to the estate might be fuelled in part by her desire to see Rajan again. If indeed that was the case, Mei Ling chided herself, it was unconscionable. She was risking the whole guerrilla force if she was caught and tortured into giving away their location. Of course, she hoped to have the strength not to tell. But the Kempetai was feared by every man, woman and child in Malaya for good reason.

Mei Ling kept a sharp lookout for Japanese troops and anyone from the estate. The Japanese flag was flying from the flagpole in front of the manager's bungalow. The whole building was ablaze with light. Mei Ling guessed that the Japanese had commandeered the building. The new colonialists had adopted the comforts of the old. Mei Ling crept away. She needed to get close to the staff quarters. Perhaps her father was back. Maybe her mother in her weak state had sensed something, his presence, calling to her. The bond between them was very great. She shook her head. She was being fanciful. If her father had returned, he would have traced them through his communist friends.

Mei Ling experienced a wave of doubt so strong she felt her knees buckle. She put a hand against a tree to steady herself. What if she could not find Rajan? What if he was away? What, her heart turned over with a sudden cold fear, if he was dead, killed by the Japanese because he had been rebellious? She knew Rajan so well. He was easy going and tactful – not in the least confrontational – unless he was upset and then his temper flared red hot like a bonfire of dry leaves. She remembered how he had stood up for his father on the first day of the Japanese arrival. She hoped and prayed that Thomas had kept his son away from their new masters. Mei Ling felt a stab of longing so acute it felt like a wound. She had to see Rajan.

As if the fates were her subjects, her heart's wish was answered. She saw a slim figure ambling towards the neat, small bungalow that had been Rajan's home all the while she had known him. There too she could see changes. The beautiful flowers that his mother had tended to so assiduously were gone. In their place were the ubiquitous tapioca plants, standing tall and straight, as if they took pride in having vanquished the merely decorative from garden plots all over Malaya.

Mei Ling thought Rajan looked taller and thinner. His hair was cut very short – the wavy black locks that would fall over his face or stand up on end when he was animated were gone. She couldn't see his face. He was walking away from her.

Mei Ling picked up a smooth oval rubber seed and flung it at him. She missed but it struck a pot. He stopped and looked around, his body language nervous and tense. Mei Ling knew that Rajan did not fear anything that nature could throw at him. It must be the Japanese who had turned him into this suspicious, watchful creature.

'Rajan,' she hissed.

He didn't hear her. She was too far away. Mei Ling was worried that he would walk away and her last chance to see him, to speak to him, would be lost. She grabbed a handful of small brown pebbles and threw them hard. They scattered about his feet like hailstones. He stared at her hiding place in the trees.

She whispered again, 'Rajan!'

This time he walked over until he was at the edge of the rubber trees. Mei Ling slipped out from behind a broad, mottled trunk and said, her voice carrying in the semi-darkness, 'It's me! It's Mei Ling.'

Rajan started like a deer and stood stock still, staring at her.

'Is it really you?' he asked, his voice shaking.

For perhaps the first and last time in her young life, Mei Ling felt like an uncertain teenager. Had she changed so much? Had he forgotten her? It had only been a few months since she had fled to the jungles although, in that moment, it felt like a couple of lifetimes.

But then he glanced around to ensure there was no one in the vicinity and ducked between the rubber trees. He grabbed her by the hands and she looked up at him. His eyes glowed in his dark, shadowed face.

'Mei Ling? Where have you been? I've been worried sick about you!'

She looked down at her feet. 'I'm sorry. I wanted to tell you that I was leaving. But I thought it would put you in danger if you knew too much.'

He waved his hand, dismissing her concerns for him as being irrelevant to his desire to know where she had gone. 'Where have you been? I looked everywhere!'

'In the jungle with the MPAJA.'

***

He sat down on a fallen log as if the strength had abandoned his legs. Mei Ling sat down next to him.

'I wanted to tell you but I just couldn't.'

'You were right to go. The Japanese are,' he shook his

head, 'beyond words. If they had found out about your father, you would have been in terrible trouble.' He added, locking his long fingers together, 'I'm not sure that you could have trusted everyone on the estate or in town. Someone might have given you away.'

She changed the subject. He was not surprised. It was not pleasant to dwell on the possibility that she could not have relied on her father's friends.

She asked, the tremor in her voice giving away the faint unquenchable hope that she was carrying in her heart, 'Has my father returned?'

Rajan shook his head. 'Is that why you came back?'

She nodded. He noticed that her hair was rougher, less glossy than when she had lived on the estate. Her face was thin, her cheekbones protruded like blades. There were deep shadows under her eyes. He could not imagine what she had been through, living in the jungle. Where had she found the strength?

'My mother is not well,' explained Mei Ling. 'She has malaria. She's been adamant that father is looking for us … I agreed to come here and find out whether he had returned. I'm hoping that my visit here will give her some peace of mind so that she finds the strength to recover.'

Rajan nodded his understanding.

'Has there been any word at all?' she asked.

Rajan put his arm around her and felt her shoulder blades jut out from her slim back. His voice broke like that of an adolescent boy. 'It's not good news. Rumours are flying, carried back from Singapore by those who have been allowed to return to Malaya. A while back, my father heard that he was rounded up as part of the *Sook Ching*, the purge of Chinese dissidents. He stood up for some lady who was being beaten by the Japanese. The Japanese took him away. He's not been seen since.'

'He could be a prisoner?'

Rajan nodded. 'It's possible.'

He looked at her and knew that it was his responsibility to be honest. 'Mei Ling, there are terrible stories about what the Japanese have done in Singapore and other big towns, even here in Johore. A lot of the people who were rounded up have disappeared without trace. Many suspect that the Japanese have murdered them.'

Mei Ling stiffened as if his words were body blows that she was warding off physically. And then she collapsed against his shoulder, buried her face in her hands and sobbed as if her heart was breaking. Rajan knew that it probably was and he regretted having been so truthful.

'I always feared this but I kept hoping,' she whispered.

'You can still hope …'

She shook her head. 'It is better to be honest. We do not defeat our enemies if we are afraid to confront the truth.'

Rajan smiled. She looked different but this was the same girl he remembered, with the strength of character and commitment to her ideals that had always left him embarrassed at his own free and easy ways. But she was right. The way to combat the horror that had been visited upon them by the Japanese was to remain true to their beliefs and to show personal courage in the face of danger. 'What are you going to do?' he asked.

'I have to go back.'

He took her hands in his and felt the calluses that hard labour had left on her palms. 'Can I come with you?' It was not the question he had intended. He was no longer sure what he had planned to say. Instead, he had blurted out his deepest, most secret wish.

Mei Ling shook her head and smiled at him. 'No!' she said.

'Why not?' He was insistent now, demanding the right to be by her side. So much unspoken and yet understood between them.

'It's dangerous.'

'Do you think I am a coward?'

'No, I don't. But I do know that you will endanger yourself as well as the whole camp. Your parents will raise the alarm if you go. You cannot do that to your father. You know how much he loves you.'

Rajan, on the verge of protesting, paused. She was right. He acknowledged that by letting go of her hands.

Mei Ling put a hand on his cheek, feeling the stubble on his chin. It reminded her of the rough bark of a rubber tree, familiar and comforting. 'This war will end soon. I will come back.'

Rajan noted this blind optimism from the most unlikely source. She was trying to make him feel better and he was grateful for the attempt. He wanted to ask her whether she would come back *to him* but he held back the words. If they were to part, as it seemed they must, he didn't want to make it harder for her – for either of them.

Mei Ling got to her feet and dusted herself. 'I have to go now.'

'How will you get back?'

'One of the guerrillas is waiting for me. He has a motorbike. After that, we have to trek for a few hours.'

'I'm here if you need me.'

She smiled, 'I know that.' She stood on tip-toe, kissed him on the cheek and walked away into the trees.

***

Rajan watched Mei Ling go. He wondered whether he was making the biggest mistake of his life not going with her. There was no way to know. But he could not leave his parents without telling them where he was going and he could not tell them without endangering their lives. So he would stay and let the girl he loved disappear back into the jungles of the hinterland.

He realised he had not asked her very much about her life. There had been no time. She would have refused to tell him anyway. It might endanger him to have too much information if the Kempetai came calling. He would have liked to be able to picture what she was doing, to feel the closeness of knowing her routine. He remembered the calloused hands. Life in the jungle was hard. That much was obvious. He thought about her mother, dying of malaria. The news he had given Mei Ling about her father would not work as a cure. He wondered if she would tell her mother the truth or leave her with the faint hope that Chan was alive. Rajan did not doubt that Mei Ling's father was dead. He had not told her, there was no need to spell out the full horror, but there had been rumours swirling of massacres and mass graves. People spoke in hushed tones of hearing machine gun fire and seeing newly turned earth. The Japanese were visiting vengeance on the Chinese population, not just for their resistance during the invasion of Malaya and Singapore but also for their support of China in the years leading up to the Pacific War.

His father had been right, thought Rajan. Each ethnic group in Malaya was being treated differently. On the estate, the Japanese were recruiting Tamil workers for the Indian National Army that was supposed to overthrow the British in India under the leadership of Subhas Chandra Bose. His father was enthusiastic. He was convinced that the hardships of life under the Japanese would be worth every kick and slap if only the motherland could throw off its colonial yoke. Sergeant Hashim, who had been the sidekick of that large Scot, Commander Murray, was now in charge of the police force in Bukit Pagoh, reporting to his new masters as he had once done to the old. Rajan had a sudden fear that even if the Japanese were defeated, the people of Malaya, each dealing with the Japanese occupiers in a different way, would find it almost impossible to work and live together again.

Rajan slipped into his house through the back door. He hoped that no one would notice he had been out so late. His head was full of his encounter with Mei Ling. He did not think he was capable of obfuscating if anyone asked him where he had been.

Rajan heard strident voices from the front room. It was his father and Das. He took off his sandals and arranged them beside the door. In times of trouble, he thought, habit often governed behaviour. He went to see what the commotion was about. He found the two men standing on the carpet in the living room. He pushed aside the curtain of stringed shells that hung across the doorway. The men turned at the sound of rattling. His mother was seated on the sofa, her cheeks stained with tears. The black tea she had made for the men was untouched on the low table.

Rajan went to sit by her. He looked up at his father and Das. The tension in the room was like a physical presence. 'What's the matter?' he asked.

When neither man replied, he asked again, 'Pappa, what's the matter?'

It was Das who answered. He turned away from Thomas and looked at the boy. 'You are old enough to have a view and advise your father. The Japanese want us to join the Indian National Army. Apparently,' there was a wealth of sarcasm in his voice, 'the INA is going to liberate India.'

'Why are you such a sceptic?' demanded Thomas. 'I know as well as you, *better* than you, that the Japanese are not altruistic. But our interests coincide with theirs. All Indians should desire a free India. Japan can make it happen.'

'Are you questioning my patriotism?' snapped Das. 'I want a free India – *not* one that exchanges one colonial master for another, infinitely worse. Has our experience here taught you nothing?'

'But it is Indians that are being called upon to fight! Indians troops have defected from the British and joined the INA. It is not the same situation at all. Japan is arming and training Indians, not fighting.'

'Yes, I have seen the regiment of Indian soldiers garrisoned in town. I think that they are just as likely to have switched sides to avoid being prisoners of war than from any change of heart.'

'Pappa, do they want you to *fight*?' demanded Rajan. He left unsaid that his father was too old for such activity.

'No, son. I think they're recruiting people like Das and me to reassure the Tamil labourers that this is the fight for them.'

'Already we have lost many workers to the promise of better wages and better conditions if they go north to Thailand to work on the railway line. Can we afford to lose a bunch of men as soldiers? We will not be able to keep the estate running.' Das had returned to the practical arguments that were his forte.

'This is more important.'

'I don't believe that the Japanese will liberate India,' said Rajan, daring to look his father in the eye as he contradicted him. 'They just want to keep the British tied up fighting so that they do not have the resources to attack any Japanese-held territory.'

'See! Even your son sees through the Japs,' expostulated Das. 'Only you are prepared to believe that they can be of use to anyone except themselves.'

'Well, I am going to join the Indian National Army!'

'And I am not!' Das was adamant.

The two men glowered at each other, unable to find the words to convince the other that they were misguided in their decision.

'What about me?' asked Rajan.

'What about you?'

'What if they want me to join up too?'

His mother let out a sudden wail. All three men had forgotten she was there, sitting and dabbing her eyes with the frayed edge of her worn *saree*. Rajan felt sorry for his mother. She was a simple, comfortable woman whose life had been turned upside down. He noticed how much weight she had lost. She was not the happy creature of six months ago. Now she worried whether there was enough food to feed the family. She was apprehensive that her precious son was not getting enough to eat. She was convinced that her husband would fall foul of his new Japanese masters, and now this – the possibility that Rajan would be called upon to join an army. She could not stop crying, her shoulders heaving, the tears falling like the first few splatters before a massive storm.

'Enough! There is no reason for this display,' said Thomas. 'Rajan is too young. I will tell the Japanese that I will join but he need not.'

There was a silence in the room, punctuated by the sobbing woman, now wringing her hands in the air in despair. All of them knew that no one told the Japanese anything.

Whether Rajan was compelled to join up depended entirely on the whim of Colonel Hidojo.

***

A few days later, with a change of clothes, tin plate, tin cup and hat packed into a kitbag, Coleman climbed on a truck with other prisoners, mostly military personnel, both British and Australian. At the main railway station in Singapore, his bag was searched by Japanese soldiers. Their methods were simple. They tipped the contents of kitbags on the floor and kicked them around to see if there was any contraband. Coleman picked up his things and repacked the bag without a murmur. He had a few cigarettes under his belt but the Japanese had not found them. They hardly ever did body searches. He supposed they were reluctant to touch the prisoners, who were not particularly hygienic in the circumstances. Or it might have been a cultural inhibition. Coleman didn't care. He had his small stash of cigarettes that he might be able to trade for food, or in an emergency, actually smoke.

The transport to Thailand was not what he'd been expecting. Instead of passenger carriages, all the prisoners were crammed into freight cars for the passage north. Despite this, Coleman was pleased to be underway. He didn't mind the cramped conditions at first but they soon became unbearable. There was no room to lie down. He sat crouched with his back against the wall. As the sun got higher in the sky, the metal container became unbearably hot, like a large steel coffin, and he thought he might faint from the waves of heat radiating from the sides. He was thirstier than he had ever been in his life. There was very little water to go around. A few men had brought leather bottles and they shared their water. It didn't amount to more than an opportunity to wet his mouth. It made him feel worse, reminding him of the taste and smell of fresh water, without slaking his thirst. From time to time, the train would stop and the Japanese would hand out a pint of soggy rice to each prisoner, sometimes with strands of stringy meat floating in it. Coleman and a few other prisoners kept back some of each day's ration for the following day to ease their gnawing hunger. Many succumbed to dysentery. Coleman was overwhelmed by the indignity. Unlike the soldiers who were more accustomed to the privations and lack of privacy, Coleman was humiliated by his weakness. There were no toilets in their boxcar. The train made occasional toilet stops but those were a misnomer. There were no facilities. Anyone who had to relieve themselves just found a spot and did so. At first, Coleman tried to find some privacy in the bushes or behind a wall. He soon abandoned such niceties. There was no time. His stomach was too bad.

On the train, the other prisoners had to help. Coleman found himself held by his fellow prisoners at the only open door, his shorts around his knees and his bottom hanging over the side of the moving train. But it was better than soiling the limited space that they had.

One dawn, as the grey light crept in, Coleman saw a

young soldier sitting in the corner. His knees were bent so that he could rest his chin on them. Tears streamed down his cheeks as he stared away into the middle distance, lost in his own unhappy thoughts. Unaware that the pitch darkness was about to give way to a hint of daylight, he had let himself go. Looking at the thin, freckled face and the lank yellow hair he realised that the boy could not be more than a year or two older than Matthew. He felt a sudden panic that the war would go on long enough for his son to end up like this. He was glad that it was him on that train despite the misery of it. Maybe, the gods would decide that the family had suffered enough and leave Matthew alone.

At last the train journey came to an end. The prisoners were told to disembark. The Japanese demanded an inspection. Men who had been forced to sit hunched up for four days had to persuade their weakened limbs to hold them upright. The Japanese counted heads and made sure that none had escaped. A few prisoners had not survived the trip. Their bodies – Coleman counted seven – were laid out on the platform. He did not know any of them and might not have recognised them if he had.

The Japanese explained that they were in Thailand, at Ban Pong. A few, including Coleman, were told to carry the dead men into the jungle and leave them there. A Japanese soldier with a gun escorted them into the wilderness. They laid out the men in rows, trying to provide some dignity in death that had been absent in their passing. As they left to march back, Coleman, who was last in line, grabbed the hat from the body closest to him. It felt terrible, stealing from the dead, but the reality was that if they were to do any marching, his own threadbare cap might not last the trip.

The camp at Ban Pong was the most disgusting place Coleman had ever seen. From a distance, all the men were relieved to see the rows of long *attap* and bamboo huts. It appeared welcoming and restful after days sitting up in the train. On getting closer, the filth of the place was evident. The ground was knee deep in mud, a result of the monsoon rains. There were food scraps, rubbish and piles of excrement outside and within the huts. Despite this, the exhausted men lay down on the bamboo beds, spreading a piece of ground cloth on the slats if they had one but otherwise lying directly on the surface, and did their best to sleep.

The next morning, an officer amongst the prisoners ordered the men to clean up the camp. But before they could begin work, the guards indicated that they would march that evening. The Japanese made the crew trek at night because it was cooler. They hoped the prisoners would make quicker progress. It was a miserable passage through virgin forest. They crossed streams and rivers. They were soaked by the rains. There was hardly any food, just pints of soggy rice. Coleman could not decide what he hated most; the swarms of mosquitoes around his head that he was too tired to brush away, the thick mud they had to wade through or being constantly wet. His clothes rotted and his shoes came apart. He developed foot rot between his toes. His heels and the balls of his feet were scraped raw. During the day, the men would strip naked and hang their clothes on every available bush, desperate to have something dry to wear. The humidity was unbearable. Coleman found that he was bathed in sweat, the perspiration rolling off his chin and down his back and legs in small rivulets. They drank from passing streams but the water was muddy and foul. It was impossible to sleep in the day.

Coleman would lie down in a patch of shade to conserve his energy for the evening march. The Japanese regularly kicked them awake and demanded they get to their feet and form up for a headcount. Coleman could not decide if this was sadism or whether they genuinely expected some of the prisoners to make a break for it. Where did they think the men could go, he wondered, with thick jungle on all sides and hardly a fit man amongst them?

Despite his doubts, a crew of six men tried to escape. At a rest stop, on a pre-arranged signal, they indicated that they were going into the undergrowth to relieve themselves. Instead, they made their way into the forest. Coleman was later told that one of the men had a compass. They believed they could make it to the sea. The sharp-eyed Japanese guards noticed that they had not returned. They went in pursuit. The prisoners sat and waited. When there was a sudden burst of prolonged gunfire, they bowed their heads. The Japanese did not bring back the bodies. They were left in the jungle to rot. Coleman realised that the young man, the boy whom he had seen weeping on the train was one of those killed. He felt a stab of guilt that he had not tried to comfort him. Trying to escape had been foolhardy to the point of suicidal and he, Coleman, might have been able to prevent it if he had lent the young man a sympathetic ear.

The Japanese ordered them to start walking. Coleman spared a last thought for the boy whose name he did not know and then put him out of his mind. There was no room for anything in the jungle except a single-minded dedication to personal survival and even that might not prove enough.

A few days later they reached Kanchanaburi. Any hope that this was their ultimate destination was soon quashed. The men were told that they would have to go on to the Three Pagoda Pass, the highest point on the proposed railway line near the Thai-Burma border. Coleman's shoes had not survived the first fifty miles to Kanchanaburi. One of the men found an old tyre. With a knife he had managed to secret on his person, he cut pieces for those who had something to offer in return. Coleman handed over his spare hat, stolen from the dead soldier, and tied the two pieces of rubber to the undersides of his feet with twine. They were his shoes for the rest of the march. He considered himself lucky. Many of the men were almost naked and barefoot, their clothing reduced to a few strips to cover their privates – the rest had disintegrated. Coleman didn't even bother to wonder if he could survive the journey to the railway line. He just put one foot in front of the other and continued on his way.

***

Mei Ling told her mother that there was no news from her father at the Kuala Reman estate. He was probably hidden in a camp somewhere just like theirs. She could almost see her mother shrink and age. The old woman shut her eyes. It had the finality of a theatre curtain coming down. 'I am sure that you are right, Mei Ling,' she said. 'Your father is a brave man and we should be proud of him.'

She didn't open her eyes again. She lay there on the bamboo *charpoy*, refusing food, agreeing only to wet her lips from time to time with fresh, boiled water from the stream. It seemed to Mei Ling that her mother had guessed the truth despite the lies she had told – her husband was not coming back. She had decided that she would prefer to die rather than battle for survival in the jungle. The young woman watched her mother. Inside, she screamed with anguish that her sole remaining parent should choose to leave her. What about me, she wanted to ask? I am your daughter. Would you leave me here, alone, an orphan? She kept these thoughts to herself. She held her mother's head up to give her water and marvelled that her glossy black hair was now deep grey and felt like the surface of a de-husked coconut, coarse, fibrous and unfamiliar.

She would have suggested that they take their chances in town but her mother was too ill to be moved. Besides, Mei Ling did not want to skulk in town, bowing to Japanese soldiers and wondering if her neighbours were traitors. She wanted to be the sort of daughter who would make her father proud. If he was dead, Mei Ling was determined to honour his memory.

She did not speak of these plans to her mother. It would have upset the old woman but would not have persuaded her to linger a little longer in their jungle hideout. Mei Ling did not doubt that her mother knew how she felt. Only the knowledge of a long and fruitful life, of contentment earned and ambitions fulfilled, could reconcile a child to the loss of a parent. Neither of her parents could provide her with that crumb of comfort. It was not their fault. The Japanese were responsible. The Japanese were to blame for the death of her father, for her mother's bereavement, for the fact that she was in the jungle, away from Rajan whom she loved, with no future to look forward to except of war and illness. And it was not just her family. She looked around the camp and spotted Chung, who had left his old parents to fight the Japanese in China and was now estranged from his children too. She caught sight of Siow who had to live every day with the knowledge that his choice to wage war was endangering the family he had left behind.

She had made choices that had led them to this place but these had been forced on her by the Japanese. She'd done the best she could with the limited options available. Her mother lay on the flat surface. Her eyes were closed to the dappled light that streamed into their jungle home. Mei Ling gently fanned her with a palm leaf, trying to make her more comfortable.

She watched her mother breathing unevenly and tears rolled down her cheeks, trickled down her neck and joined with the rivers of sweat between her breasts.

Later, when she was asked how her mother had died, Mei Ling would remember that day and answer softly, 'She made a choice to die. I could not change her mind and I did not try.'

***

Rajan was shell-shocked after Mei Ling's visit. He hadn't been able to see her clearly in the half-light of dusk. The only illumination had been from the distant yellow glow of the houses. It had merely created shadows upon shadows. That was how he felt about her visit, he decided, that a shadow had appeared – the shade of an old friend and would-be lover. He had detected changes, the coarse hair, the work-roughened hands, but the essential person had been the same. She was still Mei Ling, determined to seize life with two tight fists and shake it until it agreed to conform to her expectations.

It sounded as if her mother was in a bad way. Rajan summoned a memory of the old woman. He remembered how she would nod and smile at him, her black hair in tight curls. Mei Ling had told him that her mother spent every night in curlers when he remarked that she had not inherited her mother's wavy hair. He had felt foolish for not realising that Chinese hair, so thick and straight, could not have achieved those ringlets naturally. He had said sheepishly at the time that he preferred her smooth head of black gold. Mei Ling had laughed and told him not to be silly. Mei Ling was not a person one could flirt with – he had discovered that very quickly.

If her mother was dying, Mei Ling would soon be an orphan. There would be no one to act as a restraint if she was in one of her wild moods. He feared that she would embark on some foolhardy campaign. He wished that he had some authority over her behaviour but realised that no one had control over Mei Ling. Her parents exercised some influence because of her love for them but also because she admired their values, but that was all.

Rajan knew that she had affection for him. He had sensed it as she sat with him in the privacy of darkness and was for a brief moment reluctant to leave. But he doubted his views would carry much weight with her. Especially as his main concern was for her safety – Mei Ling valued her own life least of all when there were battles to be fought.

Rajan realised he needed advice. He sought out his father. He was sitting in his cane rocking chair wearing a faded cotton *sarong* and a snowy white vest with a patch on it. Their clothes were falling apart. There was no money to buy anything new. The Japanese currency, the banana money, was fast becoming worthless. Using Straits dollars, the old currency under the British, was punishable with death or imprisonment. Most trade was now done on a barter basis – anything valuable was used to obtain something extra in the way of food, not wasted on clothes.

'Pappa?'

Thomas did not appear to hear his son.

Rajan said again, more loudly this time, 'Pappa!'

His father looked up at him and blinked as if he had been so lost in his thoughts that he could not find his way to the present.

'Pappa, I need your advice.'

Thomas sat up in his chair and rocked it forward until his two bare feet, with neatly trimmed nails and tufts of dark hair on each big toe, were planted on the floor. Rajan saw that he had caught his father's attention. After all, he never asked for advice although it was volunteered on a regular basis.

'What is it?' asked Thomas. And then, his voice reedy with anxiety, 'I hope you're not in trouble with the Japanese.'

'No, no. It is not that.'

'Then what?'

'It's about Mei Ling.'

Rajan could see from his father's blank face that he had no idea who Rajan was talking about.

'You know, Mr. Chan's daughter!'

'Yes, of course. She and her mother went to Cameron Highlands.'

'No they didn't,' said Rajan. 'You said at the time it was just a ruse to escape from the Japanese.'

'Yes, you're probably right. I think it was a good idea that they went away. If the Japanese found out about Chan's activities – it would have been very bad for the family.'

'They're hiding in the jungle.'

'What?'

'They're with the MPAJA. Mrs. Chan is not well but Mei Ling is all right.'

Thomas was staring at his son. 'How do you know all this?'

'She was here – earlier today, she was here.'

'Who?'

'Mei Ling!'

'Why? Why did she come back?'

'To check if her father had returned. Her mother is dying

of malaria. Mei Ling said it was making her worse – the worry about Mr. Chan. So Mei Ling agreed to come and see if there was any news.'

'My God, son! If the Japanese had spotted her with you – they would have asked questions. You could have ended up in enormous trouble.'

Rajan waved away the concern. 'That's not what I wanted to ask you, Pappa.'

'What is it then?'

'I'm worried about her. I think she might join the MPAJA – try to fight. It will be so dangerous. I need to try and stop her. But I don't know how.'

Thomas stood up, tucking his *sarong* around his waist. His lanky teenage son was now six inches taller than he was. He raised a finger of admonition. 'I do not want you to have anything to do with that girl. She is trouble. You have endangered us all by talking to someone who harbours anti-Japanese feelings. If she returns, you must refuse to see her. If she is persistent, we will report her to the Japanese.'

Rajan was more shocked than he had ever been in his life. He stared at his father as if he could not recognise him. This was a stranger inhabiting his father's likeness. Was this what war did?

'Pappa, I want to help her.'

'That is the last thing you can do,' replied Thomas. 'I absolutely forbid it!'

CHAPTER 12

My word, war is boring when you're seventeen and hiding out in the English countryside. I wasn't evacuated as such, a bit too old to be part of the official exodus, but Mother insisted that we go to her village in Dorset after the V2 rockets started coming in. Hitler's last throw of the dice, but it decimated London. It was terrifying, never knowing when they would strike or where – death was as random as anything I had seen so far in the war.

In the country, life was almost 'normal' if you can call it that when all the abled-bodied men had gone to fight, the place was full to the brim with evacuated children and every bit of food depended on a ration card. I worked at various odd jobs to help the 'war effort' but mostly I just counted the days until I would be old enough to enlist.

I thought of you and Mei Ling living under Japanese occupation and hoped that you were having an uneventful time and staying out of trouble. Little could I imagine that the fates were already arranging our eventual reunion.

Colonel Hidojo was smiling. It was not a reassuring sight to Thomas and Das, standing before him like school children in the headmaster's office. Their quarrel the previous evening had ended without resolution. The two men stood next to each other, a history of co-operation behind them but at loggerheads about the future.

They had expected the summons from the Japanese colonel. They both knew what he wanted – for the men to join the Indian National Army. Das suspected that the officer did not expect any difficulty. He wondered whether there was a way of going on the offensive, of changing the dynamic of the conversation. If he was going to do something, he needed to do it now.

Das said, with the assistance of the ubiquitous interpreter, 'Colonel Hidojo – I would respectfully like to speak to you about something.'

The Colonel had thin arched eyebrows that looked as if they had been drawn with a fine pen rather than grown through the efforts of nature. He raised one eyebrow and it conveyed both permission to speak and a mild astonishment that such a request should have been put forward.

'There have been reports that the conditions on the Burma-Thai railway project are not as comfortable as was promised to the workers. In fact, we have heard that the death rate is very high. A large number of our Tamil labourers accepted your offer to go north. Is there any truth in these rumours?'

Feeling that he had couched the question too directly despite his efforts to be conciliatory and non-accusatory,

Das bowed deeply to rob his words of offence.

'What does it have to do with you?' Colonel Hidojo seemed puzzled. 'These men do not work for you anymore. Why do you care if conditions are not good?'

'I used to be their conductor, sir. I feel responsible,' answered Das.

Hidojo was dismissive. 'I was told to round up workers and I did. They are building a railway from Thailand to Burma so that we can attack India without any threat to our supply lines from sea attacks. Everyone said it could not be done – that the jungle was too inhospitable – but we are making good progress. It is true that conditions are harsh, but sometimes there must be sacrifice to achieve important goals.'

'Do those who change their minds have the option to return home? Their families are living on tapioca and vegetables they grow themselves – they are even clearing rubber trees to find space for their vegetable plots!'

Hidojo scowled. 'Those who vandalise Japanese property must be punished. As for their menfolk, I do not see why they should not return if they choose.'

Thomas had been silent during the conversation between the two men.

Das turned and asked him, 'Have *you* any concerns about conditions on the railway?'

Thomas was cross. It showed on his face. The lines on his forehead were etched deeper as if someone had run over them with a charcoal pencil. Das knew that he did not want to be involved in the discussion. The Japanese were not going to change their behaviour on the railway project because a conductor from Johore was worried about his ex-workers. At best, they would be cross that he was daring to question, even criticise, the conduct of the Imperial Army. But Das felt obliged to raise it. He had a responsibility to do what he could once he became aware of a problem. Thomas took the opposite view. If it could not be changed then it was best to leave well alone. Any protest drew attention, not to the problem, but to the messenger. And with the Japanese, the consequences for the unfortunate messenger could range from a kick to an execution.

'There are only rumours,' said Thomas. 'We have no way of knowing the truth. If conditions were that bad, some of the men would have returned by now.'

Hidojo nodded, a pleased smile on his face. Das had noticed before that the Japanese were not interested in the sentiment behind any remarks. They always took comments at face value. Thomas lacked sincerity because he, like Das, believed all the rumours. The two men had discussed it and Thomas had expressed the same unease. But he was not prepared to carry his alarm to the Japanese.

'Enough of this talk,' snapped Hidojo. We are not here to discuss the railway. I asked you both a question a few days ago and I want your answer.'

Das felt as if someone had flipped the contents of his stomach like a *chappati*.

Thomas said, standing upright in an unconscious imitation of a soldier's posture, 'It would be an honour to serve in the Indian National Army. I look forward to the

INA defeating the British in India with Japanese help.'

The colonel went so far as to come around the table and slap Thomas on the back – Thomas ducked his head at this indication of approval.

'And you?' said the Colonel, turning to Das, the remnants of his smile on his face.

'I regret that I must turn down your kind offer, Colonel Hidojo. I will not join the INA,' said Das.

'What?' The question was like a gunshot and the translation an immediate angry echo.

***

Mei Ling went to Major Chung after her mother's death and said, 'I would like to take a more active part in the fight against the Japanese.'

Chung looked at her carefully, his eyes bright, alert pinpricks in his weather beaten face. He had just had a haircut, Mei Ling noticed. It was a professional job. One of the guerrillas had been a barber before. He claimed to have joined the resistance because of his shock at discovering that one of his pre-war employees was a Japanese spy.

'I know you're upset about your mother, but you should not make any hasty decisions,' replied the Major.

'This is what I always intended to do. While my mother was alive I did not want to worry her further. Now, I am an orphan and I can risk my life with pleasure for our cause.'

The guerrilla commander steepled his stubby fingers and looked at her over the tips. Mei Ling was surprised by his apparent reluctance. She had mastered the weapons and attended courses on bomb-making and guerrilla tactics in the camp. She had worked hard to disseminate information on the communist effort, writing articles for the underground printing press that was run in the town.

'Why do you hesitate? Do you not trust me?'

'I trust you.'

'Is it because I am a woman?'

'The communists adopt a policy of equality between men and women.'

'Then what is it?' demanded Mei Ling.

'I hesitate because I fear that you might choose one day to follow your own mind rather than my orders.'

'I understand military discipline. I would be a loyal soldier to the cause,' replied Mei Ling.

'Sometimes the cause is hard to identify in these complex times, Mei Ling.' Chung clapped his hands together. 'But I have no right to stop you. You have a good mind and you are brave and dedicated.'

'Thank you, sir. I will not let you down.'

'Don't make promises you can't keep, young woman!'

In a very short while, Mei Ling was equipped with a rifle and a uniform. The khaki hat with the three stars on it gave her particular pride. She was inducted into the MPAJA with a simple oath at a ceremony in the jungle. She wished that one of her parents was there and wondered what Rajan would think if he could see her now. She doubted he would approve.

Her impatience for an active mission was viewed by

Chung with misgivings. He called her to one side and said, 'Mei Ling, your time will come. But we must protect the safety of the guerrillas and this camp. The Japanese are patrolling the forests. It is difficult to find enough food.'

'With all due respect, sir – our role here is not just to eke out survival and avoid the Japanese. We are the MPAJA. We must take the fight to them.'

'You may sit in at out next tactical meeting with the political commissar and our senior men,' said Chung.

Mei Ling was filled with excitement. This was more than she could have hoped for – to be allowed to take part in a discussion on tactics. She made up her mind that she would refrain from expressing her opinions. It was an honour to be invited along – especially as she had not been on a single active mission. It was a concession to her father's status within the party and her own impatience for action. Probably, Chung felt that if he exposed her to the planning process, she would understand why it was not possible to charge into the nearest town with all guns blazing.

The meeting was held in the hut that functioned as the headquarters of the regiment. The men filed in.

'I have invited Mei Ling to join us today as a mark of respect to her father,' said Chung.

There were a few nods, replacing the surprised looks as well as expressions of disapproval at her presence. Mei Ling smiled and tried to look innocuous and respectful.

Chung called the meeting to order. 'We need to decide on our military strategy. How do we inflict maximum damage on the Japanese with the assets at our disposal?'

'We have many weapons but not enough ammunition,' explained Siow, who was the person in charge of armaments. 'Our equipment was collected from the battlefields while the British and their allies were fighting the Japanese. Unfortunately, much of the ammo was used before the weapons were abandoned.'

A young man with spiky black hair and a patch over one eye said fervently, 'Very well then. Let us steal some from the Japanese. It would be a huge coup!'

'It would be a huge coup for the Japanese,' replied Chung, 'when they parade your head on a stick through Johore on the following morning, Keng Lian.'

'Major Chung is right,' said another man, 'we cannot be foolhardy. The ammo dumps are well-guarded.'

'We sound like cowards, not soldiers,' snorted the political commissar.

There was an angry silence.

'It is not cowardly to be prudent,' said Chung at last. 'But I agree we should take steps to remind the Japanese that they do not have it all their way. Any suggestions?'

'Assassinations!' said Mei Ling, despite her earlier resolution to be seen and not heard. When no one responded, she added, 'It has been successful in other districts. The assassination of Japanese officers and collaborators will send a strong signal.'

'It is true,' said the political commissar, rubbing his grimy hands together. 'If we can teach the Japanese to know fear as well as reassure the population that collaborators will feel our wrath ... it will be a huge propaganda coup.

And it would not require the ammunition of a large scale assault.'

'Siow?' asked Major Chung.

'We have the resources for targeted assassinations, sir,' he replied.

Keng Lian, the exuberant young man with the patch, was on his feet. 'We should form small assassination teams – and we can ask our eyes and ears in the towns to identify targets for us.'

'That is a good idea,' said Chung in a tone of mild surprise. 'Who will volunteer to be in our first team then?'

Mei Ling, Siow and Keng Lian put up their hands.

'So much enthusiasm,' said Chung. 'I have no doubt that you will find a way to get close to your targets. But the question is – how will you get away again?'

'We will have to work out the details, but I am sure there will be no problem,' insisted Keng Lian.

'No problem? You say it is no problem?' Chung was livid. 'I agree that if you kill a collaborator or a Japanese official it is worth your life in exchange. But when they capture you, hand you over to the Kempetai and torture you until even your mother will not recognise you – will that be "no problem"? When you disclose our location here, will that be "no problem"? You young folk, you are brave but you have no judgment!' Chung turned to Siow who was sitting to his right a little further down the trestle table. 'Siow, you're in charge of this operation. If anyone behaves foolishly, report to me – I will deal with them.'

Siow nodded and said, 'Yes, sir.' He rose to his feet. 'Will the comrades who volunteered for this squad please come with me?'

'There is one more thing,' said Major Chung. They all turned to him. 'Carry a handgun each. Make sure you have a bullet left for yourselves if you are captured.'

***

'Das, don't be a fool,' whispered the *kerani*. 'It's just symbolic. We're not going to fight the British or anything. You know the Japanese just want the senior men in the estates to join the INA because it makes it easier to recruit the workers!'

The interpreter looked bemused. Should he translate this half-private, half-murmured conversation? He stole a wary look at his boss. The colonel was picking at a nail, absorbed in the task.

Suddenly, Hidojo looked up. His face was suffused with blood.

He shouted something in Japanese.

The interpreter said hastily, 'You disrespect me – you disrespect the Emperor!'

'Not at all, sir,' insisted Das. 'But this is not our war. It is *your* war against the British. I do not want to fight them. They were good to me when I was a child. It does not mean that I do not esteem the Japanese. I have worked hard for you to keep this estate going.'

Despite their experience of the viciousness of the Japanese, both men were caught by surprise. Colonel Hidojo pulled his pistol out of his belt, strolled over to Das and held the muzzle to his head.

'Does this persuade you to change your mind?' he demanded.

'For God's sake, Das, it's not worth your life!' pleaded Thomas.

Das's mobile mouth was set in an obstinate line. Thomas noticed for the first time that his hair was too long. His unkemptness annoyed the clerk. He, Thomas, was smartly turned out despite the fact that his shirts were worn and threadbare. He was doing his best to maintain certain standards for himself and his family. What did it matter which marauding exploitative occupier was in charge of their estate anyway? What mattered was maintaining one's personal discipline and keeping one's family safe. And now Das, without a family, looking scruffy, was determined to be a martyr.

The Colonel dropped his gun hand. He smiled. Das exhaled. Thomas saw his chest contract. With the gun at his head, he'd been holding his breath in anticipation of the shot.

'You would die rather than fight the British?' asked Hidojo. 'So be it. But would you let your friend and colleague who whispers good advice to you die because you will not fight the British?'

And to the shock of both men, he placed the gun's point against Thomas's temple.

There was a silence in the room. Das broke it, his voice a pitch higher than normal. 'Please, no! I'm the one who is causing you trouble. It has nothing to do with him.'

Colonel Hidojo chuckled and Thomas felt the point of the gun wobble against the side of his head.

The *kerani* was shaking – not with fear but with anger.

How could Das do this to him? 'Das, I do not want to die. I have my family to consider.' His voice was crisp and clear, almost commanding despite the gun at his head or maybe because of it.

Hidojo was cackling with delight to see the tension that could be created between two friends when a pistol was pointed at one of them.

Das's lips curled in disgust. He did not bother to hide his feelings. 'Colonel Hidojo, your behaviour is not consistent with the traditions of the Japanese Imperial Army. This man has done nothing. Punish the real culprit. Leave him alone!'

Hidojo nodded to a soldier who walked over to Das and slapped him across the face. The impact sounded like a gunshot. Thomas flinched and felt his bladder give way. He was filled with embarrassment. The horror of the stain spreading across his trousers almost outweighed the imminence of death.

Hidojo pressed the gun more firmly against his head. Thomas's fears were concentrated on the circle of pain on his temple.

Das was bleeding from a split lip. He did not touch the wound. He just stared at Hidojo with an expression of revulsion on his face. He said, his voice slightly slurred from the thickened lip, 'I will not fight on the side of the Japanese against the British or anyone else. You are animals. I'm sorry about my friend Thomas, but I will not change my mind.'

Thomas, originally from Kerala and a member of the Syrian-Christian community, attended church every Sunday with his wife. In all those visits he had sat at his pew, kneeling or standing as ritual required, dropped his coin into the collection plate, wandered forward when his wife beckoned him to take communion, his head always filled with accounts and chores. He had never given over his mind to God, never spoken to him directly. Now, for the first time in his life, he tried to do so.

Hidojo moved the gun away from Thomas's head and slipped it back in his holster. No one moved. Was this some sort of trick, wondered Thomas?

'You're a brave man, Das, but very foolish,' remarked Hidojo. 'You are also selfish to sacrifice others for your beliefs. I have the best solution to this problem that you present.'

Das stared at him unblinkingly, trying not to look fearful, wondering, Thomas guessed, whether he was about to be handed over to the tender mercies of the Kempetai.

'You will go and personally check on your Tamil labourers, since you are so concerned about their wellbeing. I will put you on the next train to Burma.'

He ambled up to Das and stood looking up to his face from a distance of three inches. 'And you should know that the workers call it the Death Railway.'

'I had heard that,' said the conductor, refusing to look away.

Thomas thought that Das was getting off lightly.

However bad the railway was, it was not an immediate death sentence. Das might get through the experience. It was more than he deserved for his recalcitrance.

Hidojo turned to Thomas. 'And you? – you do not have the loyalty of your friends. You must be very disappointed. Well, I will give Das a chance to redeem himself in your eyes. I will give him the opportunity to look after your son on the journey.'

Thomas felt as if he had taken a boot to the stomach. 'What do you mean?' he gasped.

'I am sending your son to Burma too,' said the Japanese soldier. 'The experience will toughen him up.'

***

Thomas's mouth had fallen open. His hands clenched and unclenched by his sides. His dark eyes, the whites tarnished with veins, were fixed on the colonel, unblinking.

He said, 'You can't do that.' It was a protest but the tone was of complete capitulation of body and spirit – hushed and uncertain.

Colonel Hidojo looked uncomfortable. Perhaps the desperation on Thomas's face had affected him. He shuffled his feet, hitched up his trousers and scratched a protruding ear. But he was not a man to recant an order once given.

Das was silent. He wanted to intervene. But there were no words that he could think of to change the reality unfolding before him.

'Spare my son. Send me instead,' said Thomas.

'We are trying to build a railway, old man. What use would *you* be?' replied Hidojo.

'I can work!'

Hidojo grinned. His enjoyment of the situation had returned. For a brief moment the Japanese officer had been discomfited by the old man's desolation. Now he was back in the role that Das could see he enjoyed most of all – a predator playing with its prey – enjoying the victim's futile efforts to escape.

Das found his voice. 'Look, I am sorry. I will join the INA. Do not take it out on the boy.'

'You will join the INA?' Hidojo asked the question as if they were participating in a pleasant dinner conversation about the possibility of a round of golf the next day.

Das nodded, his teeth gritted together too firmly to answer, a vein throbbing in his neck. It went against everything he believed in to agree to the Japanese request. But he could not have Rajan suffer for his stubbornness. He thought about all those workers who would follow his lead. They would probably end up fighting the British in India. Many of them were parents. Some of the Tamils were teenagers like young Rajan. But Das did not change his mind – he would join the INA. He could not be responsible for sending a boy with a gentle nature like Rajan to his death.

Hidojo's grin was wide and toothy. His latest gambit had produced the result he wanted.

'I'm sorry,' he said, peering at Das carefully as if he was determined to discover what motivated the man, 'but it is too late. I see that I have found the best way to punish you for your insult to the Emperor. You are willing to sacrifice your life and that of your friend. But you will struggle every day with the knowledge that you sent a young boy to his death.'

Thomas fell to his knees and clutched at the Colonel's boots. He was sobbing. Das hurried over and tried to disentangle him. Hidojo shook his leg, seeking to dislodge Thomas as if he was a dog on heat. Thomas fell back to the ground. All the stoicism so carefully nurtured in his personal appearance was gone. His white shirt was grimy with dust and mud from the floor and the Colonel's boots. His hair was dishevelled and falling over his forehead. Hidojo kicked him as he lay on the ground. The blow caught him on the chin. Blood was added to the stains on his shirt. Time stood still for a moment and Das was filled with a sense of overwhelming dread.

Thomas propped himself up on one arm. An expression of sly cunning suffused his face.

Hidojo watched him carefully. The man on the floor had a second wind and he was curious to know its source.

'I know something.'

They all waited.

'I know something that you would like to know.'

Thomas got to his feet carefully and seemed to notice the blood on his shirt for the first time. He put a tentative hand to his chin and gazed at his blood-stained fingers. He wiped them on his trousers.

'I have information of interest to you. If you leave my

son alone, I will tell you all I know.'

Das was staring at Thomas. He had no idea what the old man was talking about. He was the estate clerk. He had no access to secrets that would interest a conquering army. Was he bluffing? That was the worst thing he could do. All three of them would end up on the train north. Not just Rajan and him.

'Thomas! What are you doing?'

The other man ignored him – did not appear to hear him. Das realised that every fibre of Thomas's being was concentrated on the man who held the power of life and death over his son.

'You're a fool,' said Hidojo. 'If you have a secret, all I need to do is hand you over to the Kempetai. You will be screaming your secret and everything else you know within a few minutes. You do not have any bargaining power here.'

'You may be right. But if I have lost my son, I can promise you that I will die at the hands of your secret police rather than tell them anything.'

Hidojo looked at him thoughtfully. Das could see that he was considering what Thomas had said. Not many withstood the methods of the Kempetai. But those who did had either extraordinary courage or nothing more to lose.

The Colonel said abruptly, 'Very well. If your story interests me, I will spare your son a trip up North.'

***

Siow, leading the way on a cool, damp evening, made for

the base of a massive tree. He perched on a large woody anchor root. The two who followed him, Mei Ling and Keng Lian, the man with the patch, squatted on the ground in front of him.

Siow introduced them formally, 'Mei Ling, this is Keng Lian. He has recently joined the MPAJA. He is not a member of the Malayan Communist Party but he is keen to fight the Japanese.'

'They raped my sister when they arrived,' stated Keng Lian matter-of-factly. 'She was working as a clerk at the local high school which they suspected of having pro-Chinese sympathies. When she discovered she was pregnant, she killed herself. I found her hanging from the mango tree in our garden.'

Mei Ling had thought the young man impulsive, possibly dangerously so. Now she understood his motivations.

'I am sorry to hear about your sister. The Japanese have a lot to answer for …'

He finished her sentence, 'And we will make them pay.'

'We are all here to fight – but it is important that we show calmness and judgment,' said Siow. 'I do not want to be on a suicide mission.'

'Do you think Major Chung meant it when he said we should be prepared to kill ourselves rather than face capture?' asked Mei Ling.

Siow nodded without hesitation. 'He is reluctant to compromise this camp. A lot of the other cadres have been forced to shift a number of times. The Japanese have found their hideouts. Someone has revealed it under torture or they have stumbled across the location because it is not well hidden. I have also heard that the Sakai have been bribed to show them where the camps are.'

Mei Ling shook her head vehemently. 'They would not do that,' she protested. The Sakai were indigenous people who lived semi-nomadic lives in the rainforests. The guerrillas relied on them for advice on the best places to find fresh water and often used their old jungle trails as a means of getting around. Mei Ling had become fond of the shy natives who seemed so generous with their time and knowledge. Once or twice she had gone with Siow to visit their temporary camps deep in the jungles. The Sakai had shared their fruit and tapioca, and roasted wild boar on a spit. Mei Ling had played with the naked, frizzy-haired children and felt at home in the jungle for the first time. It had also been the best meal she had eaten for a while and she had wrapped some of the meat in a banana leaf and carried it back to her mother. The memory of her mother brought tears to her eyes and she ducked her head and let the hair fall over her face like an opaque veil. She didn't want the others to see any weakness in her – not now when she wanted to play an active part in this new team. 'I am sure the Sakai would not betray us,' she insisted.

Siow was diplomatic in his response, 'I agree with you that it is unlikely. But right now the Colonel views *us* as his greatest security risk. I will issue each of us with handguns from the armoury.'

Mei Ling smiled a little at this. The armoury was a small hut made of the ubiquitous bamboo and *attap*. Great care had been taken to waterproof the building. The guns and ammunition were wrapped in oilskins to keep them dry. She would not have referred to the location as an 'armoury' as such, but Siow was very pleased with his status as the guerrilla in charge of weapons. Mei Ling remembered the shy young man who had escorted her mother and her into the forest for the first time. She thought how much he had matured in the time she had known him. He radiated an authority that was reinforced by his large size. He was thinner, of course, they all were on their diets of tapioca and sweet potato, but he was tall and strong. For an instant, Mei Ling regretted her loyalty to the Indian youth on the estate. Almost as a rebuke, an image of Rajan's thin, thoughtful face, eyebrows raised over dark eyes, appeared fully formed in her mind. She sighed. There could be no relationship with anyone else when Rajan had the power to interrupt her thoughts in this way.

'Yes, give me a gun – but I plan to take some Japanese with me before I use the last bullet on myself,' said Keng Lian.

'Me too,' said Mei Ling, smiling at the enthusiastic young man, glad of the distraction from her memories.

***

Thomas stared at the Japanese colonel as if trying to determine if he would keep his word. There was not much he could do to ensure it, thought Das. He would have to trust that the peculiar sense of honour of the Japanese would not allow Hidojo to break his promise.

'There was a man on this estate – his name was Chan,' whispered Thomas. 'He was a communist, always telling the labourers about their rights, urging them to join the communist party even though the British had banned the organisation.'

Das could not believe that Thomas was telling the Japanese about Chan. But he could understand why he was doing it. Besides, Chan was almost certainly dead and his wife and daughter had fled. If this was the betrayal of a friend, at least it would not have concrete consequences. But would it be enough to save Rajan?

Hidojo was paying careful attention, his head to one side as he watched the expression on Thomas's face and listened to his interpreter at the same time.

'Chan left the estate to train with the British at their Special Forces school in Kuala Lumpur and then went to Singapore. We heard that he joined the Singapore volunteers and fought with distinction.'

'Where is he now?' asked the colonel.

'No one knows,' said Thomas. 'We heard rumours that he was rounded up with the other Chinese during the mass screening in Singapore. There has been no word from him since then.'

'He is dead, I think,' said Hidojo. 'We punished those that fought against us in Malaya and Singapore. He would not have escaped. This means that your information has no value to me. I cannot spare your son.'

Thomas closed his eyes. He folded his arms. His shoulders

hunched as if he was cold.

'There is more,' he added.

Das raised his head to stare at Thomas in surprise. This was news to him. What did Thomas know that he didn't about the Chan family?

Thomas licked his lips as if he was trying to lubricate the passage of the story. 'Chan had a wife and a daughter. The day after you arrived, they left in secret. Their note said that they had gone to visit relatives in Cameron Highlands. That wasn't true.'

'Thomas, stop! You cannot do this,' said Das.

Neither Thomas nor the colonel spared him a glance.

'Your story gets more interesting,' said Hidojo, rubbing his hands together like a comic strip villain.

'I know now that the women did not go to the highlands. They fled into the jungle and are hiding out with the MPAJA. The mother is ill, probably dying. But the girl, she has her father's beliefs and is prepared to fight the Japanese – her name is Mei Ling.'

'What have you done, Thomas?' whispered Das.

Thomas hung his head. He was sacrificing another man's child to save his own. He did not believe that he had any choice. He was Rajan's father. His responsibility to the boy came first.

'Very well,' said Hidojo. 'A colonel of the Japanese Imperial Army is an honourable man. You have provided good information about anti-Japanese elements – we did not know about this girl or her whereabouts. I will spare your son.'

He turned to a soldier and growled an instruction at him. The soldier grabbed Das by his arm and led him away.

Das glanced back once at Thomas, his face accusing. He opened his mouth to speak and then closed it again.

At the door, he put a hand out and stopped their progress by gripping the wooden frame. 'God help us, Thomas, for what we have done today.'

The soldier reversed his rifle and dealt Das a blow to the small of his back. The conductor stumbled. He straightened up, his face twisted in pain. He glanced back once more at his impassive colleague and strode away with his escort in tow.

It was the last time Thomas saw him.

CHAPTER 13

I joined up the minute I turned eighteen in the dawn of 1945. I was glad to be getting in on the action. Skulking in the countryside while the whole world went to hell didn't suit me. My mother was against my signing up but I didn't hesitate. Funny how the best of good intentions can go so wrong. At the time I was indifferent to what the future held as long as I had an active part to play in its determination. I knew, of course, that it might involve death or serious injury. Despite being young, I had none of the blind faith in my own immortality that some of the other kids had. The escape from Singapore was littered with the corpses of too many young soldiers for me to feel immune from death.

I have to confess that the army wasn't quite what I'd anticipated. I assumed they would give me a gun and point me at the enemy. Instead, there was a lot of running around dusty tracks, more poor food, boot polishing and yelling sergeants. Looking back, I guess this must have been the period when Mei Ling was building her reputation as a guerrilla fighter in Johore. Say what you like about the girl, she was never one for half-measures!

'Who is the target?' demanded Siow.

'A Chinese man who has worked very hard to ingratiate himself with the Kempetai,' answered Mei Ling. 'He has informed on a large number of townsfolk – he says they contributed money to the war in China before the invasion of Malaya. Usually, these are his business rivals rather than genuine anti-Japanese elements.'

'And,' added Keng Lian, 'he operates a brothel on the high street of Bukit Pagoh for Japanese officers. There are stories that he will kidnap any wife or daughter of a resident if one of the Japanese officers has an interest in that woman.'

'Well, if even half the stories about him are true he is an ideal target,' remarked Siow.

'It will demonstrate that we have good intelligence,' said Mei Ling. 'Collaborators should know that we have our eyes and ears everywhere.'

'How did we find out about this man?' asked Keng Lian.

Siow smiled. 'We do have eyes and ears everywhere! Actually, the bicycle shop in town is opposite the brothel. The owner has seen this man fraternising with the Kempetai. He is a loyal party member so we can trust him.'

'What's the plan of attack?' asked Mei Ling.

'We know where he lives,' answered Siow. 'We could ambush him on his way to work.'

There was an emphatic shake of the head from Mei Ling.

'What's the matter?' asked Siow. 'I thought you would be pleased at the idea of assassinating this man.'

'I am! But it is not enough that we just kill him. The Japanese and townspeople might think he was the victim of a robbery or a business rivalry. The Japanese are a ruthless military power. For our efforts to be effective, it is not enough that we eliminate the target – we must do it in a spectacular manner so that it appears that the Japanese do not have control over their environment – and cannot protect those who work with them!'

Keng Lian thumped a fist into a hand. 'She is right. That is a good understanding of strategy. We must do this with style.'

Siow looked rueful. Keng Lian slapped him on the back with grinning camaraderie. Everything that Keng Lian did involved a physical gesture. He was the complete opposite of Siow, who was so self-effacing that it was almost possible to ignore his physical size and underestimate his strength.

'Siow, we are not criticising you. Your target is a valuable one. And your plan to kill him would definitely succeed. But we do not want anyone else to get credit for our good work.'

'What do you think we should do then?' asked Siow.

There was silence while they all turned the question over in their heads. Keng Lian rubbed his forehead with his thumb and index finger as if a massage would produce an idea.

'We will kill him at the brothel in front of all the Kempetai officers,' said Mei Ling.

***

When the day dawned for the raid, they set off down the

mountain. Siow and Keng Lian had spent weeks in town watching the brothel, trying to detect a pattern of behaviour in their target and making preparations at the bicycle shop, whose owner had been nervous but co-operative. The three had civilian clothes in their bags. When they reached the outskirts of town, they changed out of their uniforms and removed the caps with the three red stars. Siow had bicycles hidden in the scrub. The members of the assassination squad hopped on and pedalled energetically towards Bukit Pagoh.

When they reached the dusty high street with its rows of run down shophouses on either side, Siow climbed off his bike, cursed and started fiddling with his bike chain. He rose to his feet, pretended to explain something to the other two and then looked up and down the lane. Mei Ling thought his acting was a little theatrical, especially when he shouted in excitement that there was a bicycle shop down the road. They all made their way there with Siow pushing his bike and the others riding slowly.

Siow walked in to the gloomy interior and hollered for the owner. A short, wiry sunburnt man came out wearing a pair of baggy shorts and a white vest that was streaked with black grease. He had very dark hair combed away from his forehead but his face was lined and creased. He had a few more miles on the clock than was suggested by his coiffure, thought Mei Ling.

She glanced around the shop affectionately. It reminded her of the enterprises her father and his friends had run – dingy, badly lit shophouses scattered all over Johore where they had worked and lived, the beating heart of their sole proprietorships. This place was stacked with bicycles in various stages of repair. There were bicycle accessories for sale; baskets, pumps and bells in different sizes. Inner tubes were piled in the corners and the whole place reeked of rubber and grease and was lit by a couple of bare light bulbs hanging from the exposed wooden beams.

Siow introduced Mei Ling and Keng Lian to their host, Mr. Tan, and he beckoned them into a back room.

They perched on three legged metal stools with wooden seats around a small Formica-topped table with coffee rings and cigarette burns on the surface. 'Did you get everything we requested?' asked Siow.

The man nodded and grinned, exposing a row of gleaming gold teeth. 'My wife's sister runs a laundry business. She lent me the uniforms. But we must return them. It does not matter if they are dirty but they must not be damaged – bullet holes are very difficult to disguise.'

'If there are bullet holes in the uniform, it will not be the only thing that is damaged,' said Siow.

Mr. Tan seemed to find this very funny. He cackled and thumped the table.

'And the dress?' she asked.

'A pretty dress for a pretty girl?'

Mei Ling smiled – the man was comical but he meant well. Besides, there was no point antagonising him. Their lives were very much in his hands.

He went to a chest in the corner. Mei Ling noticed that it was a beautiful piece of furniture, glossy, polished rosewood with a butterfly-shaped metal clasp. It was quite out of place in that grubby room. Mr. Tan opened the lid and drew out a red silk *cheong sam*, delicately embroidered with peonies. He held it up for them to see and Mei Ling exclaimed, 'That is a beautiful dress!'

Mr. Tan nodded once and then placed the frock gently back in the chest. 'It belonged to my wife,' he said. 'She was killed in a bombing raid in Singapore. She was visiting relatives. When the Japanese invaded Malaya, I told her to stay there. I was sure it would be safer. But later they told me that her brother's shophouse in Chinatown took a direct hit from a Japanese plane. They found her under the rubble and dragged her out but she was already dead.'

There was a silence in the room. Mei Ling could not help thinking that it was better to die as her father had done, standing up for what he believed in, than to be snuffed out by an unseen enemy dropping bombs from on high.

As if he had read her thoughts, Mr. Tan said, 'I decided to do what I could to fight the Japanese. It is better to die for what you believe than to be afraid and hungry and grow old without companionship.'

'Your help is invaluable to us,' said Siow. 'We will do our best to deal a blow to the Japanese and those who collaborate with them.'

They huddled in the back room the whole day. Mei Ling felt hot and stuffy. The ventilation was not good. The only air circulation was from a stand fan in the corner that rotated in an arc, blowing warm air on the back of her hot neck and then moving past. Mr. Tan brought them a loaf of bread which they ate with *kaya*, a coconut jam. He apologised for the meagre rations – supplies had grown scarce and he did not want to raise eyebrows by departing from his usual practice and buying a large amount on the black market. Mei Ling, who had not tasted the fluffy, white sweet bread baked in clay ovens by Chinese bakers since she had fled to the jungles, devoured a slice. She felt the sugar hit her bloodstream like an injection of energy.

As the night grew late, shops switched off their lights one by one. Soon the only noise was from the brothel across the road. Mei Ling peered through the cracks in the shutters. She could see that the place was brightly lit. There were sounds of music and laughter coming from within.

She went back to the room. The men had already changed. Both were dressed in Japanese uniforms; a shirt, jacket, jodhpurs and boots. Siow unwrapped a parcel he had brought with him and took out three Nambu pistols with wooden handles and slender barrels. He passed one to Keng Lian and slipped the other into his belt. Mei Ling took the third gun and tied it to her thigh with a handkerchief. She slipped on the dress and paraded around the room, feeling self-conscious but also enjoying the admiring looks from her colleagues.

'You are very beautiful,' said Siow.

Mei Ling laughed but stopped playing the fool. She slipped on a pair of shoes and tidied her hair.

Siow opened a small bottle of whisky, took a swig and then tipped some down the front of his uniform. He passed the bottle to Keng Lian who did the same. They waited for Mr. Tan's signal.

Mei Ling had just reached the conclusion that their prey had chosen that night to change his routine and not visit his brothel when Mr. Tan came rushing in whispering, 'He is here! He has arrived.'

The three of them slipped out the back door and jogged around the building. When they were within sight of the brothel, Keng Lian and Siow began dragging Mei Ling between them while she resisted fiercely.

Siow shouted the little bit of Japanese he had learnt for the role, 'Come on! Come on.'

Keng Lian was laughing out loud, stumbling as he walked but keeping a firm hand on Mei Ling's arm. He slapped Mei Ling hard on the cheek as they arrived at the brothel, and she screamed.

A grotesquely fat Chinese man was at the entrance. He watched them approach with an expression of benevolent pleasure. Mei Ling knew this was their target. She had been apprehensive that they would not recognise him but Siow had assured her that if she saw the most obese man she had ever laid eyes on, that was the collaborator.

Mei Ling fought harder as she got to the door and the man said, 'My, you're a wild thing!'

'Will you help me please? They took me from my family. I have a husband and a baby,' she pleaded, the words interspersed with painful gasps.

The Chinese man shrugged and his fat cheeks wobbled like the pink, transparent jellies her mother had made for tea once upon a time. 'If you know what is good for you, you will not fight these men.'

He flung open the double doors with a flourish and ushered the 'officers' and their prey inside. Mei Ling was almost blinded by the brightness of the lights. She blinked and saw that she was in a big hall with thick carpets, plump cushions and deep armchairs. The walls were painted red and gold and the women were almost as brightly coloured. They formed a contrast to the dull-coloured uniforms of the Japanese officers. There was much music, laughter and loud conversation. The place stank of alcohol, cigarettes and cheap perfume. Mei Ling barely had to act. She *was* terrified. Especially that the disguise of her Chinese comrades would not pass muster under the bright lights. As she pulled herself together and looked around, she was relieved to see that most of the Japanese officers were too drunk to have noticed even if she had walked in with two Indian communists.

Siow and Keng Lian nodded their drunken approval at the scene. Siow shook the Chinese man by the hand. He patted them on the back and ushered them in. He pointed to a check-in desk where they had to leave their guns. The two men placed their pistols in a cubby-hole, grabbed a cardboard square with a number on it and wandered further in. Mei Ling had her gun – she could feel its heavy barrel cold against her thigh. The whole group was now in the middle of the room.

Suddenly, Keng Lian turned on the Chinese man, screaming with anger. Siow leapt forward and they both started to hit and slap him. Anyone watching, they hoped, would assume he had managed to annoy the notoriously hot-tempered Kempetai officers. The Chinese man's face was a picture of shock. He warded off the blows with his flabby arms, careful not to hit back, all the while shouting that he had not done anything wrong. The drunken Japanese men lounging around with their comfort women shouted encouragement, enjoying the spectacle. All eyes were on the fight. Mei Ling was unattended, her erstwhile kidnappers raining blows on the collaborator. She slipped the gun out and shouted, 'Move away from the collaborator!'

On cue, Siow and Keng Lian jumped back. In that second, when she pulled the trigger, Mei Ling realised that she had never killed a man before. She emptied the entire magazine into the fat belly of the Chinese man. He fell to the floor, blood seeping into the thick carpet. Keng Lian kicked him once. The three members of the guerrilla army turned and dashed away as fast as they could. The Japanese gave chase, of course. But they were drunk and in shock that their inner sanctum had been breached. By the time a proper pursuit was organised, Mei Ling and her fellow assassins had melted into the jungles.

***

'My God – it's filthy,' whispered Coleman, his face sagging with shock. They had reached the camp at the Three Pagodas pass.

'Coolies from all over Asia, Tamils from Malaya, Indonesians and even handfuls of Vietnamese and Cambodians,' explained one of the prisoners, a British officer. 'No military discipline.'

Coleman stumbled forward with his fellow prisoners. The workers had left the camp in uninhabitable condition. The *attap* roofs had rotted through and the long huts were exposed to the vicious sun and monsoon rains.

'You have one day to clean this place up. Tomorrow work begins on the railway,' barked a Japanese soldier.

Coleman rubbed his tired eyes and began to work, his fingers clumsy with tiredness. The Japanese would not provide any roofing. They had to remove the bamboo walls and use them as makeshift roofs. The wind and rain lashed the sides and drenched everything.

Coleman had hoped the food situation would improve once they reached a static camp, especially if they were supposed to work on the railway, but that was not the case. If anything, it was worse.

Rice was transported to the camp but rationed. The first time there was an announcement that a shipment of meat and fish had been sent for the prisoners, he had hurried forward with the other men, anxious to view this miracle for himself. But nothing had been refrigerated so the meat was seething with maggots. The medical staff, gagging with disgust, boiled the meat for hours on an open fire made from driftwood. Eventually, after scooping away the maggots that floated to the surface, the meat was pronounced fit to eat. At least, thought Coleman, it changed the taste of the rice slightly.

There were hardly any vegetables. The desperate men experimented with different leaves from the shrubs and trees, trying to identify edible greens to add to their diet. Many of them broke out in hives and rashes. The discomfort of terrible constipation followed by weeks of gut wrenching dysentery afflicted Coleman as well the other men.

The Japanese removed the quota of food from prisoners who were too ill to work. Men who could not labour on the railway were of no use to them. There was no point wasting food. The prisoners shared their rice with the sick rather than let them starve to death so there was even less to go around.

The work on the railway was monotonous and dangerous. The men cleared trees using handheld tools, built roads for vehicles, dug and cleared land using the Malay *changkul*, a device with a long wooden handle and an iron blade at right angles to the wood. It had to be heaved up and brought down in a looping action from over the shoulder so that it would cleave through the earth. They worked from dawn to dusk to shore up embankments. Earth was carried from point to point in double-handled wicker baskets. The rough-hewn wooden rails and the cross beams of teak were laid out by hand. Coleman, half-starved, exhausted to the point of collapse but unable to sleep on the bamboo platforms, was soon emaciated. Every rib protruded through the loose skin on his concave chest. In contrast, his legs were swollen – the same thickness from thigh to ankle – and excruciatingly painful, as a result of beri-beri. He had nasty tropical ulcers that he surveyed with care every day, praying they would not spread. He had seen men with ulcers that had eaten right though to the bone. Hundreds of tiny, white slimy maggots infested the wounds and fed on rotten stinking flesh. These men would beg the camp medical officer to amputate the leg because they could not stand the pain and had no hope of arresting the spread of the ulcers. Once, Coleman was called upon to help.

'Hold him down,' shouted the Irish doctor, who was trying to remove the man's leg from just above the knee with a knife sharpened on a stone and disinfected in boiling water.

In the absence of anaesthetics, the prisoner fought and writhed and screamed, eventually fainting from shock and pain. Sweat dripped from the doctor's brow into the open wound. The prisoner did not survive the procedure. Coleman did not know of many who had suffered surgery on that wooden bamboo table and lived to tell the tale, but men still volunteered to go under the knife rather than watch their bodies be consumed by maggots.

Finally, as a last almost-hopeless measure, Coleman agreed to have the ulcers on his own legs excavated to remove the rotting flesh within. The medical officer, a cheerful Irishman who'd been captured in Singapore, warned him that it would hurt like nothing he had experienced before and then set about to prove his point. Coleman passed out after a few agonising minutes. When he came to the medic was grinning and assuring him that he had as much chance as anyone of surviving a jungle operation without anaesthesia or disinfectant. The treatment seemed to work and the ulcers did not deteriorate.

Coleman was also lucky, he knew, not to get cholera although he had several severe bouts of malaria. The cholera sufferers were moved to a separate tent. There was no effective medication and many died in a few days from dehydration after constant vomiting and diarrhoea. The bodies were gathered together and regularly cremated just beyond the confines of the camp. The stench of burning flesh filled the camp for weeks.

Coleman was amazed at the tenacity with which he clung to life. He would lie on his cot shivering with malarial fever, or stand knee deep in water heaving his *changkul* rhythmically, and wonder why he was working so hard to fend off death. Death at the camp was cunning and cruel, picking out the young, the strong and the healthy and marking them for a painful and unpleasant end, far from family and friends. Grown men wept, missing their wives and their sweethearts. Coleman smiled at the thought of missing Sarah to the point of tears. He was not fighting for survival because he pictured a reunion with his wife.

Was it for Matthew, he wondered? He loved his son and was proud of him. But it would be an exaggeration to say they had been close. Matthew had preferred the company of that Indian boy on the estate to that of his parents. No, if he was battling to survive his wartime experiences it was because he, Andrew Coleman, was not yet ready to die. He had not yet given up hope of finding some happiness and he didn't want the possibility taken from him by the Emperor of Japan and his minions.

***

The assassination of the obese Chinese collaborator in the front room of his brothel was the beginning of numerous successful attacks.

Their most daring raid, conducted by Mei Ling and her small but determined group, was on a police station. The gang arrived at the station in an unmarked van wearing the uniforms of Japanese soldiers. Mei Ling stayed in the vehicle. The Japanese had no women in their ranks so her presence would give the game away. She was the designated getaway driver.

The two policemen at the station, completely unsuspecting, were soon disarmed and trussed up with twine, handkerchiefs stuffed in their mouths to prevent them raising the alarm.

Keng Lian would have executed them but Siow refused.

'But they work for the Japanese!' insisted the younger man.

'Yes, but they're just doing their job. Everyone has to make a living in these hard times. There is no record that they are collaborating with the Kempetai.'

One of the policemen was Chinese and able to understand the discussion on whether he should be executed – his eyes were fixed on the guerrillas, his pupils dilated with fear, his mouth working behind the gag, trying to beg for his life. The other policeman, Sergeant Hashim, a Malay, could not understand the dialect so he was less fearful. He watched them thoughtfully and lay perfectly still.

Keng Lian kicked one of the policemen in frustration and Siow glared at him. 'We do not further our cause if we behave like our enemies,' he said.

The two guerrillas, maintaining an antagonistic silence, went to the glass case where the weaponry was kept and in a couple of relays, had loaded the entire collection of machine guns, pistols and grenades in the back of the van. They were pleased that there was a large cache of ammunition as well.

Mei Ling drove away hurriedly. They sped to a pre-arranged drop off point where they had dug a large hole and lined it with waterproof tarpaulin to store the weapons until they were transported back to the jungle hideout in batches.

Mei Ling was delighted. 'Comrades, this raid will make the front page news!'

She was met with a deep silence. Keng Lian was chewing on his fingernails. Siow sat in the passenger seat, staring out of the window as if he was interested in the repetitive scenery of ageing rubber trees.

'What's the matter?' asked Mei Ling.

It was Keng Lian who, still aggrieved, answered, 'Siow would not let me execute the two policemen.'

'They're not really collaborators,' insisted Siow.

They both turned to Mei Ling as if theirs was a democracy rather than a military unit and her casting vote could determine the rightness or wrongness of leaving the men alive.

Two vertical lines appeared between her thick, dark eyebrows. 'It is difficult. Everyone is trying to survive. There is not enough food. The "banana" money is worthless. The towns, even the villages, need a police force to keep the peace between ordinary folk, especially when they are all pushed to the edge of desperation because of food shortages.'

Siow smiled eagerly, his desire for her approval

outweighing his natural reticence. 'You agree with me then?'

'No. I understand why there are some who work for the Japanese. But if we are to win this war, we must make any co-operation punishable by death. Anything else empowers the enemy.'

Her remarks were met with disquiet on the part of Siow. Even Keng Lian, who in the heat of the moment would have been delighted to shoot the policemen, was taken aback by Mei Ling's cold-blooded analysis.

She laughed. 'Don't look so horrified. This is war! Anyway, we didn't kill them. If we have a reputation for compassion, it might also help us with our recruitment efforts and generate support from the population.'

Mei Ling was grinning as they tramped through the rubber trees back towards the camp. She was enjoying her active role in the war against the Japanese. They had made quite a name for themselves, the three of them, for meticulously planned, daringly executed raids. Mei Ling knew quite well that a lot of their success was due to her efforts. Keng Lian was an effective action man but lacked the mental discipline to map out their forays in advance. He would long since have ended up in Kempetai hands if left to his own devices. Siow was too cautious. He didn't have the imagination for the bold plans she devised and they carried out as a team. Mei Ling acknowledged to herself that she was enjoying the notoriety she had achieved as well. There were rumours all over town about the *femme fatale* who led the guerrillas. Tales were circulating of her beauty and her facility with weapons. Back at the camp, the other guerrillas treated her with a combination of amusement and grudging respect. She was taking the fight to the enemy.

***

Coleman was on camp duty. He was assigned to do odd jobs like repair huts, wash what little clothing the prisoners had left, carry water from the well and generally do chores. One of the cooks had heard that there was an edible mushroom growing in the surrounding jungles. Coleman was sent out to collect a few samples. Relative to the work on the railway line, this was all quite restful. Coleman set out in good spirits. He wandered about looking at toadstools and mushrooms sprouting from rotten tree trunks and along the ground and collected those that seemed less self-evidently toxic. They were all desperate for diet supplements at the camp but Coleman doubted that this particular experiment was going to work. He decided, as he selected fungi, that he would not partake of the first serving of mushroom soup.

He was picking a brown toadstool when he heard movement in the undergrowth. He stood very still. It might be a mouse deer or a wild boar. If it was not too large he would tackle it. Meat would be a much more useful addition to their diet than mushrooms. The sounds of a creature crashing through the undergrowth grew closer. A Tamil worker loped into the clearing, wild-eyed with fright. He saw Coleman and drew up short, motioning with a finger to his lips that Coleman was to keep quiet. Coleman did. There was a camp of Tamil workers from Malaya nearby. He didn't want to be implicated in an attempted escape by a labourer.

There was complete silence in the jungle, none of the hollering and crackling of leaves that signalled pursuit. The fugitive relaxed slightly. His Japanese pursuers had lost the trail.

'There is nowhere to go even if you can get away. It is better to go back.' Coleman spoke in the Tamil he had picked up on the estates of Malaya and Ceylon.

The man looked at him full in the face and the flash of recognition hit them both simultaneously.

It was the Tamil who spoke first, haltingly in English as if he had not used the language for months, 'Sir – is it you?'

'Das, what are you doing here?'

'The Japanese have been rounding up workers from the plantations to work on their railway here.'

'And they got you too?'

'They insisted that I join the Indian National Army. When I refused, they sent me here.'

Coleman didn't inquire any further – this was not the time for small talk. Instead, he said again, 'There is nowhere to go. It is all jungle around here.'

Das was staring at his old manager, an expression of genuine concern on his face. 'Look at you, sir. I didn't realise that the Japanese would treat the whites as badly as us. I see the prisoners of war working as hard as the coolies. It is a very shocking thing.'

Coleman looked around nervously. It would not do to be caught talking to someone from another camp. The Japanese were capricious and cruel and punishment might involve anything from a beating to immediate decapitation.

'Why are you running away?' he asked.

'They asked me to do something – I couldn't do it.'

Coleman grinned, the expression almost a caricature in his gaunt face. 'You're going to have to learn to follow instructions sometime, Das.'

There was an answering smile from the tall Tamil. But then his face sobered. 'We have terrible cholera at our camp.'

Coleman nodded. 'Us too.'

'They wanted me to burn some of the victims.'

Coleman was surprised. 'We're doing that too. It is awful but better than the disease spreading. Those poor sods have turned up their toes. It doesn't matter to them.'

Das shook his head, his expression sickened. 'You don't understand. They wanted me to set fire to one of the huts. The men inside – they have cholera – but they're not dead.'

Coleman pressed a finger and thumb against his eyeballs. In the silence between them, they both heard the sounds of Japanese voices.

'I told them I was going to get more firewood,' said Das. 'Now I'm trying to get away. I cannot do what they ask. I cannot do it.'

He held out a hand and Coleman shook it. 'Good luck, sir. I hope you survive this.'

Das disappeared into the bushes. The ferns sprang back and obscured his passage. A few minutes later a group of six

Japanese soldiers burst into the clearing. They gesticulated and shouted at Coleman. He guessed that they were asking whether he'd seen Das. He thought of the years they had worked together on the estates, him with Das as his conductor, and what Das had been asked to do by these men in front of him.

One of the Japanese soldiers slapped him and shouted in Japanese again, his spittle spraying Coleman in the face like a fine rain. Coleman pointed in the direction that Das had gone. They all turned and rushed after him. Coleman felt bad. He did not have the courage of his Tamil employee. But Das was as good as dead. There was no point annoying the Japanese for a lost cause.

In the distance he heard a burst of gunfire.

He waited till there was silence and then moved cautiously in the direction of the shots. Das was lying spread-eagled on the forest floor. His chest was a hollow, bloody mess. He had caught a direct burst of machine gun fire. He must have turned and faced his killers as they caught up with him. Coleman knelt down beside his erstwhile employee and arranged his gangly limbs until he was laid out neatly, arms folded across his chest and legs straight. He shut his eyes so that the dead man's expression was peaceful, the last frightened gaze hidden. Coleman wished that he believed in a God so that he could think that this man, so brave in his refusal to act against his conscience, would have a reward. But he feared that the only recompense for Das for his acts of courage was this jungle grave.

Coleman hoisted the bag of mushrooms on his shoulder

and walked back to the camp.

***

Colonel Hidojo was at the Kempetai headquarters. It was housed in what had once been a Roman Catholic boys' school run by brothers of the La Sallian order. The priests had been evacuated, still dressed in their white cassocks, to Singapore. Some had obtained safe passage out but many now inhabited Changi prison. The school was closed. The Kempetai had taken over the building. Townspeople in Bukit Pagoh crossed the road so as not to walk alongside the beautiful, low, whitewashed structure.

The Kempetai officer sat behind the polished sandalwood desk that had once belonged to the school headmaster, while Hidojo stood before him. The spicy scent of wood filled the air. Colonel Onada wore a high-collared cavalry uniform with insignia and tall black leather boots. He had a prominent white armband on his left arm with the characters *ken* (law) and *hei* (soldier). He was armed with a cavalry sabre and pistol.

In theory, Hidojo and the man on the other side of the table were of similar rank. But Hidojo stood before the desk while the other man sat. The Kempetai was feared even by their own and Hidojo was already in the bad books of the man in front of him. Colonel Onada was a squat, thick-necked man with full pouting lips. His hair was cropped close to a head that could have been carved from stone. His broad forehead, wide flat nose and narrow eyes barely registered in profile. Wire-rimmed spectacles were curled around small neat ears. He was deeply tanned. Onada's favourite sport was fishing. He spent long hours on a jetty by the river, his line drifting on the surface as he waited for a bite.

'Why did you not come to me with this information earlier?' demanded Onada. 'You heard this months ago.'

'I did not think it was of much importance,' explained Hidojo.

'Did not think it was of much importance? This girl has made us a laughing stock!'

Hidojo nodded, then hastily spoke again, nervous that Onada would assume he was agreeing with the assessment that the Japanese Imperial Army was a source of amusement. 'The minute I heard that there was a female guerrilla involved in these attacks on us, I realised it could be this girl I was told about – Mei Ling. I came immediately.'

Onada sighed. 'There is no way of knowing for sure it is the same girl, of course. But it seems likely. There can't be dozens of female terrorists in the jungles. Her parentage suggests that she would have the courage.'

'Did you find out any more about the family?' asked Hidojo.

'The mother disappeared at the same time as the daughter. The father was executed at Changi beach.'

'That is good news at least,' said Hidojo. He added, 'I also have this,' and handed over a photo of Mei Ling. He had kept it back as a peace offering to placate the Kempetai officer. 'It was taken a few years ago. If she has been camping in the jungle she might have changed quite a lot, but it is a start.'

Onada stared at the black and white photo in his hand. It was a studio shot. The girl was looking straight at the camera. Her gaze was challenging, as if putting the photographer under pressure to hurry and not take up her time. In contrast, her smile was half-formed, as if she had been instructed to smile for the cameras but had taken just that instant too long to comply. Her hair was thick and shoulder length, the symmetry of a ruler-straight middle parting undone by an unruly lock of hair.

'Where did you get this?' asked Onada.

'I had the house they used to live in on the Kuala Reman plantation searched from top to bottom. This had fallen behind a cabinet.'

Onada nodded. It was diligent work on the part of Hidojo. He had shown courage in bringing the information provided by Thomas and the photo to the Kempetai. Onada had no illusions. He knew there were many officers of the Japanese army who would have preferred to stay out of trouble and act as if they had not received any valuable news. He said, 'You have done good work today. I will not forget.'

Hidojo bowed. He knew what that meant. Onada was offering him a single favour. He could collect at any time. It was the way the Kempetai embedded themselves into the fabric of the Japanese army. Hidojo could inform Onada if he fancied a local girl, if he had an enemy that needed dealing with, if his wife had a boyfriend whom he wanted eliminated, and Onada would see that it was done. He bowed again to indicate his gratitude for Onada's generosity.

'I will have posters made. We will catch this bandit queen,' said Onada. 'And when we do – I pity her.'

CHAPTER 14

Someone – one of the higher-ups – caught on that I had lived in Malaya. I was taken aside and asked if I wanted to volunteer for a special operations job, to be parachuted into Malaya to prepare the ground for an invasion. As you can imagine, I was delighted. I exaggerated my knowledge of local languages and my experience of the geography of Malaya and was flown out to Ceylon. There was an emphasis on jungle warfare and guerrilla skills and the part I liked the least – leaping off wooden platforms simulating parachute drops.

They were desperate for men with knowledge of Malaya. The British had signed some sort of deal with Chin Peng, the head of the MPAJA, that the commies would co-operate with the British to fight the Japanese. We'd agreed to send in large caches of weapons, uniforms, food packets and anything else we thought the MPAJA would need – plus a few troops (like me) to make sure the MPAJA were sticking to their end of the bargain and not secreting the supplies away to use against the British when we turned up to liberate Malaya from the Japs.

I soon persuaded them I was ready to go.

The Liberator B-24 was one of the few aircraft that had the range to get from Ceylon to Malaya and back again. The men from Force 136 who were to be parachuted behind enemy lines sat along the fuselage and felt their teeth and their bones rattle with the plane's violent vibrations. Matthew had his parachute on the ground between his feet. From time to time he would finger it gently, trying to convince himself that a jump into hostile terrain in Japanese-held territory would not be that different from the practice jumps he had done in Ceylon. Matthew realised that he was afraid. Not so afraid that he was going to embarrass himself by refusing to jump, but scared enough to make it unpleasant.

It could have been worse. One of the men in Ceylon had described to them what it was like to be crammed into a submarine for weeks, breathing stale air, given only a small allocation of water, fed dry army rations, with no space to stand or work or sleep comfortably. All this before being dumped on a beach in Malaya, struggling ashore wet, bedraggled and cramped only to be met by a hail of bullets. Matthew comforted himself that at least he would arrive fighting fit – unless he got shot on the way down, of course. He realised, looking at his long legs stretched out ahead of him, that he had changed a lot since leaving Malaya. He'd grown tall. His yellow hair had darkened. After his army training, he'd developed a wiry strength. Few would recognise him as the skinny teenager who had fled Malaya with his mother.

Matthew wondered whether he would meet Rajan. His instructions were to remain in the deep jungle to organise the resistance and train the guerrillas for a British counter-offensive – he was not to enter the towns or villages. Malaya was well and truly in Japanese hands and Matthew didn't intend to be paraded around Bukit Pagoh and the other town centres in chains and then publicly beheaded. It was a pity, but he would not see Rajan until after the war. He hoped that Rajan had kept his head down and stayed out of trouble. Matthew was optimistic. Rajan was on the Kuala Reman estate with his family. It was unlikely that there would be a huge military presence on a rubber plantation, or much opportunity to get on the wrong side of the Japanese.

***

The blows from the ivory-handled cane were raining down on his body. Rajan fell to his knees and then to the ground. He curled up in a foetal position, trying to protect his head and face with his arms. The toad-like officer with the grizzled hair was beating him with all the force he could muster. Rajan felt the skin split on his forearms and back. The assault stopped as suddenly as it had begun. Rajan did not move. His whole body throbbed with pain. He had bitten his tongue. Blood filled his mouth. The Japanese colonel loomed over him.

'Get up!' he shouted.

Rajan didn't move. He was not sure he could. He was catatonic with shock. He was rewarded with a kick from a heavy boot that caught him on the side of the jaw. Another explosion of pain, this time coursing through the nerves in his face like monsoon rains on a dry river bed. Rajan staggered to his feet, desperate to avoid further punishment. He was not sure how he was able to keep his balance. The human body did by instinct what he could not have achieved by an act of will.

'Where is Mei Ling?' asked Colonel Onada, his tone deceptively casual.

Rajan tried to speak. He found it difficult to move his mouth. Blood trickled down his chin. 'I've told you, I don't know. There was a note – when they left – it said she was going to Cameron Highlands to visit her relatives.'

'Liar!'

The colonel spat the word at Rajan who rocked backwards on his heels. It was at this point in their previous conversation that Onada had laid into him with the cane that he was now twirling in his right hand as if he was a band leader on parade. Rajan could see that there was blood – his blood – on the polished length of it.

'I swear it's true!'

This time there was no accusation, just the cane wielded like a baseball bat. Rajan put up a hand to protect himself. The blow hit him on his wrist. He doubled over in pain. His wrist was fractured. But this time he did not fall to the ground.

Onada stepped back and looked at the boy in disgust. 'All of you – you just want to be heroes. But Colonel Onada always knows when you are lying … and how to make you tell the truth. In the end you beg for mercy and tell me everything you know. But at first, you have to be stubborn.'

'Mei Ling lived on the estate,' said Rajan, as convincingly as he could. 'I didn't know her very well. Her father ran the sundry shop for a few years. He left to go to Singapore. I don't know why. Just after the Japanese arrived, she and her mother left – I have not seen them since.'

Onada giggled. It was a chilling sound, issued from between fleshy lips.

Rajan realised that this nightmare might be one without end, except in his death. It was a difficult leap of the imagination. Despite the pain throbbing in his arms and legs, now eclipsed by the agony in his wrist, Rajan was an eighteen-year-old with a teenager's optimism. Even when the Japanese soldiers had arrived and dragged him from the house in the middle of lunch, his mother crying and screaming and tearing at her hair and his father shouting that it was all some mistake, that he had a deal with Colonel Hidojo, Rajan had not been unduly troubled. He had no idea what his father was talking about but he knew that he had led a depressingly blameless existence as far as the Japanese were concerned, growing tapioca on the plot behind their small house and running errands for his father. He had accompanied the guards to a military vehicle and sat between two soldiers at the back, his hands cuffed together in front of him. It had been an uncomfortable ride. Neither soldier had been prepared to answer any questions. Rajan had given up asking them where he was being taken and why. Quite possibly they didn't speak Malay or English, he decided.

They had driven right past the old wooden police station. His initial surprise had turned to fear when they drew up outside the Catholic school that was now infamous as the headquarters of the Kempetai. He found himself in a plush office, facing a man whose grotesqueness reminded him of a *hantu* of myth. Rajan bowed. Everything about the officer reeked of power. Antagonising him was just foolish. The man said in perfect unaccented English, 'It is good that you are here. I have some questions to ask you. You have been assisting the bandits.'

Rajan was perplexed. 'Excuse me, sir, but I have no idea what you are talking about. I have never done such a thing.'

'Liar!'

That was when the beatings started.

***

Matthew got the signal and slipped on his 'chute, tightening all the straps. He was to be dropped, along with a bunch of supplies and a radio operator, into Johore. He had insisted on this. It was the region of Malaya he was most familiar with – the location of the Kuala Reman estate where he had spent the pre-war years. The plan was that the guerrillas in Johore, all part of the MPAJA regiment in the area, would prepare a drop zone and meet him on the ground. Matthew perched alongside the open door, holding on to the leather strap attached to the fuselage for dear life. He didn't want to jump early. It was daylight. The Japanese air defences in Malaya were so inadequate at this stage of the war that it was believed by senior command that the risks of a daytime jump were outweighed by the advantages of being able to see. It appeared to Matthew as if he was planning to leap into impenetrable jungle. He would probably spend the rest of his short life dying of starvation hanging from a tree branch. Or he would impale himself on some bamboo spike and that would be the end.

Matthew spotted the drop zone. He couldn't believe his eyes. It was about the size of the bandana he had tied around his head under his helmet. He could see that trees had been cleared in a small square. White strips of cloth had been used to mark the boundaries. It was visible from the air but it was just too small.

But there was no more time for thought. The sergeant yelled, 'Go, go, go!' Matthew opened his blue eyes wide and leapt out of the aircraft. He took a precious moment to regret that his parachute was white and therefore visible to reconnaissance aircraft, and pulled the cord. To his relief, his 'chute shot out, a thin trailing thing that billowed open within seconds. He felt a sharp, painful jerk. His descent slowed abruptly and he concentrated on hitting the drop zone. He was caught in cross winds high above the foliage. He yanked on the control ropes. The trees were coming up fast. At least there was no gunfire. The Japanese had not spotted his descent. He glanced around. He could see his radio operator some distance away. He was likely to miss the target too. He hoped the guerrillas were prepared to hunt for them. This was not going to be a convenient gathering in one spot.

Matthew hit the trees. The leaves and twigs grabbed at him like greedy fingers. He felt his neck jolt as the parachute caught on a branch and then he was dangling twenty feet off the ground wondering how he was going to get down. He didn't think he was injured – scratches and bruises and a bit of whiplash but nothing that would impede his mission, assuming he could get out of the tree. He looked around. He recognised the species from the brown, coiled pods, some split in two to reveal tiny bright red seeds. He and Rajan had used the seeds of the *saga* tree as bullets in their catapults.

Matthew tried to undo his harness but his position was too awkward and the straps too tight. He remembered that he had tightened them just before jumping, and grimaced. He couldn't reach the knife strapped to his belt either. Besides, if he cut the cords, it was a long way to the ground. He would be lucky if he didn't break a leg, or his neck.

A voice said in Malay, 'Need help up there?'

He looked down. A young Chinese man in the full uniform of the MPAJA, khaki top and bottom, black boots and the ubiquitous three-cornered cap with the three stars, was looking up at him, a broad grin on his face.

***

Thomas tracked Colonel Hidojo down to the big house on the hill and asked for permission to speak with the officer. He had never had any dealings with the Japanese in their place of residence. Indeed, he had not been to the manager's bungalow since Colonel Hidojo had moved in. He noticed, with that small part of his brain which was functioning, that very little had changed. The furniture, furnishings and even the paintings on the wall were the same. Hidojo did not seem to find it incongruous that a hunting scene with men in red coats on horses with their guns and dogs, should adorn his walls. The only addition that Thomas could see was a glass fronted cabinet with a row of *katana,* the main weapon of the samurai. Their vicious long, curved blades were hidden in scabbards. He was debating entering the living room and demanding that Hidojo see him when the servant returned and ushered him in.

Thomas bowed, a perfunctory effort. 'They've taken my son! Soldiers have taken my son.'

Hidojo put down the Japanese language newspaper he was reading and gazed at Thomas thoughtfully. He was in uniform but had removed his boots. They sat by his footstool, polished and shining and ready for him to wear. Thomas opened his mouth to speak again and Hidojo put up a hand to forestall him.

'I know they have your son.'

The colour drained from Thomas's face. In that instant, the *kerani* knew that his belief, his profound hope, that there had been some sort of mistake, was misplaced.

'Why have they taken him?' he asked, voice trembling.

'To find out what he knows about the girl.'

'The girl? Mei Ling?'

Hidojo nodded.

'But he doesn't know anything. I told you everything he

told me. That was our deal!' Thomas's voice had risen to a scream.

'That was why I did not send him to Burma,' corrected Hidojo. 'Unfortunately, when I passed the information about the girl to Colonel Onada at the Kempetai, he wanted to make sure that nothing had been omitted.'

'The Kempetai have Rajan? Oh my God! Oh my God!'

Hidojo said, almost as if he was trying to comfort the distraught father, 'If he tells everything he knows, I am sure they will let him go.'

Thomas was in a daze. 'I must go to him,' he said.

He walked away, his movements erratic. The shock had robbed him of the power to order his limbs. Nothing was natural or came naturally in a world where the Kempetai had his son. Since the colonel had co-opted his motorbike, Thomas had relied on a bicycle to get around. Now he saw the motorcycle in front of the building, spotlessly clean and gleaming. Without a second thought he hopped on and raced off. Somewhere at the back of his mind he knew that the Japanese had executed people for less than the repossession of a motorbike, but he didn't care. That was a problem for another day. Right now he had to get to his son.

He travelled as swiftly as he could along the laterite road. The dust from the baked and cracked red clay covered him in a fine coat. Stones, spat up by the spinning tyres, hit him from time to time. Thomas did not notice the sharp stings. His trousers flapped in the wind. Spots of rain were falling, streaking and congealing the dust on his white shirt. Thomas turned towards the main tar road and remembered that he had not told his wife where he was going. She was worried sick already but nothing would compare to the knowledge that the Kempetai had his son – their son. Her present state was blissful ignorance relative to the anguish that was to come.

He reached the outskirts of town. A few heads turned to see the old man race by as fast as his two-stroke engine would carry him. In the era of the Japanese occupation, people operated their vehicles at a moderate speed. There was a twofold reason for this. One was practical, fuel was scarce and black market prices exorbitant. The other was born of fear – under the Japanese it was best not to attract attention. Thomas, who had regularly cautioned Rajan to keep his head down, ignored his own advice in his urgency.

He reached the Kempetai HQ and stopped at the guardhouse. 'What do you want?' demanded the soldier.

'My son is in there.'

'So?'

'I need to see him.'

'That is not allowed.'

'I must see someone in charge. I need to explain that there has been a terrible mistake.'

The sentry burst out laughing, his body arching backwards and his eyes tearing with amusement. 'That is what they all say, the relatives of the prisoners.' He imitated Thomas's voice, 'There's been a terrible mistake.'

'Colonel Hidojo sent me. I have a message.'

The look of enjoyment was wiped off the guard's face. Thomas had gambled on the Japanese fear of authority.

In the hierarchical military that followed the pattern of their society, each rank had complete authority over lower ranks. When others had complained of Japanese treatment, Thomas had said that it did not differ much from the way their soldiers treated each other. Das had pointed out that the entire population of Malaya had less status in the eyes of the Japanese forces than the lowliest foot soldier, so they were going to be very uncomfortable while the occupation lasted.

'You can go in – ask for Colonel Onada,' barked the guard.

Thomas rode his scooter into the compound and parked it on the grass. He ran towards the main building and found his way to a reception area. There were other tired, troubled relatives sitting or standing in small clusters, clutching bundles of food and clothing for the inmates to their chests, begging for permission to hand them over. A Japanese sentry was shaking his head emphatically.

'I have to see Colonel Onada,' said Thomas.

The sentry looked at him, startled. Thomas had no idea what a wild looking figure he cut with his grey hair standing on end and streaked with red dust, his trousers muddy from ankle to knee and his white shirtfront patterned with mud.

'I have to see Colonel Onada. I have urgent information for him.'

A booming voice shouted from inside, 'Send that man in.'

The sentry stood aside. Thomas tottered past him, his steps hesitant for the first time. He was here. He was being granted an audience. He could feel the stares of the others. The back of his neck was prickling. He walked into the office. The light from the windows caught Onada's glasses and they gleamed, opaque and gold. The Japanese officer was standing upright, belly protruding. He held a cane that he'd been using to beat the creature on the ground in front of him. Thomas looked at the figure with pity. At the same instant as his brain registered that the youth's back and shoulders were a bloody mess and blood was trickling from one ear, his heart screamed with recognition. Thomas gasped with the pain in his chest.

'Rajan ...' he whispered and collapsed on his knees by the boy. He turned him over and almost wept with relief to see the mild fluttering of a pulse in his neck like a trapped bird trying to escape. Rajan had fainted. Thomas was glad. It was the only way he could bear the bruises and the cuts on his son's body, the knowledge that he was temporarily relieved of pain. He laid the boy gently down and got to his feet like an old man. He pushed against his own thighs with shaking hands to gain the momentum to stand upright. His knees straightened slowly.

Thomas asked and, in contrast to his trembling hands, his voice was steady, 'Why are you doing this?'

Onada perched on the edge of his table, one leg swinging in a relaxed pendulum, ignoring the bloodied figure on the floor and indifferent to the suffering in the old man's eyes.

'Your family seems to be familiar with this famous terrorist, Mei Ling.'

'We know nothing about her present activities,' answered

Thomas, never taking his eyes off his son.

'But that is not what I hear. Colonel Hidojo tells me that she visits your son in the evenings – quite the little romance.'

'She came once. To find out about her father. The boy told me and I told Hidojo. He knows there is nothing else to tell. Ask him.'

'Ahh, I understand what you are saying, of course. But I prefer to be sure. I thought I would ask your son a few questions.'

'I made a deal with Colonel Hidojo …' Thomas's voice sounded like he was squeezing the words through a narrow gap in his throat – thin and strained.

'The Kempetai does not recognise any deal with anti-Japanese elements,' said Onada.

'But I'm not anti-Japanese! I've joined the Indian National Army. I've rounded up labourers for your railway. I *told* you about that girl's visit. What more do you want?'

'I want that girl! She causes me great embarrassment with her stunts.' His face contorted with rage and he slammed the walking stick on the table. It splintered down the middle.

Thomas hung his head. 'I don't know where she is!'

'But maybe your son does!'

'I swear to you he doesn't. I forbade him from having any more contact with the girl. I told him she was trouble.'

They both looked at Rajan and saw for the first time that he was conscious, trying to raise himself on one elbow. Thomas rushed to him, crouching low to cradle Rajan's head. 'Wait, son. Don't try and get up.'

Despite his injuries, Rajan shrugged off his father's hands. He said, his voice a faint whisper but a wealth of emotion contained in the soft words, 'Don't touch me. Leave me alone.'

Thomas was stunned. His eyes widened. His hands fell to his sides and then reached out again, unsure of what his son was saying, choosing not to understand the clear meaning of the words spat out and mingled with blood.

Onada watched developments, his eyes bright with interest behind the round wire-rimmed glasses.

'What's the matter? What is it?' asked Thomas.

'I heard you. I heard you tell … him. You betrayed me. You betrayed Mei Ling.'

CHAPTER 15

I was a young man on an adventure, fighting for a good cause, ready to do my utmost for Malaya – to free her people from the tyranny of the Japanese. I can almost smile at the memory of my youthful idealism. It's true that I was filled with admiration for those young communists, their camaraderie and courage. I had been so lonely in England ... and now I was back in Malaya ... with Mei Ling.

Matthew, grateful and relieved to have been cut down from his unwanted perch high in the foliage, fell into step with the young communist. At first, he was silent and watchful, mindful of the danger of Japanese patrols. But as his companion tramped through the undergrowth without any apparent trepidation, he asked in English, 'No Japanese here?'

'No, no! We are very deep in the jungle. Japanese too scared to come here. They are terrified of an ambush. Also, we have scouts and sentries all over so they cannot sneak up. Do not worry.'

Matthew decided to take the reassurance at face value. The guerrillas had tracked him down pretty quickly. They seemed to know their jungle. The young man, Matthew thought they must be about the same age, with a patch over one eye and a shock of black hair peeping out from under his three cornered cap, looked very competent in the casual way he shouldered his rifle, a knife and a canteen. He even had a few grenades strapped to his belt.

'What about the radio operator and the supplies?'

'All blown off course. Other teams are out looking for them. You British provide very good equipment,' he continued and patted his gun.

'Well, I hope you're putting them to good use.'

'The Japanese and the collaborators all over Johore fear us.'

Matthew nodded his approval. The young man's enthusiasm for the fight was infectious. He said, 'My name is Matthew Coleman.'

'I am Keng Lian.' They walked on in silence for a few minutes and then Keng Lian, who seemed a talkative fellow, said, 'I will introduce you to the rest of our main strike team. Our most successful member is a female. She is feared by all the Japanese. They think she might be a spirit of the forest because she cannot be stopped and she cannot be fought. She is a dedicated warrior …' He stopped as if embarrassed and Matthew decided he'd stumbled on a romance, remarkable really in this dense hot jungle. The sweat was trickling down his back like a swarm of long-legged insects running down his spine. But apparently there was still the opportunity and the wish to fall in love.

'I look forward to meeting her,' said Matthew, to fill the gap in the conversation.

Keng Lian grinned and suddenly they were two young men on an adventure – the serious nature of their work overwhelmed by the spirit of youth and companionship and the dappling of sun through the trees like little gifts of light under the bottle green roof. It reminded Matthew of the long hot days tramping through the plantation with Rajan and playing cricket outside the rubber factory.

There was a flame of the forest tree in the distance, its entire canopy hidden under a molten layer of flaming flowers.

'We used to have one of those on the estate where I grew up,' said Matthew. 'I had forgotten how beautiful they are.'

'The tree?'

Matthew nodded.

'For us it also marks the camp. We can find our way back from almost anywhere in the forest when the flames of the tree are burning.'

'What about the Japanese?'

'We are always in danger, of course. But,' he shrugged, 'we have no choice – we have to fight.'

Matthew realised that this was not bravado. It was pure, undiluted courage. He felt his respect for the young man grow. He, Matthew, was finally taking part in the war – but the tide had turned and he knew success was possible, even likely after a sequence of Japanese military defeats from Midway to the Philippines. The real question for him was whether he could execute his military duties without losing his life in the time the war had left to run. But these men and women in the jungle had commenced fighting when there was no hope and continued it through three years of barbaric reprisals. And what did victory hold out for them? Matthew knew full well this arrangement of convenience that allowed the communists and the British to work together would not survive very long after the war. He did not think the communist leadership was green enough to think otherwise. Matthew wondered about the personal relationships forged between the men at arms, like himself and this gutsy young Chinese man for instance. Time would tell if such bonds would be severed by necessity.

They had almost reached the site. As if by magic, guards materialised and hailed a greeting. Matthew had not caught a glimpse of them as he marched towards the camp. These communists were well trained. Matthew glanced at the bamboo and *attap* huts, the small campfire and the sandy clearing in the middle that bore the imprints of boots. He guessed it was the parade ground of the regiment. Altogether it was professional and orderly.

He met Major Chung who was well-briefed about the new addition to his team and delighted that Matthew had a Malayan background. Matthew saluted Chung smartly and gave his name and rank in a respectful tone. This man had forgotten more about fighting than he would ever learn.

'We are not so formal here, young man,' said Chung,

smiling, the crow's feet radiating from the corners of his eyes like a fan. 'I hope you had an uneventful journey?'

'Yes, sir. I got stuck in a tree, but your men found me and cut me down before I got too anxious.'

'That is very good. I will arrange for you to be shown to your quarters and then perhaps we can meet to discuss a few things. And,' he twinkled at Matthew like a favourite uncle, 'you will find that you and our escort share a history.'

Matthew stared at him in puzzlement and then his face broke into a wide smile. Could it be that Rajan was here in the jungle? Had he joined the communists? Who else did he know well in Johore? He was grinning when Chung said, 'And here is your tour guide.'

Matthew turned around and stared at the young woman, his expression changing to bewilderment. She looked familiar. She was very attractive if a trifle thin and tired.

'You don't remember me, Matthew? Or have I changed so much?'

He noted the short hair peeping out from under the hat, the delicate features, the high cheekbones accentuated by the thinness of her young face, the seriousness that underlay her amused expression as if humour was something that she wore as a mask but which could not disguise the foundations of grim purpose that defined her life.

It was that last that gave her away. He breathed, 'Mei Ling,' combining recognition and pleasure in the speaking of her name.

She did a little skip forward and hugged him tight. He

was astonished at the warmth of his reception. And touched. Then, with an insight that was rare for him, he realised that she was not so much wrapping her arms around him as embracing a happier past in which he had figured, albeit as a bit player in the friendship between her and Rajan.

'Do you know how Rajan is?' he asked.

She took a step back and shook her head. He saw that there was a brightness about her eyes. It hinted at a sadness that ran deep but was rarely acknowledged.

She answered in a tone that strived for normality. 'I last saw him about a year and a half ago. He was fine then. I hope he is still.'

'I would love to see him again. He was my best friend.'

Mei Ling gestured for Matthew to walk with her. 'Yes, I remember you two being as thick as thieves. All we have to do is win this war and we can have a grand reunion.'

Matthew laughed. 'I think we may be well on our way to victory. I am here to make sure that all is in place for when the British return to Malaya.'

'Yes, things are going as well as can be expected,' said Mei Ling. 'We in the MPAJA have harassed the Japanese. The local population has remained loyal to our cause.' She continued in a cold voice, 'We have made collaborators think twice about their actions.'

Matthew glanced at the woman next to him curiously. It was difficult to get accustomed to such martial talk from the slight figure in baggy greens. And yet her reputation, if Keng Lian was to be believed, was fearsome.

'This must have been a very hard time for you,' he said.

'I might not have chosen this path if choices had been offered to me,' she answered. 'But once my father threw in his lot with the Singapore volunteer army, there was not much that my mother and I could do but try to escape. This was the only possible refuge.'

'How are your parents? I remember so well your father in his shirt sleeves talking politics with Thomas and Das while your mother got on with the work.' Matthew's face broke into a smile as memories came rushing back.

Mei Ling could not rein in her emotion. Teardrops trembled in the corners of her eyes and she sat down on a rough bamboo *charpoy*. She folded her arms and rested her head on them. He sat down next to her and put an arm around her. He could feel her sharp shoulder blades through the rough cotton of her uniform. He sat there for a while and felt the tide turn as she once again reached deep for the strength that had kept her in the jungle and at war for three years.

She sat up, dried her eyes on her sleeve and said matter of factly, 'My father did not return from Singapore. We suspect that he was murdered during the Sook Ching, the round up of the Chinese. My mother came with me into the jungle. But she struggled with the conditions and caught malaria. In the end, I think what killed her was the knowledge that my father was probably dead. She did not accept it at first. In fact, I last saw Rajan when she sent me back to the Kuala Reman estate to see if my father had returned. I knew it was not possible, but I went anyway to try and give her some peace of mind.'

And because it gave you a chance to see Rajan, thought Matthew.

'When I got back and she realised that there was no hope, not really, she just died – as if it was a matter of choice.'

There was silence as they sat lost in their respective thoughts. Matthew felt a strong bond of kinship with Mei Ling, forged from their shared memories.

'What about your parents?' asked Mei Ling.

'My mother is back in England. She is fine though not that happy that I volunteered for this mission.' It was his turn to have emotions force their way to the surface and reveal themselves in his cracking voice. 'My father was taken prisoner. We heard that much but nothing more. He might have been sent to the Burma-Thai border to build some railway but that was never confirmed. I don't even know if he's dead or alive.'

'It is so easy in these times to feel sorry for oneself,' said Mei Ling. 'But we're all in the same boat. There are dead and missing relatives amongst everyone here. No one has been untouched by the viciousness of the Japanese.'

'Well, that's why I'm here,' said Matthew with a flash of boyish optimism. 'We need to kick those bastards back into the sea.'

***

The next couple of weeks were the happiest that Matthew had known since he left Malaya. It rained incessantly, the mosquitoes followed him everywhere in a dark cloud and the food was awful but the camaraderie between the communists, the infectious idea of victory and, most of all, the companionship of his old friend Mei Ling trumped the hardships. He could feel that she respected his new status – he was not the white manager's son any more, he was a soldier in her cause. As for him, he was overwhelmed with admiration for this diminutive bandit who took the fight to the Japanese.

Late one evening, as was his habit, he sought out Mei Ling. It was his personal reward after a hard day patrolling the jungles to sit with her as the heavy dusk descended into velvet black until all she was to him was a husky voice in the shadow of the torches. She was talking about Rajan, remembering some episode involving the three of them, when a harsh voice called her name. It was Siow and he sounded upset. Mei Ling stood up and walked out into the open. She beckoned to Matthew through the open door and he came and stood with her, watching the burly Chinese soldier hurry across the dusty parade ground.

He said, the minute he was within earshot, 'Mei Ling, there have been some developments.'

'What is it?'

'There was a message from the plantation where you used to live.'

'Who sent it? Was it Rajan?'

'No, it was one of our informers amongst the labourers. The Japanese have arrested your friend Rajan.'

'What?' exclaimed Matthew.

'He was taken to the old school – to Colonel Onada.'

Mei Ling turned pale. Her skin was almost translucent with fear.

'What does that mean? Who is Colonel Onada?' asked Matthew.

It was Siow who answered, looking at Mei Ling with concern. 'He is Kempetai. His cruelty is legendary.'

'But why? Why have they arrested Rajan?'

Siow replied, his eyes fixed on Mei Ling and his voice hoarse with apprehension, 'It is about you.'

'Me? What do you mean?' she asked.

'Our information is limited. But it seems Rajan's father, Thomas, tried to find out what was happening to his son. Our informer heard his conversation with Colonel Hidojo when he got back to the estate – in fact, everyone heard it because the father was wild with grief and anger. Your visit to the plantation, the Japanese know about it. Now they want to find out if Rajan knows where you are hiding.'

Mei Ling looked devastated. She swayed on her feet like a boxer who had taken a clean hit to the jaw. Matthew put a hand on her arm to steady her.

'Well, does he?' demanded Siow.

'What?'

'Does your friend know where this camp is – did you tell him?'

'Of course not. Besides, he would never tell.'

'Everyone talks, you know that; and he has already been in Kempetai hands for two weeks.'

'Not Rajan.' Mei Ling spoke with complete confidence.

Her lips pursed into a stubborn line to emphasise her confidence.

Siow was angry. 'You are being naïve. Who told the Japanese that you had gone to the estate in the first place? You told me you only spoke to this fellow Rajan.'

Mei Ling was silent, trying to find an explanation to fit the facts that was not the obvious tale of betrayal, although that was the commonest story of the times.

'Is that right? Did you only see Rajan?' asked Matthew.

Mei Ling nodded. 'But I swear to you he would not have told the Japanese. I cannot imagine him telling *anyone*, but he must have done so – and that person betrayed him to the Kempetai.'

'I don't care how word got to the Japanese,' said Siow. 'But we have to assume that he will tell what he knows – he's been beaten very badly.' He turned to Mei Ling and said roughly, trying to hide his worry for her in his duties as her superior officer, 'Does this man Rajan know where the camp is?'

'I did not tell him because I knew it might endanger him.'

Siow's open, honest face broke into a wide smile of relief. 'Well, that is good news indeed.'

'But what about Rajan?' interrupted Matthew.

'What about him?'

'What will happen to him?'

'He will count himself lucky when he is dead. The important thing is that he cannot betray us even if he wanted to – so we are safe.'

Matthew flushed with resentment, the mottled colour at odds with his yellow hair. 'This man is my friend. Is that all you have to say?'

Siow looked at the Englishman in genuine puzzlement. 'I am sorry for your friend, but what do you expect me to say? I have to put the safety of the camp first. I never suspected Mei Ling of any inappropriate disclosure but the fact is the Japanese now know that the girl who lived on your plantation is the same one they are hunting high and low.'

Matthew's pale lashes framed accusing eyes. Siow continued, garrulous in his own defence. 'The Japanese have a photo of her that is being widely circulated. They must have got that from someone on the estate. Your friend has, unwittingly or otherwise, got Mei Ling and all of us into a lot of trouble. *His* situation is worse but we are not responsible for that.'

'That's not true.'

The two men turned to Mei Ling. She had been so quiet as they argued that both of them had almost forgotten she was there.

'*We* may not be responsible for his fate, but I am. I went to see him and the Kempetai are holding him as a direct result of that visit.'

'You can't blame yourself for that,' said Siow.

'It is my fault – and I need to get him out of there.'

'Don't be ridiculous.'

'I do not expect the regiment to get involved,' explained Mei Ling. 'It is my problem and I will solve it myself.'

'You mean get yourself killed.'

'If that is the outcome, so be it.'

'I forbid it!'

Mei Ling laughed with genuine amusement. She put her hand on Siow's arm, her thin fingers barely encircling his muscular forearm. 'Siow, it is very kind of you to try and protect me – but this is my choice to make.'

'I am the leader of our force. I can prevent you doing this.'

'Only by imprisoning me. Are you prepared to do that – to turn me into a prisoner after all I have done for the MPAJA?'

Matthew watched the two of them squaring off, uncertain of the rights and wrongs of the situation. A woman he felt a powerful desire to protect was debating whether to rescue his best friend. He felt profoundly ignorant and unable to understand or assess the risks.

'I cannot prevent you from throwing your life away.' Siow was almost begging now. 'But we need you – you have a responsibility to your cause, to this war.'

'Yes, but the war is almost won. My strengths were in attacks that attracted publicity, embarrassed the Japanese, gave the population something to believe in ... *that* phase is over. Now we must fight to free Malaya – open warfare against the Japanese together with the British soldiers. You don't need me for that.' She nodded at Matthew. 'You have him.'

As Mei Ling walked away, Siow addressed a question to her receding back, 'What do you plan to do?'

She turned her head and smiled pensively. 'I have no idea.'

Thomas returned to the estate to beg Hidojo for help. Despite what Onada had said, Thomas could not think of anyone else who might be able to influence the Kempetai colonel. He tracked Hidojo down to the labourers' quarters where he was conducting a surprise inspection. Thomas begged and pleaded and eventually confronted the Japanese officer. He raised his voice and screamed his anger and frustration at what he saw as Hidojo's treachery. The Japanese colonel was restrained in his reaction, merely instructing his men to remove Thomas from the vicinity and send him back to his house.

His wife, weak with shock since she had been told the news about Rajan, collapsed. Her heart, not very strong after the years of carrying excessive weight around followed by the three lean years when her diet had been reduced to subsistence level, was unable to take the strain. Thomas shouted for help and realised that Das, his closest neighbour and friend, was gone, sent to the Burma-Thai border. The only other inhabited house was a hundred yards down the road. Thomas half-dragged and half-carried his wife to their marital bed with its thin mattress and shabby but freshly-laundered sheets. Thomas felt tears wet his eyes. His wife had done her best to maintain the household through these miserable war years. He had never acknowledged her efforts or thanked her and now her eyes were closed, the lids bluish and her breathing laboured.

Thomas ran down the road until he reached the other

house and yelled for Ibrahim, the estate medical officer. He was in the middle of dinner but he ran out in his checked sarong and singlet, a mug of hot tea in his hand.

'What is it? What is the matter?'

'My wife! She has collapsed.'

Ibrahim stopped only long enough to grab his equipment bag and sprinted after Thomas who was already on the way back to his own home.

'What happened?' he panted.

'My son has been taken by the Kempetai. When she heard the news …' Thomas trailed off and Ibrahim did not pursue it. There was no need.

Mrs. Thomas was on the bed, her eyes shut. Thomas thought her breathing was a little easier. Ibrahim checked her quickly and then beckoned to Thomas and they both stepped out of the door.

'She has had a mild heart attack. I think she will be all right as long as she does not become anxious or have a shock.'

Thomas grimaced.

'I know that is impossible, so I think we should sedate her,' said Ibrahim. 'It will keep her asleep – even when she awakes, she will be calmer under the influence of the drugs.'

Thomas nodded. 'You have such medicine? I thought you had run out of everything.'

'I have saved a bit for emergencies.'

Thomas grasped Ibrahim's right hand in both of his own. 'I have to go back to town and see what I can do for Rajan. Will you keep an eye on her?'

'Of course.'

Thomas turned to leave the house, a dishevelled, tired old man, a stark contrast to the immaculate creature Ibrahim had known for so many years. His face creased with sympathy, Ibrahim said, 'I will pray that you can help Rajan.'

Thomas clutched at his thinning grey hair, feeling as if he was on the verge of madness. He wanted to say so much to the Malay man looking at him with such sympathy – to beg for reassurance that a God did exist despite a world ravaged by war, to ask Ibrahim how he maintained his simple faith in such pressing times, to seek some way to believe that to trust to God was to leave his son in safe hands. Instead, he raised a hand in a gesture that was partly a plea for some sort of succour and part farewell, climbed back on Colonel Hidojo's bike and set off for town once more.

***

'What can I do to help?' Matthew's own mission to forge military ties with the communists was forgotten.

'There is nothing you can do, Matthew,' said Mei Ling.

'Rajan is my best friend!'

Keng Lian laughed out loud.

'What's so funny,' demanded Matthew, prickly with resentment.

'A white man will not last ten minutes in a town crawling with Japanese soldiers, informers and people who are just trying to survive until the end of the war,' explained Keng Lian.

Matthew acknowledged this with a reluctant nod.

'I can help,' said Keng Lian.

Mei Ling shook her head. 'This is a personal quest. We cannot waste good men on it.'

'How are you going to manage it on your own? You need to find out what's going on.'

Mei Ling bit her bottom lip.

'You cannot turn up in person – not with your picture on "wanted" posters all over town.'

Matthew listened to this exchange with growing irritation. He could see that Mei Ling was swayed by Keng Lian's offer as she had not been by his. There were good practical reasons for this but it did not make Matthew feel less aggrieved.

Mei Ling slipped an arm through his and explained in her quiet, deep voice that she understood that Matthew wanted to help. She was only considering Keng Lian because he might be able to obtain useful information – like the whereabouts of Rajan within the prison complex. Matthew was sick with worry about Rajan. The stories that Siow and Keng Lian had told him, when Mei Ling was out of earshot, about Colonel Onada and the Kempetai had filled him with horror. But a large part of his stomach-churning terror was the thought of Mei Ling ending up in the hands of these people. He had only been in the jungle a few weeks but this woman had got under his skin. She was relying on him, turning to him in her worry because she thought that they had their common history and mutual affection for Rajan to bind them together. This was not the time to tell her that the threesome was a triangle. There was time enough to compete for her affections when Rajan was safe and the war was over. He just had to try and ensure that outcome. But Matthew had absolutely no idea how he was going to do it. He felt as helpless as when he'd huddled on the deck of the Empress of Japan, praying that the Japanese would not spot them.

***

Keng Lian went to town to investigate. He left with a cheerful wave, his insouciance typical of the man but at odds with the danger he faced. He had changed into civilian clothing. He spent the day with his family. He carried the false papers that they procured for him through a friend who worked for the Japanese department in charge of the permits that every person was supposed to carry and have ready to display at checkpoints and whenever challenged by a Japanese soldier. All the communists who came into town on missions had them. The Japanese had instituted a vast bureaucracy to deal with every contingency that could result from a resentful population. This had merely created opportunities for corruption and cronyism amongst the non-Japanese who worked for them. Driven by need, anger, greed or fellow feeling, there was always someone who knew someone who could arrange for the latest piece of paper that gave one as much freedom to travel as was available under the Japanese regime.

Keng Lian went to the Kempetai headquarters and asked whether he could see if a missing cousin of his was within its walls – the mother was frantic, he explained, although in his view his cousin had run off with a pretty girl. The Malay guard was amused and let him through, pointing out that his relative would be in much better shape if indeed he had found himself a woman rather than a spot behind the white walls. Keng Lian entered the main building. The relatives of prisoners were begging for access or information or to be allowed to hand over some medication or a blanket or a boiled egg. A number were resigned to sitting with their backs to the walls along low wooden benches, hoping that someone would give them some news. Their eyes were red-rimmed and exhausted, their spines curved with fatigue. Keng Lian sat down too and watched events, wondering how he was going to find Rajan.

An old man marched in. He walked straight over to the counter, ignoring everyone else in the waiting area and said in a loud voice, 'I want to see Colonel Onada.'

This request was met with a laugh. The man was adamant. He wanted to see Onada about his son Rajan. At the mention of Rajan's name, Keng Lian sat up and paid attention. He felt a pang of sympathy. Rajan's father was at the end of his tether if he thought that he could bully his way in to see either the dreaded Colonel Onada or his own son. He watched the soldier get impatient and cuff the old man. It was a hard blow. Rajan's father shook his head, as if he was trying to clear the ringing in his ears. He put both hands, with fingers splayed, on the table. 'I must see my son. He is innocent, I tell you. He has done nothing.'

Keng Lian could see that his assertive pose with hands on the table was mostly to hold himself up.

Thomas had succeeded in annoying the soldier behind the desk. At a quick barked command in Japanese, two sentries grabbed him by his arms and dragged him out of the building. His legs were trailing in the dirt. They reached the main gate and threw him to the ground.

Keng Lian moved to the door. He saw that Thomas just lay there, by the side of the road, unable or unwilling to get up. Nobody stopped to help. Anyone in trouble outside Kempetai headquarters was toxic. The people of Bukit Pagoh averted their eyes and strode past as swiftly as they could, pretending not to notice the thin, bruised man lying with his face in the thick carpet of sunny flowers that had fallen from a yellow flame tree by the gates. Eventually, Thomas sat up and tottered towards his motorbike.

CHAPTER 16

I've often wondered if my feelings first developed on the Kuala Reman estate and I was just too naïve to recognise them or whether it really was 'love at first sight' in the jungles of Malaya. All I can tell you, dear friend, is that I loved Mei Ling with my whole being (however pathetic that sounds) and I have never loved anyone since with even a quarter of that intensity. Everything I did – and this is my only excuse – was borne of that overwhelming emotion.

Thomas was sitting in his rocking chair swaying back and forth. His wife was in bed, fast asleep. There were dinner dishes on the dining room table and a candle burning on a sideboard. To Mei Ling, peering in at a window, it was a cosy domestic scene. She knew better, of course. Keng Lian had reported Thomas's attempts to see his son. Ever resourceful, Keng Lian had managed to bribe one of the Indian soldiers, formerly with the British Army, now in the Indian National Army and responsible for patrolling the prison at night. He reported that it would be impossible to rescue Rajan by force. He was in a terrible state, badly beaten and starved, locked in a small cell with a number of other prisoners and well guarded. Colonel Onada viewed him as an important source of information about the notorious female communist terrorist, Mei Ling, and was determined to wring every last piece of information from him, even if it was accompanied by every last drop of blood in his body. Mei Ling had closed her eyes when she heard this. Matthew put two big hands on her thin shoulders and held her close. It did not seem that there was much that could be done. Mei Ling knew that Rajan would not survive his interrogation for the simple reason that he had nothing of value to tell the Japanese. If Onada was convinced that Rajan knew more, he would be tortured until death rescued him.

Mei Ling, sitting in darkness outside the window, remembered the many times she had sauntered through the estate on some errand for her father. Rajan would materialise out of nowhere and walk with her. She smiled a little when she realised that he must have been lying in wait for her – at the time she'd thought their meetings were happy coincidences. She had talked about her father's beliefs and he had listened and nodded, his dark eyes twinkling with pleasure, she had assumed because of the worthiness of her ideals. Now, her understanding sharpened by fear for Rajan's life, she realised it had been the simple pleasure of listening to her speak and not the content of her conversation that had cleft his cheeks with vertical laughter lines.

Matthew and the others did not know – yet – that she had come here, to Rajan's home. She had crept away in the dead of night. They would have urged her not to be so foolish, perhaps even detained her. She was about to risk the safety of the entire camp.

Mei Ling rapped on the window with her knuckles. There was no response from Thomas within. She tapped again, a little harder. This time he sat up. His movements were ungainly as if he had some wasting nervous disease and his mind had to remind his body how to do the simple things. New lines were engraved into his skin as if each day of his son's incarceration was being recorded on his father's face. Perhaps Rajan was doing the same on the prison walls, marking the days of his imprisonment.

Thomas came to the window and opened it, blinking into the night.

Mei Ling stepped out from the shadows and said, 'Good evening, Mr. Thomas. I am here about Rajan.'

He stared at her as if she was an apparition. His eyes were bloodshot. Mei Ling noticed that he smelt of unwashed clothes and stale sweat. One of his cheeks was cut and scratched. There was mud and dirt in the wounds.

'Mr. Thomas,' she said again. 'I'm here about Rajan. I want to help.'

He opened the window and she climbed in. She was wearing her military uniform. Thomas stared at her in genuine confusion. At last he whispered, 'Mei Ling, is it you?'

She nodded and his eyes were drawn to the three stars on her cap.

'Rajan has been arrested by the Kempetai.'

'That's why I am here.'

'It is your fault – you should never have come to see him.'

The words were angry and accusatory, but the tone was unchanged. Mei Ling assumed that he had played over and over in his head what he would like to say to her, given the chance. But now that she was standing before him, the futility of wasting words and emotions was apparent. His son was in the hands of the Kempetai. Nothing else mattered.

'I know it is my fault, Mr. Thomas. I am very sorry for what he's been through because of me.' The emotion oozed like pus from an infected wound.

He must have sensed her regret was genuine because he said, 'I believe you, but that does not help my son.'

'I have a plan to help Rajan.'

'What can you do – a rescue? With your soldier friends?' Hope, like a forgotten memory, dawned on Thomas's face.

'I was hoping that we would be able to do that. The MPAJA is well-armed and well-trained and the tide of war is turning.'

'Can you do it?'

She shook her head. 'There is no way. He's too well-guarded. The Kempetai think he might know where I am and they want to get their hands on me very badly.'

'Then what is your plan if you cannot rescue my son by force?'

'I want you to arrange a trade with Colonel Onada.'

'Trade? What do I have to offer him? I have nothing that he wants!'

'You have me.'

***

Mei Ling's letter was written in a firm, sloping hand. Matthew wanted to scream and shout and rip the piece of paper to shreds. Instead, he just sat on the log that was his seat, reading and re-reading it. It was not a long letter. There had not been that much to say. Her decision was conveyed with a few concise strokes of the pen. He was sworn to secrecy, of course. Her reasoning was sensible and showed yet again her ability to see the big picture even when her personal life was diverging from her cause. Matthew would have ignored her command that he tell no one of her plan if he had any hope that there was time to stop her. But when he had read the letter the first time, his heart sinking into his heavy boots, he had run over to the hut where she slept only to discover that she'd left the previous night on a mission. The female soldier with whom she shared the hut explained that this was not uncommon – too much information exchange risked the group and the individual. Mei Ling operated on a 'need to know' basis.

He had walked back to his spot and read the letter again. On a 'need to know' basis? That was not entirely correct. There was no *need* for this letter that she had written to him. The contents would have become self-evident once her actions became known. But Matthew knew why she'd committed her thoughts to paper. Once she'd made her decision, there must have been a desire on her part to tell someone, to leave knowledge of her sacrifice with another human being. Perhaps, although there was an overt prohibition in the letter on informing Rajan of her decision, she hoped that there would come a time when Matthew could tell him what she had done. Some part of her must have wanted Rajan to know the strength of her love. A love never spoken of between them, but a knot that tied their destinies together while ensuring that their lives and deaths were to be forever on parallel paths.

Matthew tried to analyse his own emotions, an intellectual exercise to rationalise his fear. His predominant feeling was rage. He was furious with Rajan. His imprisonment was the root of Mei Ling's sacrifice. After all, he must have told someone, even if not the Japanese, about her visit to the estate, otherwise he would never have been arrested in the first place.

He was mad at himself for not telling Mei Ling how he felt. He knew that it would not have affected her decision in any way, but for the words never to be spoken left him with a deep feeling of frustration. But most of all he was angry with Mei Ling that she had chosen to throw her life away. Matthew wondered how, if and when this war ended, he would be able to face Rajan again. His emotions were now too conflicted to imagine such a meeting, although once upon a time he had considered that possibility his chief reward in coming to Malaya again.

The sun travelled slowly through the sky and a shaft of light threaded its way through the leaves and fell like a benediction on the letter in Matthew's hand. The paper turned golden, as if it was an ancient parchment rather than two damp pages torn out of a cheap notebook. He looked at the last line once more – 'Promise me you'll never tell Rajan that I exchanged myself for him. He would never forgive himself – or me.'

Matthew folded the letter and buttoned it into his breast pocket.

***

Thomas got in to see Onada.

Explaining that he had information on the whereabouts of Mei Ling was a passport straight into his presence. Thomas had washed, shaved and changed into fresh clothes. In many ways, Mei Ling, hidden in his house, thought it accentuated his suffering – there was no disguise of dirt and sweat now. His face had aged a year for every day that his son had been taken from him. She watched him go and warned him of the possibility of a Japanese double-cross. He nodded as he got on his bike. Leaning to one side, a foot on the ground, the other on the starter, Thomas gazed at the girl who was prepared to deliver herself into the hands of Onada to save his son.

'It was my fault – I told Hidojo, the colonel in charge of Kuala Reman estate, about your visit,' said Thomas.

'Rajan told you?'

'Yes – so that I would give him permission to join you in the jungles. I said no, that it would kill his mother.' His hands gripped the handles so tight that his knuckles were white and bloodless. 'It looks like I've managed to do that on my own.'

'She will recover once Rajan is safe,' said Mei Ling, finding compassion enough to comfort the man who had just confessed to betraying her. She continued in a tone of mild curiosity as if she was discussing something trivial, 'Why did you do it?'

'Hidojo threatened to send the boy to the Death Railway. So I traded him the information about your visit in return for him allowing Rajan to stay.'

'I can understand that. He is your son and you love him.'

Thomas was determined to get the whole sorry tale off his chest. He continued, 'But Hidojo told Onada, and once they realised that you were behind all the assassinations, Onada was certain there was more to the story. That's why they seized Rajan.'

'I see,' said Mei Ling. 'Well, it all began with my visit. I wanted to see him and did not have the self-discipline to stay away. I pretended it was for my mother's sake but it is too late for lies and self-deception now.' She looked at the old man sharply and said, 'Do you remember every detail of our plan?'

He nodded respectfully, responding to the core of steel in the guerrilla fighter and not to the thin young girl who stood before him.

'Go then, and good luck.'

Thomas rode straight back to the school and this time he was ushered into the presence of Colonel Onada. The Japanese man was sitting behind his big desk. He was a little too short for it, which would have been comic if the man did not come with Onada's reputation.

'This better be good, old man. I'm bored with your stubborn son.'

'I have information about the girl, Mei Ling, and I will trade it for my boy.'

'What is to stop me beating it out of you? The Kempetai does not make deals.'

'You can try, of course,' acknowledged Thomas. 'But I am an old man. If you have my son, I have no reason to live. I think I will take my secret to the grave. Are you prepared to take that risk?'

Onada twined his fingers together and rested his chin on them. Thomas noticed that his fingers were short and thick, with the nails cut so short that a red line appeared between nail and fingertip. 'What sort of information?'

'I can give her to you.'

Onada stood up and came around the desk. He was shorter than Thomas, even in his riding boots, but almost twice as wide. He thrust his chin, stubbly with grey, at Rajan's father.

'You know where she is?'

'Not exactly.'

Onada struck him so suddenly that it took a moment for the blow to register. It was an open-handed slap. Thomas could feel the imprint of every single one of the stubby fingers on his cheek. He did not acknowledge the attack. The Japanese colonel was breathing heavily, a result of the rush of temper.

Thomas knew he was within seconds of having Onada try and extract his secret by more direct methods. 'I don't know where Mei Ling is because it would be too tempting for you to try and beat it out of me. But I can arrange an exchange – you release my son and she will turn herself in.'

'Turn herself in? Why would she do that?'

'She blames herself for his arrest.'

Onada sniggered.

It was a repulsive sound. Thomas felt sick to the stomach that he was planning to deliver a young girl to this parody of a human being. The Kempetai colonel took off his round glasses and wiped them on a white handkerchief. He looked at Thomas myopically, eyes blinking in an effort to focus without his spectacles. 'Do I detect a romance?' he asked and giggled again. 'At least that explains the estate visit, the boy's stubbornness and now this offer. Very well – you have a deal. Colonel Onada will not stand in the way of love's supreme sacrifice.' He began to laugh so hard that tears rolled down his cheeks, his eyes narrowed to slits, and he had to lean on the desk to steady himself. He wiped his eyes, slipped on his glasses, winding the frame around his ears, and then looked at Thomas again. 'You have a deal,' he repeated.

***

When Rajan was brought out, Thomas wept. The boy had no fingernails left on his right hand, just bloody stumps where they had been. He was shirtless and his back was a mass of cuts and bruises. He had been beaten with a blunt instrument like a truncheon but also with something that cut the flesh in strips, perhaps a thin bamboo cane. He was thinner, his ribs showing through, although he'd been in captivity for no more than a couple of weeks. His shorts were soiled. He must have done it while being tortured and not been permitted a change. Livid burn marks, the skin charred and black around large fluid-filled blisters, pocked his calves, and there were deep holes in the backs of his knees that must have been made with a sharpened stick. A number of his teeth were missing and his lips were dry and chapped. His wrist was swollen and black, the blood congealed just under the surface. His face and arms were covered in mosquito bites, each one an inflamed welt. One eye was swollen shut but the other saved its hostile, bloodshot glance for his father rather than for the man who had reduced him to this state.

'Here is your son. Looks like you got here just in time,' said Onada.

Rajan said, barely audible as he tried to wield his swollen, bitten tongue to make the sounds he sought, 'I do not wish to go with this man. He is not my father.'

It was a brave gesture but ignored by all present. Thomas helped Rajan to the Land Rover he had borrowed from Hidojo for the trip. Rajan fainted as he was manhandled into the vehicle, and Thomas laid the boy on the mattress he had put in the back. He was grateful that Rajan would not feel the drive back to the estate on roads that had fallen into disrepair under the watchful eyes of the Japanese administration.

He left the engine running and went back in to see Onada. 'The girl will turn herself in later today,' he said. 'I beg of you to remember that this war is ending and that you will be held accountable for whatever you do to her.'

Onada did not appear to be listening but as Thomas reached the door, he said, 'If she is not here by the end of the day, you and you son will be – in adjoining cells.'

Thomas walked out without deigning to respond.

He drove Rajan straight home. Ibrahim was waiting for him. They took the boy out and washed him and changed him. Ibrahim dressed his wounds, tut-tutted over his fingernails and shook his head over the wrist. Rajan was heavily sedated so he did not, for once, feel the pain of his wounds.

***

Mei Ling waited in the trees long enough to see that Thomas was not followed home by Japanese troops and then ran swiftly into the small house. She slipped into Rajan's bedroom and stared at the sleeping youth. She bit her lip. She had seen worse wounds in the jungle – gunshots, snake bite, tiger attack, native spears, some green with gangrene, others oozing pus and maggots – but they had not affected her as did the sight of Rajan's broken body. Mei Ling looked at Rajan and reminded herself that she was a warrior.

'He will make a full recovery, I think,' said Ibrahim. 'Only the wrist might have permanent damage ...'

She nodded. Ibrahim and Thomas shuffled out of the room and went to check on Mrs. Thomas who was stirring. There was no need to prevent her regaining consciousness now that Rajan was home.

Mei Ling, left alone with Rajan, moved forward and sat on the edge of the bed. She fingered the blanket that had been drawn up to his chest. It was made of thin cotton and she hoped he was warm enough. The ceiling fan overhead turned slowly. The lights were switched off but the room was bright; the curtains were too fine to keep out the afternoon sunshine. She wondered whether to speak. Would her words register in his subconscious somehow? She doubted it. Mei Ling had a strong practical streak that prevented her from romantic flights of fancy. She stared at Rajan, determined to have a recent image of him in her mind to take to prison. She noted the thin face, the shadowed eyelids and the long lashes resting on pale cheeks. Rajan's eyes remained shut. Mei Ling felt regret that she could not look into his brown eyes one more time. Still, it was best that he was unconscious. He would not appreciate her plan, of that she was sure. She laid a palm on Rajan's cheek. He murmured something and turned towards the hand. She smiled at him, thought for an instant of a time after the war was won, dismissed it as the stuff of fantasies – she knew that Colonel Onada would not allow a happy ending – and slipped out of the room.

***

Thomas and Mei Ling walked into the school that was now Kempetai headquarters – she for the first time ever, although many of her comrades had made the trip – he for the second time that day. The first time, Thomas had bought the freedom of his son. This time he was making payment with the life of Mei Ling.

Thomas was doing his best to avoid thinking about Chan, his onetime friend and the girl's father. What would he say to the choices that Thomas had made? Thomas knew that Chan could never have brought himself to save his own life or that of his family at the expense of someone else. His existence had been an exercise of sacrifice for principle. He, Thomas, had fallen well short of that ideal. He was prepared to give up anyone, including himself, for the good of his son. Unfortunately, his life was not worth anything to the Japanese. But this girl was valuable and she was the price of Rajan's life. Thomas tried to take some comfort from the fact that the girl was doing this voluntarily, that in some ways her affection for his son was a stronger, purer force than his own. Mei Ling was acting true to the principles that Rajan believed in to save him while he, the boy's father, was compromising them.

He had tied Mei Ling's hands behind her back at her own insistence. It was better if her communist comrades did not know she had given herself up, she explained. It might affect their resolve to fight the war through to its end if one of their leaders showed such weakness as she now did.

'Weakness?' asked Thomas in confusion.

'Yes, no communist should put the individual over the collective good. It is better if they believe that I was captured. That is a fate that we all understand – there is a certain inevitability and honour about it.'

Thomas wished the girl would not talk about honour.

Colonel Onada came out immediately. He looked Mei Ling up and down and his face broke into a wide smile, his full lips stretched thin in his glee.

'Well done, Thomas!'

Thomas did not answer.

Onada marched up to the girl. They were about the same height, a few inches above five feet, and now he stared at her carefully, examining her features as if to confirm that she was the girl in the photograph and not some last-minute substitute.

Onada turned to Thomas, 'You – get out. Your work is done.'

'My son is safe? You guarantee it?'

Onada glanced at Mei Ling again. Then he turned to Thomas, 'Yes, I guarantee it.'

Thomas turned to Mei Ling. He was at a loss for words. How could he articulate his thanks? What could he say to this girl?

'Don't worry, Mr. Thomas. This is my choice.'

He put out a hand and touched her shoulder. He left the room.

***

The Indian policeman on guard duty by the door was watching proceedings. His pocket was plump with the cash that Keng Lian had given him along with a promise of more if information was forthcoming about Rajan, his father or anyone else connected with the case. He had already sent word that Rajan was free but this was an interesting new development and bound to be worth some money.

***

'They have Mei Ling! The Kempetai have Mei Ling!'

Keng Lian burst into the meeting of senior cadres without ceremony. They were all seated around a bamboo table with maps of Malaya open in front of them. Matthew was briefing them about the likely invasion routes that his radio operator had just received from Ceylon. The invasion was being brought forward to August. The war in the Pacific was going sufficiently well that the Allies were confident that there was no need to delay. The plan, called Operation Zipper, involved British troops sweeping through Malaya from the north in a loose imitation of the Japanese tactics that had driven them out in the first place. They would be joined at every juncture by soldiers of the MPAJA who would assist in the fighting, provide the necessary local knowledge, brief the invading forces on Japanese positions and troop strength and keep civil order in the immediate aftermath of Japanese defeat before civilian British rule could resume.

Matthew had known Mei Ling's capture was inevitable since he received her letter. It was burning a hole in the breast pocket directly over his heart. But to hear confirmation, to know that she had gone ahead with her plan to rescue Rajan, was devastating.

Chung stood up. His skin, grey with shock, was almost

the same colour as his hair. 'How did this happen? What do you know?'

Keng Lian, who had brought the news, was unable to stand still. He marched to the head of the table, looked at his comrades, waved his hands in the air to indicate his own helplessness and said, 'I don't have much information. My informant, an Indian policeman, sent word that Rajan had been released to his father. He was in bad shape – beaten up but alive. I was in the bicycle shop in town.'

'Later,' continued Keng Lian, putting his hands on his hips, 'I got another message – this time it was that the father, Thomas, had brought a girl to the Kempetai HQ. She was bound.' Keng Lian bowed his head and his voice trailed off into a whisper. 'She admitted to being Mei Ling and a member of the MPAJA.'

'She left yesterday. She told no one where she was going,' said Siow.

Matthew knew how much the big man was hurting. He admired the iron discipline that meant he could contribute to the discussion in a sensible way.

'She has signed her own death warrant,' said the Major.

'She did nothing,' shouted Keng Lian. 'It was the father, Rajan's father, who betrayed her. This Thomas – he has cost us dearly!'

'We can ill-afford to lose someone like Mei Ling. The Japanese will paint this as a triumph.' It was the political commissar, speaking in his thin precise voice.

'Perhaps we can mourn our comrade before we discuss the propaganda aspects?' said Siow, his voice trembling with rage and his hands bunched into fists.

Chung put up his hands, palms forward, a gesture asking for restraint, for pause. 'We are all in shock because of this news. But from the moment that Mei Ling decided to try and rescue this childhood friend of hers, we knew that she was at risk.'

'But she was betrayed!' Keng Lian was shouting, his anger boiling over at Mei Ling's fate.

Chung nodded his agreement. 'There is an ugliness about what happened. But she put herself in a position where treachery was possible. She must have gone to see the boy's father and he captured her and exchanged her for the boy – it was a tactical error. The question now is whether this camp is secure.'

'We must move – this hideout is compromised,' said the political officer.

'She would never reveal our location,' insisted Siow.

'She would never do so willingly,' said Chung, 'and I don't doubt she has the courage of ten men. But we cannot take the chance. We must move.'

Matthew had not spoken since Keng Lian had burst in with the news. He was coming to grips with the knowledge that Mei Ling was lost to him. He knew that Thomas had not compromised Mei Ling's safety. It had been a willing exchange – her life for Rajan's. She had walked into the old school building with full knowledge of the consequences, knowing it was the only way to get Rajan away from the Kempetai. But Matthew did not speak. She had placed the burden of secrecy on him and he would respect her wishes.

It was all he could do for her. He asked in a measured tone that was in contrast to the raised voices around him, 'Can she be rescued?'

'No, I do not think so. Mei Ling is such a valuable prisoner. They will have her closely guarded at all times.' It was Keng Lian who spelt out in stark words what they already knew.

'We cannot waste good men on a futile errand. Matthew, what is your view on relocating our base?' said Chung.

Matthew raised his shoulders to signify that he did not know the answer. 'I don't believe that Mei Ling will talk. Anyway, your perimeters are well guarded and you will have time to retreat if the Japanese do find out about this place. That is my best advice – but the reality is that I have only been here for a short while. I will be guided by you in this matter.'

Chung acknowledged the burden of leadership with a quick nod to Matthew. 'We will stay for now. We will post sentries up and down the mountain so that we have ample warning of a Japanese encroachment. The arms cache must be moved away from this site so that we do not lose our weapons if we have to leave in a hurry.'

There were nods all around signalling concurrence. They would place their faith in the stoicism of a young girl. But they would have an escape plan if the Kempetai was able to persuade her to divulge the location of their jungle home.

'We will continue our other discussions at a later time,' said Chung. 'Keng Lian, go back to town and keep an eye on the situation in case there is an opportunity to help Mei

Ling.' He added, 'Even if it is only the means to end her suffering once and for all.'

***

The cell was about eight feet square, estimated Mei Ling. It had been formed by partitioning classrooms with unplastered brick walls that stopped three feet short of the ceiling. There was a wooden platform covering one third of the area. It was crowded with sleeping forms – men and women both. The place stank of faeces and urine. Mei Ling tracked a sickly rotting smell to a prisoner, a young man with an abscess in the back of his knee, infected and oozing yellow pus. The latrine was a bucket in the corner that was already overflowing. There was no privacy. Mei Ling had her uniform. The other prisoners, from what little she could see of them in the half darkness, were dressed in filthy rags, their bodies grimy and bearing signs of torture, their hair hanging in limp knots.

Mei Ling huddled in a corner and waited for Onada to turn his attention to her. She did not have to wait long. A Sikh policeman unlocked the door and snapped her name. She got to her feet and came willingly. There was no point being dragged kicking and screaming into his presence. She was determined to show courage. She noticed as she was led out that her name had been written in chalk on a small board nailed to the door.

Onada was waiting in a small room with high windows covered in grills. It was below ground level because she could see booted feet marching by. A single flickering light bulb lit the room, its intermittent flashes reflected in her jailor's spectacles. There were two other soldiers in the room. Their presence was overshadowed by the grim visage of the most feared man in Johore. Mei Ling did not waste a glance on them.

'You are Mei Ling?' asked Onada.

'Yes.'

'You are a member of the Malayan People's Anti-Japanese Army?' He spat out the words as if he had bitten into a rotten fruit.

'Yes.'

'You have been conducting a campaign of murder against the Japanese and their allies from your jungle hideout?'

'I have been fighting a war, yes.' She was defiant. 'I have killed Japanese soldiers and collaborators and I'm not ashamed of it.'

'You are not ashamed of it, maybe – but I will make you regret it.'

The suddenness of his fury was terrifying. He slapped her on both cheeks repeatedly with his open palms, screaming obscenities.

Mei Ling kept her hands by her sides although her cheeks were on fire. The big signet ring Onada wore on his left hand had gashed her face from ear to lip.

Breathing heavily he asked, 'Where is the guerrilla hideout?'

'I will not betray my comrades.'

'If you know what is good for you, you will tell me. Where is the guerrilla hideout?'

'I will not betray my comrades.'

A rattan cane was on a side table. Onada grabbed it and hit her repeatedly on the back and shoulders with it. When she collapsed to her knees, he picked up a wooden plank and continued raining down blows. Mei Ling caught the final knock to the side of her head and fainted.

When she recovered consciousness she was back in her cell, lying on the filthy floor. A guard appeared and handed her a coconut shell with a bit of rice and dried fish in it. It was her first meal in prison. Even as she held it she realised that there was a hole in the bottom. She caught what she could and then ate the grains off the floor, chasing away rats the size of her feet. She could barely finish the meal, her face a mass of pain from that final blow, but she forced herself to swallow.

Within hours she was dragged back to the same cell. This time Onada was friendly, offering her a chair and a cigarette. She accepted the chair but shook her head at the smoke. She wondered if he expected her to be overcome with gratitude and tell him everything. If so, he'd have to think again.

'Where is the guerrilla hideout?'

'I will not betray my comrades.'

'We will see about that.'

Mei Ling knew all about the water torture, of course. It was a well-known Kempetai method of extracting information. But forewarned was not forearmed in any way. They bound her ankles with twine and tied her hands together in front of her. They laid her on the floor. A soldier wedged her mouth open and forced a length of garden hose down her throat while the other held her head steady in a vice-like grip. She was choking. The pain of the twine cutting into her ankles and wrists helped her focus on breathing.

Another soldier poured water down the tube using a tin funnel. The pain of her expanding stomach was excruciating. But there was worse to come. A soldier placed a plank on her distended belly. Mei Ling shut her eyes. In his boots, Onada jumped on the plank bringing all the weight of his grotesque form down on her. She felt water burst out of every orifice. She vomited and the water ran into her nose. Mei Ling gasped and choked and struggled for breath. Water flowed from her eyes, not tears but liquid seeking ways to escape the build up of pressure. Mei Ling was soaked through. The two guards dragged her limp form back to the prison.

Time had no meaning in the cell with the muttering, suffering inmates. Mei Ling estimated that many hours had passed. It was almost morning. She had not been able to sleep despite her physical and mental exhaustion. Soaking wet and without a change of clothes, she had begun to feel the chill of a cool night. She shivered. Her teeth were chattering. She knew more punishment would follow but she still longed for an end to the interminable night. Mei Ling wondered how she was to survive. Indeed, she acknowledged, survival was the least of her concerns, the least of her desires. She would rather die quickly, before Colonel Onada broke her will and she revealed the location of the camp. It was possible that Chung had moved the hideout but Mei Ling was not certain that he would have done so at this late stage in the preparations for a British invasion. She could not take the chance. She did not want to give Onada the victory.

The prison door opened and Mei Ling was called. She got to her feet and tottered out, pleased that she was able to show this independence. She knew that soon enough they would have to carry her to the interrogations. This time she was taken to Onada's office. He looked at her in disgust.

'You are filthy and you stink – do you communists have no self-respect?' He picked up a small mirror and held it up to Mei Ling. 'See what you look like!' Mei Ling had a brief glance of livid bruises and puffy eyes.

'I would be happy to bathe if provided some soap and water and a change of clothes,' she mumbled.

He walked up to her and pinched her bottom lip between forefinger and thumb, squeezing and twisting until hot tears sprang to Mei Ling's eyes.

He let go and pulled up a chair. Mei Ling almost collapsed into it. He nodded to a guard who obviously knew what was expected of him. He grabbed Mei Ling's right hand and held it splayed against Onada's polished sandalwood desk. Onada opened a few drawers, grumbling under his breath as he could not find the implement he was looking for. At last, he popped up triumphant, pliers in his hand. He asked, 'Where is the guerrilla camp?'

'I will not betray my comrades.'

Onada grasped the nail on her index finger with the metal jaws of the pliers and pulled. Mei Ling screamed.

'Where is the guerrilla camp?'

'I ... will not ... betray ... my comrades.'

CHAPTER 17

When Emperor Hirohito surrendered as a result of what he called the 'new and most cruel bomb', my first thought was that there might be a chance to save Mei Ling. Unfortunately the higher ups decided that the troops of Operation Zipper wouldn't land in Singapore and Malaya until after the formal surrender of Japanese troops in South East Asia. I remember the sheer frustration of knowing that the Pacific war was won but having no way to impose our will on the Japanese. In the meantime, their soldiers were executing prisoners, destroying evidence and making overtures to the MPAJA on whether they would be open to the possibility of fighting the British – a belated revival of their 'Asia for the Asians' propaganda. I didn't care. Perhaps I had 'gone native' but it didn't seem to me such a terrible thing if the MPAJA took over Malaya. They had fought long and hard for the privilege.

My only real concern was Mei Ling. Keng Lian's spies indicated she was alive – barely. I was desperate to get her out of the Kempetai's hands. And that, I suppose, is the point where our two stories became one.

'We have to get Mei Ling out of there.' Matthew was determined to have his way. He stood up, much taller than the Asians in the hut, and thumped the table to emphasise his point.

'You have heard Keng Lian,' said Major Chung. 'She is close to death, perhaps already dead. We cannot concentrate on the liberation of an individual. We do not know how the Japanese will react. I do not see Colonel Onada surrendering.'

'They have lost the war. We have *won* it. Why should one more person from our side die?' Met with silence, Matthew continued, 'If we go in with a large force, I wager that we will not have to fire a shot. Surely, the Japanese will let us free the prisoners. What choice do they have?'

'I agree with Matthew,' said Siow. 'It can be done. Mei Ling deserves that we try.'

Chung sighed and lowered himself on a bench like an old man. Matthew could see how tired the guerrilla leader was. He had a sudden vision of the long, arduous struggle in the jungle, the lack of food, the constant danger, the planning and execution of strategy after strategy in what must have felt like a futile war. Matthew knew from the others that Chung had suffered from beri-beri in the early days of the war. He had also caught malaria and it still flared up from time to time, rendering him incapacitated by fever, aches and pains. Through it all he had provided prudent, pragmatic, determined leadership that was occasionally inspired, especially in his decision to let Mei Ling and her small band create havoc in the Japanese community and amongst collaborators. But now he was taking a false step.

Matthew needed him to understand that.

'Mei Ling is a Malayan heroine!' he said.

'She is like a daughter to me,' snapped Chung.

'Her story will be told for years and years,' continued Matthew. 'If the MPAJA rescue her – save her life – you will be feted by the townspeople. You will be well-placed to provide leadership in Johore. The communists have a golden opportunity to take over Malaya and impede the return of the British. They are not due to land for at least two to three weeks.' Matthew knew that his words were those of a traitor but he was focused on saving Mei Ling.

'Our co-operation with the British is based on having a common enemy – the Japanese,' replied Chung. 'I had high hopes we would consolidate our position and take over the administration of Malaya. But you should know that instructions have arrived from Lai Tek, Secretary General of the Communist Party of Malaya. No military moves against the British are permitted – from now on our fight for power will be political.'

'What?' shouted Keng Lian.

'I too am disappointed,' agreed Chung. 'The Central Committee feels that our efforts against the Japanese and support amongst the Malayan population will give us sufficient bargaining power with the British that we can further our ideals without bloodshed.'

'We have fought for so long … why must we just hand over this land to the British?' Keng Lian was almost in tears.

'Any decision that seeks our ends by peaceful means should be respected,' said Siow. 'I for one would not be comfortable fighting the British.' He glanced over at Matthew. 'They have been our allies. Besides, I am tired of the suffering caused by war.'

Chung slumped back against the wall. 'I too am tired of fighting.'

'Are you telling me that these British,' demanded Keng Lian, 'who have arrived here in the last few weeks of war just in time to drink and dance and celebrate victory, who have not fired a shot in anger or self-defence, who have not had their family members raped and murdered, should be handed this land that has absorbed the blood, sweat and tears of so many comrades?' He spat on the ground.

'I understand your anger, Keng Lian, but orders are orders.'

'I know this war has been fought and won without my help,' said Matthew, 'but the true mark of your success has been the steadfastness and comradeship I have seen amongst you. I have been privileged to share it for a short while. Now we should demonstrate our loyalty to our fellow soldiers … by rescuing Mei Ling.'

'Very well,' said Chung, rubbing his eyes with the palms of his hands, '– we will do it.'

***

Rajan was recovered in body, except for the wrist that was stiff and painful. But he was deeply affected by his stint as a guest of Colonel Onada. His father watched over him like a mother hen and kept him away from the Japanese on the estate. His mother cooked for him, waited on him and occasionally got a small smile of thanks or a nod of appreciation, but Rajan did not speak much to her or anyone else.

He knew that Mei Ling had been captured. The Japanese had not been slow to announce that they had ended the reign of the woman they termed a bandit queen and a murderess. Gloating pamphlets were distributed. It was the lead article for days in the local newspapers. Her whereabouts were not disclosed but it was an open secret that she was at the old school, and at the mercy of Colonel Onada.

Thomas had not told Rajan that her incarceration had been in exchange for his freedom. He did not believe that his son would be able to cope with the information. Rajan had asked how it was that Onada had released him. Thomas had lied and suggested that Hidojo had intervened on his behalf. Rajan did not question his father's explanation. All his heart and mind was concentrated on Mei Ling. He sat for long hours in his room with the 'wanted' poster of her. She looked just as she had in the old days, not like the thin and tired guerrilla he had met that fateful night when she had come to the estate seeking news of her father.

Rajan had forgiven his own father for revealing Mei Ling's visit to Colonel Hidojo. He'd only been trying to save him from a trip to the Death Railway. It had backfired when Onada had tortured him for more information about Mei Ling's whereabouts. Rajan knew that his father had suffered as much as he had, perhaps even more, during that episode. He could see it in the rounded shoulders of a man who had previously stood as upright as a soldier. He had not been in a position to reveal Mei Ling's jungle hiding place even if he had wanted to, so there had been no consequences to her from that betrayal by his father.

But Mei Ling had been caught. Rajan had no idea how they had got her in the end. Her life as a guerrilla leader meant she was in constant danger. Perhaps a comrade had betrayed her or an informant had played both sides. Maybe she had fallen into a trap. It was impossible to know. Mei Ling was in the hands of the Kempetai and there was nothing that he could do about it.

***

Matthew, Keng Lian and Siow led a team of fully armed MPAJA soldiers into town. It was the first time Matthew had been out of the jungle since parachuting into Malaya. He was struck by how unchanged Bukit Pagoh seemed. The usual rows of Chinese shophouses lined the streets, selling everything from hardware to provisions. Creepers grew from fissures in the walls and pavements. He caught the familiar whiff of wild cinnamon from the tree at the bottom of the road. The streets were dusty, the drains clogged and stinking. Old cars and bicycles rushed to and fro. The pavements were busy with people going about their business.

It was only when he looked closer that he spotted changes. Each shop had a signboard in the Japanese language on the front. As he peered into one that he remembered, an old bicycle shop, he saw that the picture of George VI had been replaced with a portrait of Emperor Hirohito. The men of the town were thin and kept their eyes on the pavement, as if to avoid the attention of others, although when they recognised that an MPAJA contingent was marching past, there were grins and nervous waves.

Matthew marched along with Siow and Keng Lian at the head of the column. He was in his British army uniform; the rest were smartly turned out in khaki, wearing their three-star caps. They were mostly young men from the surrounding areas and were pleased to be able to put on a display of force. Only the weapons were incongruous. There was no uniformity; they ranged from Japanese machine guns to British-supplied equipment. Chung had decided that the guerrillas should continue with whichever weapon they felt most comfortable. Matthew had a holstered Webley pistol. He also had a Sten gun slung over his shoulder. He hoped he would not have to use it. Siow and Keng Lian both gripped Japanese pistols although Siow also carried a tommy gun.

They reached the school compound. There was a Malay policeman on guard at the main entrance. He smiled when he saw the troops and lowered his weapon.

'They've released some of the prisoners, but many are still being held. There are rumours that the Kempetai will kill them and burn their bodies to hide their crimes.'

'Is Colonel Onada here?' asked Siow.

'Yes, that is his staff car,' explained the soldier, pointing to a gleaming Rolls Royce. 'He came in this morning and has not left yet.'

The men advanced slowly. They doubted that there would be much resistance, not from the Malay and Sikh guards, but the Japanese were unpredictable in defeat.

Siow motioned for his men to surround the complex. He marched into the building flanked by Matthew and Keng Lian.

Onada was waiting for them. He stood in the middle of the polished wooden floor in the full dress uniform of the Kempetai – a red képi, a gold and red waist sash, a dark blue tunic, trousers with black facings and knee-length glossy black boots.

When they entered, he bowed.

'You are Colonel Onada?' demanded Matthew.

Again the man bowed. He seemed a comic character in his pantomime outfit – as short as he was wide, thought Matthew – until one looked into his eyes behind their glistening spectacles and recognised the malevolence within.

'Colonel Onada, your Emperor has surrendered unconditionally. I am part of the British army – we are here to re-establish control of Johore together with the Malayan People's Anti-Japanese Army. Please surrender this compound together with all prisoners. You and your men will be incarcerated until such time as military tribunals are set up to try you for war crimes.'

'It shall be as you wish,' said Onada.

'Order that Mei Ling be brought out – then we will decide if you should live,' said Keng Lian, unable to contain himself.

Onada issued an instruction in Japanese and a couple of

soldiers stood to attention. 'These men will take you to her,' he said.

As Matthew set off with the men, he hardly dared to believe that he might soon be with Mei Ling. It was almost too good to be true. Even as the thought formed in his mind, it was punctuated with gunshots in the distance.

Shouting at Siow to watch Onada, he ran towards the sounds with Keng Lian in hot pursuit. He'd been delayed by what appeared to be Onada in surrender mode. But it was quite possible that the opportunity had been taken to eliminate some of the prisoners. If even half the stories told about him were true, the colonel was a vindictive man – and Mei Ling was his most hated prisoner. Matthew cursed himself for having been so naïve. They burst through a door and found themselves in front of a row of small cells. One of the doors was ajar. A Japanese soldier was sprawled across the entrance. There was a gunshot wound to the middle of his forehead. Keng Lian pushed the door open. Matthew almost gagged at the stink that hit him. It took a moment for his eyes to adjust to the gloom.

A Malay policeman in a cobbled-together uniform who looked familiar to Matthew sat on the edge of a small *charpoy*, a rifle across his knees. A thin, wasted figure lay on the bed – it was not obvious whether she was alive or dead. On the floor, his head resting against a small tin that had functioned as the toilet in the cell, lay another Japanese soldier. He was alive, writhing a little. His pistol was close to his outstretched hand.

Matthew hurried over to the creature on the bed.

'What happened?' asked Keng Lian.

'They wanted to kill her – to cover their tracks,' said the policeman.

'You stopped them?'

'Yes.'

'Why?'

Sergeant Hashim, formerly police chief of Bukit Pagoh under the Japanese, said non-committally, 'I'd had enough.'

'If we don't get her some assistance, it will be too late anyway,' said Matthew, his voice constricted and echoing in the small stinking cell.

'I will go for help,' said Keng Lian. On his way out he stopped at the door, took out his pistol and shot the Japanese guard who was still alive in the back of the head. The noise exploded in the room and Mei Ling whimpered in her semi-conscious state. Neither of the other men flinched.

***

Siow watched the Japanese colonel. His mind was chasing after Matthew and Keng Lian, wondering what had happened. Onada stood unmoving in front of his desk, like a squat brooding statue.

Keng Lian came in panting and said, 'I am going for an ambulance and medical help. Mei Ling is alive but in a bad way. He,' Keng Lian pointed at Onada with a trembling finger, 'ordered her killed. A policeman saved her.'

Siow turned away from the colonel long enough to watch Keng Lian hurry out into the street and then fixed his eyes once more on the Kempetai boss. Onada had not batted an eyelid when Keng Lian made his disclosure, continuing to stare into the distance as if he were a soldier on a parade ground, waiting for a senior officer to complete his inspection.

'Is that right?' asked Siow.

'What does it matter?'

'It matters to me. It also matters to you as it could mean the difference between life and death.'

'You talk to me of death?' said Onada, with sudden passion. 'What is death compared to the dishonour of surrender? The world is a shameful place to me. There can be no better time for an officer of the Japanese Imperial Army to die than now!'

The colonel resumed his pose of silent passivity, his reddened face the only evidence of his sudden outburst.

Unable to stand his apparent equanimity, Siow walked over to him and hit him across the face with the butt of his rifle. Onada's glasses shattered, the fragments falling to the ground around his feet. He blinked at the sudden loss of clear sight. He turned a blank stare at Siow but did not say anything. A trickle of blood ran down from a cut in the corner of his eye. Siow resumed his previous position. He saw through the open door that a group of people was coming through the gates. They ran in but stopped short when they saw Siow and Onada. 'We heard the MPAJA was here. Is that you? Can we see the prisoners?' asked a middle-aged Malay man.

'You are welcome to find your relatives and take them

away from this filthy place.'

'What about him?' The man, self-appointed leader of the group, was staring at Onada with an expression of pure hatred.

'We have not decided. But do not worry, he will be punished.'

The man strode up to Onada. He stood looking at him from a distance of six inches, as if proximity might unlock the mystery of Kempetai behaviour. 'There is no punishment that can fit his crimes,' he said at last, and spat in Onada's face. The colonel remained motionless as the saliva trickled down his cheek.

The group left. Onada and Siow were alone in the room once again. Matthew and Keng Lian joined them. Mei Ling, unconscious, barely alive the doctor had said, had been removed to a hospital with all the care and attention befitting someone who had become a hero to the townsfolk and whose injuries filled the community with horror.

The three men, brothers in arms, stared at Onada, undecided on what to do with him.

'Killing is too easy,' insisted Keng Lian. 'For what he has done, he must suffer.'

'I understand how you feel,' said Matthew. 'But the British cannot condone torture.'

'Neither can the MPAJA', added Siow.

'May I be permitted to make a suggestion?' asked Onada.

***

'Will she live?'

'Maybe.'

Matthew felt a prickly sensation behind his eyelids. At least there was hope. He had slipped into the darkened hospital room to find the doctor with Mei Ling. She was a huddled shape in the hospital bed, covered in a blanket. She had a drip attached to the back of her right hand that lay above the covers. Each finger had been separately bandaged.

'Every one of her fingernails has been pulled off with pliers,' explained the doctor when he saw the direction of Matthew's gaze.

Mei Ling's face was bruised and cut, each wound stained with antiseptic. A deep laceration had been stitched. It looked like a long centipede crawling up her cheek. Her eyes were shut although she was murmuring under her breath, an unhappy nervous sound. There was hardly any light in the room. A slight chink along the top of the tightly-drawn curtain allowed a narrow shaft of sunshine to fall at the foot of the bed.

Matthew guessed that the doctor's concern was not the visible cuts and bruises but the damage to her internal organs and her spine from the water torture and the beatings.

'It was as if they did not care about getting information,' the doctor said. 'Her injuries ... I think she would have just passed out from what they did. Onada must be a madman.'

'She humiliated them,' explained Matthew. 'Onada was motivated by revenge. He must have known the war was ending, that there was not much point in torturing anyone any more. The bastard just wanted to get his own back.'

Matthew sat on the bed and gazed at Mei Ling's sleeping form. He wished she was resting easier but she was restless, expressions of unease crossing her face. 'Does she need more pain medication?' he asked, desperate to ease the suffering.

'No,' said the doctor. 'She needs to wake up so we can assess her injuries more fully. Because of the electric shock treatment.'

Matthew knew this was 'doctor speak' for wondering whether she was in full possession of her faculties. He felt sick with horror to think that this passionate, courageous woman might be damaged beyond repair, beyond the hope of a peaceful future, beyond the reach of those who loved her. Rajan and him were both willing to offer protection, love and a healing from war but perhaps to no avail. Perhaps it was too late.

**

Keng Lian had no qualms about commandeering a scooter from the school compound. It had probably belonged to a resident anyway before the Japanese confiscated it for their own use.

It was already evening when he set out. The shadows were growing longer as he travelled along the winding roads between the neat rows of rubber trees. Keng Lian sped past a group of old Malay farmers sitting under a wooden structure that provided a bit of shade from the long reach of the evening sun as they smoked hand-rolled cheroots. They were selling fruit – durians and mangosteens were in season. The farmers bared toothless gums at him and waved, acknowledging his uniform.

Keng Lian spotted the small signboard he had been looking for and turned off the main road. The track was in a bad state of disrepair and he weaved between potholes. It would be a shame to have to walk. He reached the estate compound. There was a small guardhouse at the entrance and a makeshift barrier. No sentry was present. Keng Lian wondered if the Japanese had fled the estate for fear of being lynched by angry mobs of Tamils.

He stopped and asked for directions from a tapper who was sitting by the road with a bottle of toddy at his side. He glanced at the man on the motorbike with unfocused eyes, took a swift swig from the bottle, spluttered a little, wiped the drool off his chin and pointed down a side road. Keng Lian nodded his thanks.

He reached a cluster of small houses. Outside one of them, a tired-looking Indian lady was taking clothes from a line, folding a *saree* as she unpegged it to prevent the long cloth trailing on the ground. Keng Lian guessed that this was his destination. He got off his bike and asked in Malay, 'Is this the Thomas residence?'

She nodded, her mouth full of clothes pegs.

'Is Mr. Thomas at home?'

Again she inclined her head and gestured at the house. Keng Lian grinned at her, his most attractive boyish smile, climbed off his bike and walked towards the house. He knocked on the door but did not wait for a response before tramping in, regretting that his boots were leaving muddy tracks on the floor. He found Thomas sitting in his rocking chair reading a book. Rajan was at the sink washing vegetables. They both turned as Keng Lian marched in. Rajan dried his hands on a kitchen towel and nodded a welcome. He recognised the uniform. Thomas made to get out of his chair. Keng Lian motioned for him to stay where he was. Keng Lian noticed that the son was pale, his face drawn and thin, as if he did not eat or sleep much. The father had aged beyond the mere passage of time, as so many had done during the Japanese occupation.

'Why have you come here? Do you bring a message?' asked Rajan in his gentle voice.

'I suppose you could call it that,' said Keng Lian.

'What is this about?' Thomas was less friendly, more suspicious.

'Someone you may know – Mei Ling.'

'Mei Ling!' Rajan stepped forward, his eyes bright. He put his palms together, an unconscious gesture of prayer, of pleading. 'Is she all right? I've been to the prison every day since the surrender but they would not let her out or let me see her. They don't seem to know or care that their war is lost.'

'She's in hospital – the MPAJA obtained her release by force earlier today. She may not survive.'

Rajan shut his eyes and grasped the dining table edge.

'That does not explain why you are here,' stated Thomas flatly, almost aggressively.

'I bring a message from Mei Ling to the man who betrayed her to the Kempetai,' said Keng Lian.

Rajan's forehead was knotted with confusion. 'What do you mean? I didn't tell them anything – I didn't *know* anything!'

'I don't mean you.'

'What?'

'Look at your father – he knows what I'm talking about.'

Rajan turned to Thomas, whose fingers were interlocked in a sign of supplication – Keng Lian noticed the plea was directed towards his son and not the soldier.

'I had no choice, son.'

'What are you talking about?'

When the old man remained silent, Keng Lian answered the question, 'He betrayed Mei Ling to the Kempetai in exchange for your release.'

***

Mei Ling's lids fluttered open. She blinked a few times, trying to focus. Matthew, watching her face as he had done for all the hours since he had settled himself in a chair by her bed, leapt to his feet.

'Mei Ling?'

She turned to the sound like a plant to light, slowly but with definite, unshakeable purpose.

'Matthew? Is that you?'

'Yes, it is. You're safe now.' His first instinct was to reassure her that her ordeal with the Kempetai was over. But inside he was exultant. She had recognised his voice. She was lucid. The doctor's fears were misplaced. Onada had broken her body but had not destroyed her mind.

'I don't understand.' Her voice was puzzled, diffident.

'The war is over – the MPAJA rescued you today. You have survived, Mei Ling. You have survived!'

'Colonel Onada?'

'A prisoner.'

She blinked as if she didn't understand his words and maybe it was too much unexpected, unlikely news to process. 'May I have some water please?' she asked

Matthew almost knocked the glass over in his hurry to do her bidding. Holding her head up gently, he held the glass to her lips. She could not swallow, and after wetting her lips she indicated with a gesture that she wanted to lie down again.

'The war is over?' she whispered.

'Yes, Hirohito surrendered. Some new bomb was dropped on two Japanese cities and destroyed them. But please, Mei Ling, don't talk – rest. There will be plenty of time for answers later.'

She smiled, a caricature of the warm smile he had grown to care about so deeply. She said, 'I need … I need to see Rajan.'

Matthew understood then what jealousy was. He had thought that to see this woman out of harm's way was all he cared about, that her safety was the only subject of the prayers he had flung at unknown and capricious gods. He knew better now. 'I will get him for you, if I can,' he replied.

'Please hurry,' whispered Mei Ling.

He bent over and kissed her forehead. But her eyes were

closed again and she did not appear to notice. Matthew left the room.

Keng Lian walked into the hospital as Matthew ran out.

The Chinese man grinned at Matthew as they stopped at the top of the wooden steps leading out into the car park. 'Where are you going?' he asked.

'On an errand for Mei Ling,' said Matthew. He was not sure why he was being evasive – to avoid the truth, perhaps? That Mei Ling had asked for Rajan the minute she recovered consciousness and that any hopes he had of competing with his boyhood friend for her affections were just fantasies?

'I've just been on an errand for Mei Ling too!'

'What do you mean?'

'Nothing for you to worry about. I will inform the central committee.'

'May I borrow your bike?' asked Matthew.

'Sure – I can always find a generous Japanese soldier if I need another one.' Matthew hopped on the bike and left the other man laughing at his own joke.

He did not know it, but he was soon retracing Keng Lian's route. He passed the old men selling fruit but did not notice their friendly waves. Keng Lian had been flush with victory. Matthew knew the war was won but feared that his personal dreams were about to be thwarted. He discovered that he resented Rajan and was surprised that he had it in himself to do so. They had been such good friends. Memories washed over him – their fishing expeditions, the cricket games, the long walks exploring the estate, the awkwardness of the encounters with his parents that they had laughed about afterwards. He remembered the warmth he had always been shown in the Thomas house, where Mrs. Thomas had welcomed him with wide smiles that turned her eyes into black, twinkling pinpoints of warmth. He acknowledged that he had envied Rajan his father. The dignified, repressed man had been unable to hide his love for his son. It shone in his eyes whenever he looked at the boy – even when he was warning them both in firm tones not to break a window with the cricket ball, or to stay indoors during a thunderstorm. Matthew had envied Rajan his mother too, who expressed her love in food, clean sheets and well-ironed clothes rather than in lectures about his place in the estate hierarchy – a position he'd compromised by fraternising with 'that boy'.

Matthew turned down the estate road. He had an overwhelming feeling that the last few years had never happened. He was going to seek out Rajan and they were going to climb a tree, play a few tricks on the assistant manager and celebrate by swigging some toddy bought from a tapper. They were going to swear like adults and then giggle like children because, really, that was what they were. Rajan would find some exotic flora or fauna and show it to Matthew, whispering his discovery in an awestruck voice. Matthew would pretend to be impressed and wonder why his best friend seemed to love creepy-crawlies so much. Matthew realised suddenly that he understood Mei Ling's passion for the young man – a passion that had almost cost her her life at the hands of the Kempetai. There was something about Rajan – the stillness of the man-boy was like the eye of the whirlpool, the centre of the storm. And he too had suffered at the hands of Colonel Onada and borne it as stoically as Mei Ling had.

Matthew felt deprived of the badge of honour that was to have fought the Japanese and suffered at their hands. What had *he* done, after all? He had fled on the first available ship and, though he had endured a couple of years of boredom and deprivation in England, his physical safety had never been under threat. Then he had returned to Malaya in a blaze of glory, determined to take part in the war, only to have the Japanese surrender without his firing a shot. Matthew realised that he had won a war and lost his heart without being anything more than a bystander.

As he got closer, he could see that all the lights were on in the Thomas house. Matthew was surprised. It was just dusk after all. As he stopped the bike and the noisy two-stroke engine fell silent, he heard the sound of wailing. He thought he recognised Ibrahim, the medical assistant from pre-war days, walking into the house.

Matthew approached with some trepidation. What was going on? He reached the front door and stood there tentatively. Then he took a deep breath and stepped into the house. He made his way to the front room, his eyes adjusting to the brightness. His gaze was drawn to Rajan sitting on the couch. His friend was so thin, almost frail. His face was deeply lined despite his youth and his mouth was turned down, as if he had forgotten how to smile. Matthew remembered the big toothy grin and the irrepressible sense of humour and had a fresh sense of the toll the war had taken. Rajan's clothes were hanging on him. His bony shoulders looked as if he'd forgotten to take the clothes hanger out before slipping on his short-sleeved white shirt.

His mother sat next to him. The rolls of cheerful fat that used to fold in layers below her *saree* blouse like a rucked up carpet had disappeared. Her skin hung loosely on her, not up to the task of shrinking with the dwindling of her flesh. She held a length of *saree* to her face, her sobbing muffled by the cloth. No one in the living room had noticed him yet, standing silently by the door. Matthew realised how much he had grown in the years since he'd been away. He would have to duck to enter the room – the doorway arch was too low. He remembered skipping in when he used to visit in the old days.

Ibrahim was sitting with his back to the door on a rattan chair. He leaned back as if he expected to be there for a while, opposite the silent young man and his weeping mother. Matthew turned his attention to something that he'd been aware of in the periphery of his vision but had refused to acknowledge, as if by looking away he could postpone the inevitability of knowledge.

A bed had been moved into the room, a single bed, quite narrow; Matthew thought it looked like Rajan's. A man was lying on the bed covered with a white sheet up to his neck. His position reminded Matthew of Mei Ling in hospital.

Thomas was dead. His cheeks had hollowed into gauntness and his skin had darkened in death. His eyes were shut, a coin on each eyelid – as if otherwise

Thomas would be staring wildly at the Grim Reaper. The small circle in the middle of his forehead stained with gunpowder, the blood wiped away, made the cause of death apparent.

Rajan glanced up – like a drowning man, thought Matthew, casting around for something to cling to. He saw the tall figure by the door and stared. There was no expression on his face, as if he was convinced the figure was a spectre, a creature of his imagination. Matthew smiled – a lop-sided smile, weighed down by the presence of death – but a half-smile for an old friend. Rajan's face suddenly lit up from within. He stood up and the impression Matthew had of Rajan's frailness was emphasised by his increased height. He was a tall man now, clean shaven, his hair a little too long and curling around his collar, but with the same long face and dark eyes.

'Matthew, is that you?' he asked, just as Mei Ling had.

'Yes.' Matthew stepped into the room and the light from the single bulb lit up his yellow hair. Rajan gave his friend a bear hug, laughing out loud with delight. Matthew guessed that for an instant he had forgotten everything in the room and was transported into a happier past. It reminded him of the way Mei Ling had hugged him when he first arrived at the MPAJA camp. Was he always to be the proxy for the other with these two people he cared about above anyone else? Rajan put his hands on his friend's shoulders. 'Smart uniform, dashing moustache – but what are you doing here?'

Matthew twirled his moustache with comic emphasis. 'I

339

was parachuted into the jungle a few weeks ago, all ready to fight the Japs, and they bloody well surrendered!' Then his face sobered. 'But Rajan, old friend, what has happened here?'

Rajan's hands fell to his sides. He led the way to the bed and they both stared down at Thomas. He said, his voice almost inaudible, 'It was a reprisal killing. My father betrayed one of the communist leaders … it was a terrible thing to do but he thought it was the only way to save me, to save my life. The Kempetai had me, you see.'

Matthew felt as if someone had plunged a hand though his chest and wrapped cold fingers around his heart. 'When did this happen?'

'Not that long ago. A young Chinese man came in – he seemed to know everything about what my father had done – and shot him in cold blood. I can't believe it. Just when we thought it was all over, these horrible fear-filled, tortured years.'

'Who was the guerrilla leader that your father betrayed?'

Rajan did not answer at first. He stood silently, his fingernails digging into his palms. Finally, he whispered, 'Mei Ling. She ended up in the hands of the Kempetai as a consequence of what my father did. I can't forgive him for that. I would never have chosen to be exchanged for her. I only found out about it this evening.'

He paused and then continued in a bitter tone, 'But I can't forgive *her* for this!' He gestured at the body on the bed. 'Mei Ling must have known that my father did it for me – war leads people to make terrible choices. I would have died a thousand times at Onada's hands rather than have my father betray her – but I didn't know ...'

'But why do you think she had anything to do with it?'

'The guerrilla who did this ... he said he had come with a message from Mei Ling.'

Matthew nodded. It made sense to him now. Keng Lian had decided to act on his understanding of the facts and execute the man he held responsible for Mei Ling's incarceration and suffering. He had wanted the old man to know why he was being singled out for death. Of course Mei Ling hadn't ordered the killing; she was unconscious in hospital. If she had not been, she would have told Keng Lian that she had gone voluntarily – that it was in fact her idea, had been her idea all along, to exchange herself for Rajan. Thomas had done no more than go along with her sacrifice.

Matthew opened his mouth to speak. He needed to explain to Rajan, make him see the whole convoluted truth. Instead he heard himself say, as if he were a stranger uttering the words, 'I am here from Mei Ling. She's in hospital, in a bad way although she might survive. She's asking for you.'

Rajan closed his eyes and swayed on his feet as if he was being pulled in all directions at once. He fell to his knees next to the bed and held his father's cold hand to his cheek. After a few seconds, he released the hand and slumped back against the bed. Matthew towered over him, gazing down at his friend – wondering what his decision would be.

'I love her,' said Rajan.

Matthew nodded, watching his friend, feeling his own

hopes ebb away.

Rajan buried his face in his hands. 'This whole war, all I have hoped for – every moment of every day – was that somehow we would get through to the other side, Mei Ling and I, alive. It kept me going when Onada had me. I hoped it would keep her going too …'

He stood up and squared his thin shoulders, the boy grown into a man who was first and foremost a creature of principle.

'I cannot come. She has killed my father. I am sorry. I love her but I cannot come.'

***

When Matthew got back, night had fallen and Mei Ling's room was in pitch darkness. She was awake and seemed to sense his presence as he slipped in through the door. She had been waiting, he realised, confident that Matthew would return with the man she loved and for whom she had sacrificed so much. She must have anticipated this moment, the first moment when the two of them might have a future as well as a past.

Matthew was unable to speak but Mei Ling asked, her voice a ghostly, disembodied thing in the dark room, 'He did not come?'

Matthew cleared his throat, struggling to find his voice, wondering what he had done. He was glad she could not see his face. 'Keng Lian carried out a reprisal killing … of Rajan's father.'

She must have been propping herself up on an elbow because he heard the bed creak and the sheets rustle as she lay back. There was a silence. His eyes adjusted to the blackness and he could see her outline, the long forehead, the thin nose and the full lips.

She said, 'Oh God …'

Matthew walked over to the bed. The die was cast. 'Rajan would not come. I'm sorry, Mei Ling, but he blames you for his father's death.'

There was silence from the bed. When he put out a hand and touched her cheek it was wet with tears.

***

But there is one more thing you need to know. The reason I have written this letter – God knows it has taken me long enough to find the courage to tell you the truth. Mei Ling never ordered the reprisal killing. She would never have sought retribution against your father. It was Keng Lian, acting on his own. I could have told you that evening – I should have told you that evening that I came to see you. I just felt a sudden desperate need to take the opportunity to create a rift between you and Mei Ling – so that maybe, just maybe, she would turn to me again as she did in the jungle when you were first arrested. I loved her, you see. But not enough it seems to sacrifice my happiness for yours and hers.

And your father? Well, perhaps he should have refused the deal she offered. But the reality was that she volunteered to be exchanged for you. She volunteered to put herself in the hands of the cruellest man in Malaya because she loved you. I enclose her letter to me, the one she wrote just before meeting your father and arranging to be turned over to Onada – I have carried it around with me all these years. In many ways though, it belongs to you.

I wonder often, if she had not died, whether I would have spoken – in the cold light of day when my own hopes had petrified and crumbled. But she slipped into a coma soon after I returned that night without you and never recovered. She died of her broken body, the doctors said. I know she died of a broken heart.

When she was gone and it was too late for happy endings – well, I didn't have the courage to tell you.

I am going to die soon, the cancer has spread – it has been a lingering painful death after a long, lonely existence but I have embraced it as a fitting punishment. It will not comfort you to know this – but the process of dying for me started that fateful evening when I walked away from the truth. I suspect it was the same for you. I don't ask for your forgiveness or your understanding, I barely dare to apologise. It seems such a trivial thing to say that I am sorry, although I am and have been every single day since Mei Ling died.

I write this letter in order that you know the truth of what happened in Malaya all those years ago … so that when your time comes to face death, you will have less to regret in your conduct than I.

Farewell,
Matthew Coleman

EPILOGUE

Rajan let the letter slip from between his fingers. He raised an unsteady hand and felt the wetness on his cheek. He looked around at the small living room, rocked backwards in his father's old chair. He had stayed on the estate, nursed his mother and eventually, when the British returned, taken over his father's old job. It hadn't been that bad, really. The British, cowed from their beating at the hands of the Japanese, had been largely benevolent taskmasters until Malayan independence in 1957. He'd never married, never had children or grandchildren, his life an airless narrow tunnel from which there was no escape. When he looked at another woman, even fleetingly, Mei Ling's features would superimpose themselves on her face and he would realise again, as if he had ever forgotten, that the war had taken his future away.

He glanced at the letter that was fluttering on the floor under the mild breeze from the ceiling fan. Mei Ling had volunteered to be exchanged for him. His father had fallen in with her wishes; he had not betrayed her. Not a second time, anyway. Was there some comfort in that? He pictured the upright *kerani* who had been brought low by the war and then murdered by Keng Lian. No, he could find no comfort there. He turned to face the doorway, almost expecting Matthew to be standing there again, young and handsome, a halo around his golden head from the light bulb, in love with the same girl – his girl. If only he had known.

Rajan closed his eyes and tried to blame his friend. Tried to find the solace that Matthew had offered as his penance, that it was not his fault that Mei Ling had died. He had refused to go to her that night when she had asked for him because of the mendacity of a man he would have trusted with his life.

The thin old man with the deep eyes and lined face shook his head and flexed his arthritic wrist. He could blame Matthew and did, but the truth was that he should have trusted Mei Ling more, so much more than he had. He picked up the letter and read the last line again – 'Promise me you'll never tell Rajan that I exchanged myself for him. He would never forgive himself – or me.'

He walked outside and stood in the small garden where his mother used to tend flowers. He looked up at the skies – it was a clear night and the glittering twinkling stars formed a vast band in the heavenly vault. He felt his cheeks cool in the light breeze and knew that they were wet with tears. He conjured up a picture of Mei Ling in his mind's eye as he had done countless times over the years. But this time – for the first time – she was young again in his imagination, and so

346

was he. Untainted by war, unravished by fate, unburdened with knowledge of the future. Rajan smiled. Childhood sweetheart, communist, bandit queen – it was a privilege to have known her and loved her.

He walked back indoors and sat once more in the old rocking chair. He spared a thought for Matthew and found that he was not angry any more. Rajan waited for the release of death with a lighter heart.

ABOUT THE AUTHOR

Shamini Flint lives in Singapore with her husband and two children. She is an ex-lawyer, ex-lecturer, stay-at-home mum and writer.

Shamini's first five crime novels, 'Inspector Singh Investigates – A Most Peculiar Malaysian Murder', 'Inspector Singh Investigates – A Bali Conspiracy Most Foul', 'Inspector Singh Investigates – The Singapore School of Villainy', 'Inspector Singh Investigates – A Deadly Cambodian Crime Spree' and 'Inspector Singh Investigates – A Curious Indian Cadaver' are published by Little, Brown and translated into numerous languages.

Shamini has written many children's picture books including 'Jungle Blues', 'Turtle Takes a Trip' and 'A T-Rex Ate my Homework'. She is also the author of the highly-acclaimed 'Sasha' series of children's travel books.

Shamini's website is www.shaminiflint.com.
Please find Shamini on Facebook (Shamini Flint) or follow her on Twitter (@ShaminiFlint)